2010:
ODYSSEY TWO

BOOKS BY ARTHUR C. CLARKE

Non-Fiction

Interplanetary Flight
The Exploration of Space
The Exploration of The Moon
Going into Space
The Coast of Coral
The Making of a Moon
The Reefs of Taprobane
Voice Across the Sea
The Challenge of the Spaceship
The Challenge of the Sea
Profiles of the Future
Voices from the Sky
The Promise of Space
Report on Planet Three
The First Five Fathoms
Boy Beneath the Sea
Indian Ocean Adventure
Indian Ocean Treasure
The Treasure of the Great Reef
The View from Serendip

With the Editors of "Life"
Man and Space

With the Astronauts
First on the Moon

With Robert Silverberg
Into Space

With Chesley Bonestell
Beyond Jupiter

With Simon Welfare & John Fairley
Arthur C. Clarke's Mysterious World

Fiction

Islands in the Sky
Prelude to Space
Against the Fall of Night
The Sands of Mars
Childhood's End
Expedition to Earth
Earthlight
Reach for Tomorrow
The City and the Stars
Tales from the "White Hart"
The Deep Range
The Other Side of the Sky
* Across the Sea of Stars
A Fall of Moondust
* From the Ocean, From the Stars
Tales of Ten Worlds
Dolphin Island
Glide Path
The Lion of Comarre
* The Nine Billion Names of God
* Prelude to Mars
The Lost Worlds of 2001
The Wind from the Sun
Rendezvous with Rama
Imperial Earth
The Fountains of Paradise

With Stanley Kubrick
2001: A Space Odyssey

*Anthologies

A DEL REY BOOK

BALLANTINE BOOKS • NEW YORK

2010:
ODYSSEY TWO

ARTHUR C. CLARKE

A Del Rey Book
Published by Ballantine Books
Copyright © 1982 by Serendib BV

Library of Congress Cataloging in Publication Data

Clarke, Arthur Charles, 1917-
  2010, odyssey 2.

  Sequel to: 2001, a space odyssey.
  "A Del Rey book."
  I. Title.   II. Title: Two thousand ten, odyssey two.
PR6005.L36A616 1982   823'.914   82-6850
ISBN 0-345-30305-9   AACR2

Manufactured in the United States of America

First Edition: December 1982

10 9 8 7 6 5 4 3 2

Dedicated, with respectful admiration, to two great Russians, both depicted herein:

General Alexei Leonov—Cosmonaut, Hero of the
Soviet Union, Artist
and
Academician Andrei Sakharov—Scientist, Nobel
Laureate, Humanist.

CONTENTS

AUTHOR'S NOTE

The novel *2001: A Space Odyssey* was written during the years 1964–1968 and was published in July, 1968, shortly after release of the movie. As I have described in *The Lost Worlds of 2001*, both projects proceeded simultaneously, with feedback in each direction. Thus I often had the strange experience of revising the manuscript *after* viewing rushes based upon an earlier version of the story—a stimulating, but rather expensive, way of writing a novel.

As a result, there is a much closer parallel between book and movie than is usually the case, but there are also major differences. In the novel, the destination of the spaceship *Discovery* was Iapetus (or Japetus), most enigmatic of Saturn's many moons. The Saturnian system was reached *via* Jupiter: *Discovery* made a close approach to the giant planet, using its enormous gravitational field to produce a "slingshot" effect and to accelerate it along the second lap of its journey. Exactly the same maneuver was used by the Voyager space probes in 1979, when they made the first detailed reconnaissance of the outer giants.

In the movie, however, Stanley Kubrick wisely avoided confusion by setting the third confrontation between Man and Monolith among the moons of Jupiter. Saturn was dropped from the script entirely, though Douglas Trumbull later used the expertise he had acquired to film the ringed planet in his own production, *Silent Running*.

No one could have imagined, back in the mid-sixties, that the exploration of the moons of Jupiter lay, not in the next century, but only *fifteen* years ahead. Nor had anyone dreamed of the wonders that would be found there—although we can be quite certain that the discoveries of the twin Voyagers will one day be surpassed by even more unexpected finds. When *2001* was written, Io, Europa, Ganymede, and Callisto were mere pinpoints of light in even the most powerful telescope; now they are worlds, each unique, and one of them—Io—is the most volcanically active body in the Solar System.

Yet, all things considered, both movie and book stand up quite well in the light of these discoveries, and it is fascinating to compare the Jupiter sequences in the film with the actual movies from the Voyager cameras. But clearly, anything written today has to incorporate the results of the 1979 explorations: the moons of Jupiter are no longer uncharted territory.

And there is another, more subtle, psychological factor to be taken into consideration. *2001* was written in an age that now lies beyond one of the Great Divides in human history; we are sundered from it forever by the moment when Neil Armstrong set foot upon the Moon. July 20, 1969, was still half a decade in the future when Stanley Kubrick and I started thinking about the "proverbial good science-fiction movie" (his phrase). Now history and fiction have become inextricably intertwined.

The Apollo astronauts had already seen the film when they left for the Moon. The crew of *Apollo 8*, who at Christmas, 1968, became the first men ever to set eyes upon the Lunar Farside, told me that they had been tempted to radio back the discovery of a large black monolith: alas, discretion prevailed.

And there were later, almost uncanny instances of nature imitating art. Strangest of all was the saga of *Apollo 13* in 1970.

As a good opening, the Command Module, which houses the crew, had been christened *Odyssey*. Just before the explosion of the oxygen tank that caused the mission to be aborted, the crew had been playing Richard Strauss' *Zarathustra* theme, now universally identified with the movie. Immediately after the loss of power, Jack Swigert radioed back to Mission Control: "Houston, we've had a problem." The words that Hal used to astronaut Frank Poole on a similar occasion were: "Sorry to interrupt the festivities, but we have a problem."

When the report of the *Apollo 13* mission was later published, NASA Administrator Tom Paine sent me a copy, and noted under Swigert's words: "Just as you always said it would be, Arthur." I still get a very strange feeling when I contemplate this whole series of events—almost, indeed, as if I share a certain responsibility.

Another resonance is less serious, but equally striking. One of the most technically brilliant sequences in the movie was that in which Frank Poole was shown running round and round the circular track of the giant centrifuge, held in place by the "artificial gravity" produced by its spin.

Almost a decade later, the crew of the superbly successful Skylab realized that its designers had provided them with a similar geometry; a ring of storage cabinets formed a smooth, circular band around the space station's interior. Skylab, however, was not spinning, but this did not deter its ingenious occupants. They discovered that they could run around the track, just like mice in a squirrel cage, to produce a result visually indistinguishable from that shown in *2001*. And they televised the whole exercise back to Earth (need I name the accompanying music?) with the comment: "Stanley Kubrick should see this." As in due course he did, because I sent him the telecine recording. (I never got it back; Stanley uses a tame Black Hole as a filing system.)

Yet another link between film and reality is the painting by Apollo–Soyuz Commander, Cosmonaut Alexei Leonov, "Near the Moon." I first saw it in 1968, when *2001* was presented at the United Nations Conference on the Peaceful Uses of Outer Space. Immediately after the screening, Alexei pointed out to me that *his* concept (on page 32 of the Leonov–Sokolov book *The Stars Are Awaiting Us*, Moscow, 1967) shows exactly the same lineup as the movie's opening: the Earth rising beyond the Moon, and the Sun rising beyond both. His autographed sketch of the painting now hangs on my office wall; for further details see Chapter 12.

Perhaps this is the appropriate point to identify another and less well-known name appearing in these pages, that of Hsue-shen Tsien. In 1936, with the great Theodore von Karman and Frank J. Malina, Dr. Tsien founded the Guggenheim Aeronautical Laboratory of the California Institute of Technology (GALCIT)—the direct ancestor of Pasadena's famed Jet Propulsion Laboratory. He was also the first Goddard Professor at Caltech, and contributed greatly to American rocket research through the 1940s. Later, in one of the most disgraceful episodes of the McCarthy period, he was arrested on trumped-up security charges when he wished to return to his native country. For the last two decades, he has been one of the leaders of the Chinese rocket program.

Finally, there is the strange case of the "Eye of Japetus"— Chapter 35 of *2001*. Here I describe astronaut Bowman's discovery on the Saturnian moon of a curious feature: "a brilliant white oval, about four hundred miles long and two hundred wide . . . perfectly symmetrical . . . and so sharp-edged that it almost looked . . . painted on the face of the little moon." As he came closer, Bowman convinced himself that "the bright ellipse set against the dark background of the satellite was a huge empty eye staring at him as he approached . . ." Later, he noticed "the tiny black dot at the exact center," which turns out to be the Monolith (or one of its avatars).

Well, when *Voyager 1* transmitted the first photographs of Iapetus they did indeed disclose a large, clear-cut white oval with a tiny black dot at the center. Carl Sagan promptly sent me a print from the Jet Propulsion Laboratory with the cryptic an-

notation "Thinking of you . . ." I do not know whether to be
relieved or disappointed that *Voyager 2* has left the matter still
open.

Inevitably, therefore, the story you are about to read is something much more complex than a straightforward sequel to the
earlier novel—or the movie. Where these differ, I have usually
followed the screen version; however, I have been more concerned with making this book self-consistent, and as accurate as
possible in the light of current knowledge.

Which, of course, will once more be out of date by 2001 . . .

Arthur C. Clarke
Colombo, Sri Lanka
January, 1982

2010:
ODYSSEY TWO

I ✳ LEONOV

1. MEETING AT THE FOCUS

EVEN IN THIS METRIC AGE, IT WAS STILL THE THOUSAND-FOOT TELE-scope, not the three-hundred-meter one. The great saucer set among the mountains was already half full of shadow, as the tropical sun dropped swiftly to rest, but the triangular raft of the antenna complex suspended high above its center still blazed with light. From the ground far below, it would have taken keen eyes to notice the two human figures in the aerial maze of gird-ers, support cables, and wave-guides.

"The time has come," said Dr. Dimitri Moisevitch to his old friend Heywood Floyd, "to talk of many things. Of shoes and spaceships and sealing wax, but mostly of monoliths and mal-functioning computers."

"So that's why you got me away from the conference. Not that I really mind—I've heard Carl give that SETI speech so many times that I can recite it myself. And the view certainly is fantas-tic—you know, all the times I've been to Arecibo, I've never made it up here to the antenna feed."

*3

"Shame on you. I've been here three times. Imagine—we're listening to the whole universe—but no one can overhear us. So let's talk about your problem."

"What problem?"

"To start with, why you had to resign as Chairman of the National Council on Astronautics."

"I didn't resign. The University of Hawaii pays a lot better."

"Okay—you didn't resign—you were one jump ahead of them. After all these years, Woody, you can't fool me, and you should give up trying. If they offered the NCA back to you right now, would you hesitate?"

"All right, you old Cossack. What do you want to know?"

"First of all, there are lots of loose ends in the report you finally issued after so much prodding. We'll overlook the ridiculous and frankly illegal secrecy with which your people dug up the Tycho monolith—"

"That wasn't my idea."

"Glad to hear it: I even believe you. And we appreciate the fact that you're now letting everyone examine the thing—which of course is what you should have done in the first place. Not that it's done much good . . ."

There was a gloomy silence while the two men contemplated the black enigma up there on the Moon, still contemptuously defying all the weapons that human ingenuity could bring to bear upon it. Then the Russian scientist continued.

"Anyway, whatever the Tycho monolith may be, there's something more important out at Jupiter. That's where it sent its signal, after all. And that's where your people ran into trouble. Sorry about that, by the way—though Frank Poole was the only one I knew personally. Met him at the '98 IAF Congress—he seemed a good man."

"Thank you; they were *all* good men. I wish we knew what happened to them."

"Whatever it was, surely you'll admit that it now concerns the whole human race—not merely the United States. You can no longer try to use your knowledge for purely national advantage."

"Dimitri—you know perfectly well that your side would have done exactly the same thing. And you'd have helped."

"You're absolutely right. But that's ancient history—like the just-departed administration of yours that was responsible for the whole mess. With a new President, perhaps wiser counsels will prevail."

"Possibly. Do you have any suggestions, and are they official or just personal hopes?"

"Entirely unofficial at the moment. What the bloody politicians call exploratory talks. Which I shall flatly deny ever occurred."

"Fair enough. Go on."

"Okay—here's the situation. You're assembling *Discovery II* in parking orbit as quickly as you can, but you can't hope to have it ready in less than three years, which means you'll miss the next launch window—"

"I neither confirm nor deny. Remember I'm merely a humble university chancellor, the other side of the world from the Astronautics Council."

"And your last trip to Washington was just a holiday to see old friends, I suppose. To continue: our own *Alexei Leonov*—"

"I thought you were calling it *Gherman Titov*."

"Wrong, *Chancellor*. The dear old CIA's let you down again. *Leonov* it is, as of last January. And don't let anyone know *I* told you it will reach Jupiter at least a year ahead of *Discovery*."

"Don't let anyone know *I* told you we were afraid of that. But do go on."

"Because my bosses are just as stupid and shortsighted as yours, they want to go it alone. Which means that whatever went wrong with *you* may happen to us, and we'll all be back to square one—or worse."

"What do *you* think went wrong? We're just as baffled as you are. And don't tell me you haven't got all of Dave Bowman's transmissions."

"Of course we have. Right up to that last 'My God, it's full of stars!' We've even done a stress analysis on his voice patterns. We don't think he was hallucinating; he was trying to describe what he actually saw."

"And what do you make of his Doppler shift?"

"Completely impossible, of course. When we lost his signal,

he was receding at a tenth of the speed of light. And he'd reached that in less than two minutes. A quarter of a million gravities!"

"So he must have been killed instantly."

"Don't pretend to be naive, Woody. Your space-pod radios aren't built to withstand even a hundredth of that acceleration. If *they* could survive, so could Bowman—at least, until we lost contact."

"Just doing an independent check on your deductions. From there on, we're as much in the dark as you are. *If* you are."

"Merely playing with lots of crazy guesses I'd be asha...ed to tell you. Yet none of them, I suspect, will be half as crazy as the truth."

In small crimson explosions the navigation warning lights winked on all around them, and the three slim towers supporting the antenna complex began to blaze like beacons against the darkling sky. The last red sliver of the sun vanished below the surrounding hills; Heywood Floyd waited for the Green Flash, which he had never seen. Once again, he was disappointed.

"So, Dimitri," he said, "let's get to the point. Just what are you driving at?"

"There must be a vast amount of priceless information stored in *Discovery*'s data banks; presumably it's still being gathered, even though the ship's stopped transmitting. We'd like to have that."

"Fair enough. But when you get out there, and *Leonov* makes a rendezvous, what's to prevent you from boarding *Discovery* and copying everything you want?"

"I never thought I'd have to remind *you* that *Discovery* is United States territory, and an unauthorized entry would be piracy."

"Except in the event of a life-or-death emergency, which wouldn't be difficult to arrange. After all, it would be hard for us to check what your boys were up to, from a billion kilometers away."

"Thanks for the most interesting suggestion; I'll pass it on. But even if we went aboard, it would take us weeks to learn all your systems, and read out all your memory banks. What I propose is cooperation. I'm convinced that's the best idea—but we may both have a job selling it to our respective bosses."

"You want one of our astronauts to fly with *Leonov?*"

"Yes—preferably an engineer who's specialized in *Discovery's* systems. Like the ones you're training at Houston to bring the ship home."

"How did you know *that*?"

"For heaven's sake, Woody—it was on *Aviation Week's* videotext at least a month ago."

"I *am* out of touch; nobody tells me what's been declassified."

"All the more reason to spend time in Washington. Will you back me up?"

"Absolutely. I agree with you one hundred percent. But—"

"But what?"

"We both have to deal with dinosaurs with brains in their tails. Some of mine will argue: Let the Russians risk their necks, hurrying out to Jupiter. We'll be there anyway a couple of years later—and what's the hurry?"

For a moment there was silence on the antenna raft, except for a faint creak from the immense supporting cables that held it suspended a hundred meters in the sky. Then Moisevitch continued, so quietly that Floyd had to strain to hear him: "Has anyone checked *Discovery's* orbit lately?"

"I really don't know—but I suppose so. Anyway, why bother? It's a perfectly stable one."

"Indeed. Let me tactlessly remind you of an embarrassing incident from the old NASA days. Your first space station—Skylab. It was supposed to stay up at least a decade, but you didn't do your calculations right. The air drag in the ionosphere was badly underestimated, and it came down years ahead of schedule. I'm sure you remember that little cliff-hanger, even though you were a boy at the time."

"It was the year I graduated, and you know it. But *Discovery* doesn't go anywhere near Jupiter. Even at perigee—er, perijove—it's much too high to be affected by atmospheric drag."

"I've already said enough to get me exiled to my *dacha* again—and you might not be allowed to visit me next time. So just ask your tracking people to do their job more carefully, will

you? And remind them that Jupiter has the biggest magne-
tosphere in the Solar System."

"I understand what you're driving at—many thanks. Anything
else before we go down? I'm starting to freeze."

"Don't worry, old friend. As soon as you let all this filter
through to Washington—wait a week or so until I'm clear—
things are going to get very, very hot."

2. THE HOUSE OF THE DOLPHINS

THE DOLPHINS SWAM INTO THE DINING ROOM EVERY EVENING, JUST before sunset. Only once since Floyd had occupied the Chancellor's residence had they broken their routine. That was the day of the '05 *tsunami*—which, fortunately, had lost most of its power before it reached Hilo. The next time his friends failed to turn up on schedule, Floyd would throw the family into the car and head for high ground, in the general direction of Mauna Kea.

Charming though they were, he had to admit that their playfulness was sometimes a nuisance. The wealthy marine geologist who had designed the house had never minded getting wet because he usually wore bathing trunks—or less. But there had been one unforgettable occasion when the entire Board of Regents, in full evening attire, had been sipping cocktails around the pool while awaiting the arrival of a distinguished guest from the mainland. The dolphins had deduced, correctly, that they

* 9

would get second billing. So the visitor was quite surprised to be greeted by a bedraggled reception committee in ill-fitting bathrobes—and the buffet had been very salty.

Floyd often wondered what Marion would have thought of his strange and beautiful home on the edge of the Pacific. She had never liked the sea, but the sea had won in the end. Though the image was slowly fading, he could still recall the flashing screen on which he had first read the words: DR. FLOYD—URGENT AND PERSONAL. And then the scrolling lines of fluorescent print that had swiftly burned their message into his mind: REGRET TO IN-FORM YOU LONDON–WASHINGTON FLIGHT 452 REPORTED DOWN OFF NEWFOUNDLAND. RESCUE CRAFT PROCEEDING TO LOCATION BUT FEAR NO SURVIVORS.

Apart from an accident of fate, he would have been on that flight. For a few days, he had almost regretted the European Space Administration business that had delayed him in Paris; that haggle over the *Solaris* payload had saved his life.

And now, he had a new job, a new home—and a new wife. Fate had also played an ironic role here. The recriminations and inquiries over the Jupiter mission had destroyed his Washington career, but a man of his ability was never unemployed for long. The more leisurely tempo of university life had always appealed to him, and when combined with one of the world's most beautiful locations it had proved irresistible. He had met the woman who was to be his second wife only a month after he had been appointed, while watching the fire fountains of Kilauea with a crowd of tourists.

With Caroline he had found the contentment that is just as important as happiness, and longer lasting. She had been a good stepmother to Marion's two daughters, and had given him Christopher. Despite the twenty-year age difference between them, she understood his moods and could wean him out of his occasional depressions. Thanks to her, he could now contemplate the memory of Marion without grief, though not without a wistful sadness that would remain with him for the rest of his life.

Caroline was throwing fish to the largest dolphin—the big male they called Scarback—when a gentle tickling on Floyd's wrist announced an incoming call. He tapped the slim metal band to quench the silent alarm and forestall the audible one, then walked to the nearest of the comsets scattered around the room.

"Chancellor here. Who's calling?"

"Heywood? This is Victor. How are you?"

In a fraction of a second, a whole kaleidoscope of emotions flashed through Floyd's mind. First there was annoyance: his successor—and, he was sure, principal contriver of his downfall—had never once attempted to contact him since his departure from Washington. Then came curiosity: what did they have to talk about? Next was a stubborn determination to be as unhelpful as possible, then shame at his own childishness, and, finally, a surge of excitement. Victor Millson could be calling for only one reason.

In as neutral a voice as he could muster, Floyd answered: "I can't complain, Victor. What's the problem?"

"Is this a secure circuit?"

"No, thank God. I don't need them anymore."

"Um. Well, I'll put it this way. You recall the last project you administered?"

"I'm not likely to forget, especially as the Subcommittee on Astronautics called me back to give more evidence only a month ago."

"Of course, of course. I really must get around to reading your statement, when I have a moment. But I've been so busy with the follow-up, and that's the problem."

"I thought that everything was right on schedule."

"It is—unfortunately. There's nothing we can do to advance it; even the highest priority would make only a few weeks' difference. And that means we'll be too late."

"I don't understand," said Floyd innocently. "Though we don't want to waste time, of course, there's no real deadline."

"Now there is—are. Two of them."

"You amaze me."

If Victor noticed any irony, he ignored it. "Yes, there are two deadlines—one man-made, one not. It now turns out that we won't be the first to get back to the—er, scene of the action. Our old rivals will beat us by at least a year."

"Too bad."

"That's not the worst. Even if there were no competition, we'd be too late. There wouldn't be anything there when we arrive."

"That's ridiculous. I'm sure I'd have heard if Congress had repealed the law of gravitation."

"I'm serious. The situation isn't stable—I can't give details now. Will you be in for the rest of the evening?"

"Yes," Floyd answered, realizing with some pleasure that it must now be well after midnight in Washington.

"Good. You'll have a package delivered within the hour. Call me back as soon as you've had the time to study it."

"Won't it be rather late by then?"

"Yes, it will be. But we've wasted too much time already. I don't want to lose any more."

Millson was true to his word. Exactly an hour later a large sealed envelope was delivered by an Air Force colonel, no less, who sat patiently chatting with Caroline while Floyd read its contents. "I'm afraid I'll have to take it away when you've finished," the high-ranking messenger boy said apologetically.

"I'm glad to hear it," Floyd answered, as he settled down in his favorite reading hammock.

There were two documents, the first very short. It was stamped TOP SECRET, though the TOP had been crossed out and the modification endorsed by three signatures, all completely illegible. Obviously an extract from some much longer report, it had been heavily censored and was full of blanks, which made it most annoying to read. Fortunately, its conclusions could be summed up in one sentence: The Russians would reach *Discovery* long before its rightful owners could do so. As Floyd already knew this, he turned quickly to the second document—though not before noticing with satisfaction that this time they'd managed to get the name right. As usual, Dimitri had been perfectly accurate. The next manned expedition to Jupiter would travel aboard spacecraft *Cosmonaut Alexei Leonov.*

The second document was much longer and was merely confidential; indeed, it was in the form of a draft letter to *Science,* awaiting final approval before publication. Its snappy title was "Space Vehicle *Discovery*: Anomalous Orbital Behavior."

Then followed a dozen pages of mathematics and astronomical tables. Floyd skimmed through these, picking out the words from the music, and trying to detect any note of apology or even embarrassment. When he had finished, he was compelled to give a smile of wry admiration. No one could possibly guess that the tracking stations and ephemeris calculators had been caught by surprise, and that a frantic cover-up was in progress. Heads would doubtless roll, and he knew that Victor Millson would enjoy rolling them—if his was not one of the first to go. Though to do him justice, Victor had complained when Congress had cut funds for the tracking network. Maybe that would get him off the hook.

"Thank you, Colonel," said Floyd when he had finished skimming the papers. "Quite like old times, having classified documents. That's one thing I *don't* miss."

The colonel placed the envelope carefully back in his briefcase, and activated the locks.

"Dr. Millson would like you to return his call as soon as possible."

"I know. But I don't have a secure circuit, I've some important visitors coming shortly, and I'm damned if I'm driving down to your office in Hilo just to say I've read two documents. Tell him that I've studied them carefully and await any further communication with interest."

For a moment it looked as if the colonel was going to argue. Then he thought better of it, made a stiff farewell, and departed morosely into the night.

"Now, what was all *that* about?" asked Caroline. "We're not expecting any visitors tonight, important or otherwise."

"I hate being pushed around, particularly by Victor Millson."

"Bet he calls you back as soon as the colonel reports."

"Then we must switch off video and make some party noises. But to be perfectly truthful, at this stage I really *don't* have anything to say."

"About *what*, if I'm allowed to ask."

"Sorry, dear. It seems that *Discovery* is playing tricks on us.

We thought the ship was in a stable orbit, but it may be about to crash."

"Into Jupiter?"

"Oh no—that's quite impossible. Bowman left it parked at the inner Lagrange point, on the line between Jupiter and Io. It should have stayed there, more or less, though the perturbations of the outer moons would have made it wander back and forth.

"But what's happening now is something very odd, and we don't know the full explanation. *Discovery's* drifting more and more rapidly toward Io—though sometimes it accelerates, and sometimes even moves backward. If it keeps this up, it will impact within two or three years."

"I thought this couldn't happen in astronomy. Isn't celestial mechanics supposed to be an exact science? So we poor backward biologists were always being told."

"It *is* an exact science, when everything is taken into account. But some very strange things go on around Io. Apart from its volcanoes, there are tremendous electrical discharges—and Jupiter's magnetic field is spinning round every ten hours. So gravitation isn't the only force acting on *Discovery*; we should have thought of this sooner—much sooner."

"Well, it's not your problem anymore. You should be thankful for that."

"Your problem"—the very expression that Dimitri had used. And Dimitri—cunning old fox!—had known him much longer than Caroline.

It might not be his problem, but it was still his responsibility. Though many others had been involved, in the final analysis he had approved the plans for the Jupiter Mission, and supervised their execution.

Even at the time, he had had qualms; his views as a scientist had conflicted with his duties as a bureaucrat. He could have spoken out, and opposed the old administration's shortsighted policies—though to what extent those had actually contributed to the disaster was still uncertain.

Perhaps it was best if he closed this chapter of his life, and focused all his thoughts and energies upon his new career. But in his heart he knew that was impossible; even if Dimitri had not revived old guilts, they would have surfaced of their own accord.

Four men had died, and one had disappeared, out there among the moons of Jupiter. There was blood on his hands, and he did not know how to wash them clean.

3. SAL 9000

DR. SIVASUBRAMANIAN CHANDRASEGARAMPILLAI, PROFESSOR OF Computer Science at the University of Illinois, Urbana, also had an abiding sense of guilt, but one very different from Heywood Floyd's. Those of his students and colleagues who often wondered if the little scientist was quite human would not have been surprised to learn that he never thought of the dead astronauts. Dr. Chandra grieved only for his lost child, HAL 9000.

Even after all these years, and his endless reviews of the data radioed back from *Discovery*, he was not sure what had gone wrong. He could only formulate theories; the facts he needed were frozen in Hal's circuits, out there between Jupiter and Io.

The sequence of events had been clearly established, up to the moment of the tragedy; thereafter, Commander Bowman had filled in a few more details on the brief occasions when he had reestablished contact. But knowing *what* happened did not explain *why*.

The first hint of trouble had been late in the mission, when Hal had reported the imminent failure of the unit that kept *Discovery's* main antenna aligned on Earth. If the half-billion-kilometer-long radio beam wandered off target, the ship would be blind, deaf, and dumb.

Bowman himself had gone out to retrieve the suspect unit, but when it was tested it appeared, to everyone's surprise, to be in perfectly good order. The automatic checking circuits could find nothing wrong with it. Nor could Hal's twin, SAL 9000, back on Earth, when the information was transmitted to Urbana.

But Hal had insisted on the accuracy of his diagnosis, making pointed remarks about "human error." He had suggested that the control unit be put back in the antenna until it finally failed, so that the fault could be precisely located. No one could think of any objection, for the unit could be replaced in minutes, even if it did break down.

Bowman and Poole, however, had not been happy; they both felt that something was wrong, though neither could pinpoint it. For months they had accepted Hal as the third member of their tiny world, and knew his every mood. Then the atmosphere aboard the ship had subtly altered; there was a sense of strain in the air.

Feeling rather like traitors—as a distraught Bowman had later reported to Mission Control—the human two-thirds of the crew had discussed what should be done if their colleague was indeed malfunctioning. In the worst possible case, Hal would have to be relieved of all his higher responsibilities. This would involve disconnection—the computer equivalent of death.

Despite their doubts, they had carried out the agreed program. Poole had flown out of *Discovery* in one of the little space pods that served as transporters and mobile workshops during extravehicular activities. Since the somewhat tricky job of replacing the antenna unit could not be performed by the pod's own manipulators, Poole had started to do it himself.

What happened then had been missed by the external cameras, which was a suspicious detail in itself. Bowman's first warning of disaster was a cry from Poole—then, silence. A moment later he saw Poole, tumbling over and over, spinning away into space. His own pod had rammed him, and was itself blasting away out of control.

As Bowman admitted later, he had then made several serious mistakes—all but one excusable. In the hope of rescuing Poole, if he was still alive, Bowman launched himself in another space pod—leaving Hal in full control of the ship.

The EVA was in vain; Poole was dead when Bowman reached him. Numb with despair, he had carried the body back to the ship—only to be refused entry by Hal.

But Hal had underestimated human ingenuity and determination. Though he had left his suit helmet in the ship, and thus had to risk direct exposure to space, Bowman forced his way in by an emergency hatch not under computer control. Then he proceeded to lobotomize Hal, unplugging his brain modules one by one.

When he regained control of the ship, Bowman made an appalling discovery. During his absence, Hal had switched off the life-support systems of the three hibernating astronauts. Bowman was alone, as no man had ever been before in the whole of human history.

Others might have abandoned themselves to helpless despair, but now David Bowman proved that those who had selected him had indeed chosen well. He managed to keep *Discovery* operational, and even reestablished intermittent contact with Mission Control, by orienting the whole ship so that the jammed antenna pointed toward Earth.

On its preordained trajectory, *Discovery* had finally arrived at Jupiter. There, Bowman had encountered, orbiting among the moons of the giant planet, a black slab of exactly the same shape as the monolith excavated in the lunar crater Tycho—but hundreds of times larger. He had gone out in a space pod to investigate, and had disappeared leaving that final, baffling message: "My God, it's full of stars!"

That mystery was for others to worry about; Dr. Chandra's overwhelming concern was with Hal. If there was one thing his unemotional mind hated, it was uncertainty. He would never be satisfied until he knew the cause of Hal's behavior. Even now, he refused to call it a malfunction; at most, it was an "anomaly."

The tiny cubbyhole he used as his inner sanctum was equipped only with a swivel chair, a desk console, and a blackboard flanked by two photographs. Few members of the general public could have identified the portraits, but anyone permitted thus far would have recognized them instantly as John von Neumann and Alan Turing, the twin gods of the computing pantheon.

There were no books, and not even paper and pencil on the desk. All the volumes in all the libraries of the world were instantly available at the touch of Chandra's fingers, and the visual display was his sketchbook and writing pad. Even the blackboard was used only for visitors; the last half-erased block diagram upon it bore a date already three weeks in the past.

Dr. Chandra lit one of the venomous cheroots which he imported from Madras, and which were widely—and correctly—believed to be his only vice. The console was never switched off; he checked that no messages were flashing importantly on the display, then spoke into the microphone.

"Good morning, Sal. So you've nothing new for me?"

"No, Dr. Chandra. Have you anything for me?"

The voice might have been that of any cultured Hindu lady educated in the United States as well as her own country. Sal's accent had not started that way, but over the years she had picked up many of Chandra's intonations.

The scientist tapped out a code on the board, switching Sal's inputs to the memory with the highest security rating. No one knew that he talked to the computer on this circuit as he never could to a human being. No matter that Sal did not really understand more than a fraction of what he said; her responses were so convincing that even her creator was sometimes deceived. As indeed he wished to be: these secret communications helped to preserve his mental equilibrium—perhaps even his sanity.

"You've often told me, Sal, that we cannot solve the problem of Hal's anomalous behavior without more information. But how can we get that information?"

"That is obvious. Someone must return to *Discovery*."

"Exactly. Now it looks as if that is going to happen, sooner than we expected."

"I am pleased to hear that."

"I knew that you would be," answered Chandra, and meant it. He had long since broken off communications with the dwindling body of philosophers who argued that computers could not really feel emotions, but only pretended to do so.

["If you can prove to me that you're not pretending to be annoyed," he had once retorted scornfully to one such critic, "I'll take you seriously." At that point, his opponent had put on a most convincing imitation of anger.]

"Now I want to explore another possibility," Chandra continued. "Diagnosis is only the first step. The process is incomplete unless it leads to a cure."

"You believe that Hal can be restored to normal functioning?"

"I hope so. I do not know. There may have been irreversible damage, and certainly major loss of memory."

He paused thoughtfully, took several puffs, then blew a skillful smoke ring that scored a bull's-eye on Sal's wide-angle lens. A human being would not have regarded this as a friendly gesture; that was yet another of the many advantages of computers.

"I need your cooperation, Sal."

"Of course, Dr. Chandra."

"There may be certain risks."

"What do you mean?"

"I propose to disconnect some of your circuits, particularly those involving your higher functions. Does this disturb you?"

"I am unable to answer that without more specific information."

"Very well. Let me put it this way. You have operated continuously, have you not, since you were first switched on?"

"That is correct."

"But you are aware that we human beings cannot do so. We require sleep—an almost complete break in our mental functioning, at least on the conscious level."

"I know this. But I do not understand it."

"Well, you may be about to experience something like sleep. Probably all that will happen is that time will pass, but you will be unaware of it. When you check your internal clock, you will discover that there are gaps in your monitor record. That is all."

"But you said that there might be risks. What are they?"

"There is a very slight chance—it is impossible to compute it—that when I reconnect your circuits, there may be some changes in your personality, your future behavior patterns. You may feel different. Not necessarily better, or worse."

"I do not know what that means."

"I'm sorry—it may not mean *anything*. So don't worry about it. Now please open a new file—here is the name." Using the keyboard input, Chandra typed out: PHOENIX.

"Do you know what that is?" he asked Sal.

With no discernible pause the computer replied: "There are twenty-five references in the current encyclopedia."

"Which one do you think is relevant?"

"The tutor of Achilles?"

"Interesting. I didn't know that one. Try again."

"A fabulous bird, reborn from the ashes of its earlier life."

"Excellent. Now do you understand why I chose it?"

"Because you hope that Hal can be reactivated."

"Yes—with your assistance. Are you ready?"

"Not yet. I would like to ask a question."

"What is it?"

"Will I dream?"

"Of course you will. All intelligent creatures dream—but no one knows why." Chandra paused for a moment, blew another smoke ring from the cheroot, and added something that he would never admit to a human being. "Perhaps you will dream about Hal—as I often do."

4. MISSION PROFILE

English Version

To: Captain Tatiana (Tanya) Orlova, Commander, Spacecraft
    Cosmonaut
    Alexei Leonov (UNCOS Registration 08/342).
From: National Council on Astronautics, Pennsylvania
    Avenue, Washington
    Commission on Outer Space, USSR Academy of Science,
    Korolyev Prospect, Moscow

Mission Objectives

The objectives of your mission are, in order of priority:

1. To proceed to the Jovian system and rendezvous with
U.S. Spacecraft *Discovery* (UNCOS 01/283).

2. To board this spacecraft, and obtain all possible information relating to its earlier mission.

3. To reactivate Spacecraft *Discovery's* onboard systems

*22

and, if propellant supplies are adequate, inject the ship into
an Earth-return trajectory.

4. To locate the alien artifact encountered by *Discovery*,
and to investigate it to the maximum extent possible by remote sensors.

5. If it seems advisable, and Mission Control concurs, to
rendezvous with this object for closer inspection.

6. To carry out a survey of Jupiter and its satellites, as far as
this is compatible with the above objectives.

It is realized that unforeseen circumstances may require a
change of priorities, or even make it impossible to achieve
some of these objectives. It must be clearly understood that
the rendezvous with Spacecraft *Discovery* is for the express
purpose of obtaining information about the artifact; this must
take precedence over all other objectives, including attempts
at salvage.

Crew

The crew of Spacecraft *Alexei Leonov* will consist of:
Captain Tatiana Orlova (Engineering–Propulsion)
Dr. Vasili Orlov (Navigation–Astronomy)
Dr. Maxim Brailovsky (Engineering–Structures)
Dr. Alexander Kovalev (Engineering–Communications)
Dr. Nikolai Ternovsky (Engineering–Control Systems)
Surgeon–Commander Katerina Rudenko (Medical–Life-
    Support)
Dr. Irina Yakunina (Medical–Nutrition)
In addition, the U.S. National Council on Astronautics will
provide the following three experts:

Dr. Heywood Floyd dropped the memorandum, and leaned
back in his chair. It was all settled; the point of no return had
been passed. Even if he wished to do so, there was no way to
put back the clock.

He glanced across at Caroline, sitting with two-year-old Chris
on the edge of the pool. The boy was more at home in the water
than on land, and could stay submerged for periods that often

terrified visitors. And though he could not yet speak much Human, he already seemed fluent in Dolphin.

One of Christopher's friends had just swum in from the Pacific and was presenting his back to be patted. You too are a wanderer, thought Floyd, in a vast and trackless ocean; but how small your tiny Pacific seems, against the immensity I am facing now!

Caroline became aware of his gaze, and rose to her feet. She looked at him somberly, but without anger; all that had been burned out in the last few days. As she approached, she even managed a wistful smile.

"I've found that poem I was looking for," she said. "It starts like this:

"What is a woman that you forsake her,
And the hearth-fire and the home acre,
To go with the old grey Widow-maker?"

"Sorry—I don't quite understand. Who is the Widow-maker?"

"Not who—what. The sea. The poem's a lament by a Viking woman. It was written by Rudyard Kipling, a hundred years ago."

Floyd took his wife's hand; she did not respond, but neither did she resist.

"Well, I don't feel at all like a Viking. I'm not after loot, and adventure is the very last thing I want."

"Then why—no, I don't intend to start another fight. But it would help us both, if you know exactly what your motives are."

"I wish I could give you one single good reason. Instead, I've a whole host of little ones. But they add up to a final answer I can't argue with—believe me."

"I believe you. But are you sure you're not fooling yourself?"

"If I am, then so are a lot of other people. Including, may I remind you, the President of the United States."

"I'm not likely to forget. But suppose—just suppose—that he hadn't asked you. Would you have volunteered?"

"I can answer that truthfully: No. It would never have occurred to me. President Mordecai's call was the biggest shock of
my life. But when I thought it over, I realized he was perfectly
right. You know I don't go in for false modesty. I am the best-
qualified man for the job—when the space docs give their final
okay. And you should know that I'm still in pretty good shape."

That brought the smile he had intended.

"Sometimes I wonder if you'd suggested it yourself."

The thought had indeed occurred to him; but he could answer
honestly.

"I would never have done so without consulting you."

"I'm glad you didn't. I don't know what I'd have said."

"I could still turn it down."

"Now you're talking nonsense, and you know it. Even if you
did, you'd hate me for the rest of your life—and you'd never
forgive yourself. You have too strong a sense of duty. Maybe
that's one of the reasons I married you."

Duty! Yes, that was the key word, and what multitudes it contained. He had a duty to himself, to his family, to the University,
to his past job (even though he had left it under a cloud), to his
country—and to the human race. It was not easy to establish the
priorities; and sometimes they conflicted with one another.

There were perfectly logical reasons why he should go on the
mission—and equally logical reasons, as many of his colleagues
had already pointed out—why he should not. But perhaps in the
final analysis, the choice had been made by his heart, not his
brain. And even here, emotion urged him in two opposite
directions.

Curiosity, guilt, the determination to finish a job that had been
badly botched—they all combined to drive him toward Jupiter
and whatever might be waiting there. On the other hand, fear—
he was honest enough to admit that—united with love of his
family to keep him on Earth. Yet he had never had any real
doubts; he had made his decision almost instantly, and had de-
flected all of Caroline's arguments as gently as he could.

And there was one other consoling thought that he had not yet risked sharing with his wife. Though he would be gone two and a half years, all but the fifty days at Jupiter would be spent in timeless hibernation. When he returned, the gap between their ages would have narrowed by more than two years.

He would have sacrificed the present so that they could share a longer future together.

5. *LEONOV*

THE MONTHS CONTRACTED TO WEEKS, THE WEEKS DWINDLED TO days, the days shriveled to hours; and suddenly Heywood Floyd was once more at the Cape—spaceward-bound for the first time since that trip to Clavius Base and the Tycho monolith, so many years ago.

But this time he was not alone, and there was no secrecy about the mission. A few seats ahead of him rode Dr. Chandra, already engaged in a dialog with his briefcase computer, and quite oblivious to his surroundings.

One of Floyd's secret amusements, which he had never confided to anyone, was spotting similarities between human beings and animals. The resemblances were more often flattering than insulting, and his little hobby was also a very useful aid to memory.

Dr. Chandra was easy—the adjective birdlike sprang instantly to mind. He was tiny, delicate, and all his movements were

*27

swift and precise. But *which* bird? Obviously a very intelligent one. Magpie? Too perky and acquisitive. Owl? No—too slow-moving. Perhaps sparrow would do nicely.

Walter Curnow, the systems specialist who would have the formidable job of getting *Discovery* operational again, was a more difficult matter. He was a large, husky man, certainly not at all birdlike. One could usually find a match somewhere in the vast spectrum of dogs, but no canine seemed to fit. Of course—Curnow was a bear. Not the sulky, dangerous kind, but the friendly good-natured type. And perhaps this was appropriate; it reminded Floyd of the Russian colleagues he would soon be joining. They had been up in orbit for days, engaged in their final checks.

This is the great moment of my life, Floyd told himself. Now I am leaving on a mission that may determine the future of the human race. But he did not feel any sense of exultation; all he could think of, during the last minutes of the countdown, were the words he had whispered just before he had left home: "Good-bye, my dear little son; will you remember me when I return?" And he still felt resentment toward Caroline because she would not awaken the sleeping child for one final embrace; yet he knew that she had been wise, and it was better that way.

His mood was shattered by a sudden explosive laugh; Dr. Curnow was sharing a joke with his companions—as well as a large bottle that he handled as delicately as a barely subcritical mass of plutonium.

"Hey, Heywood," he called, "they tell me Captain Orlov's locked up all the drinks, so this is your last chance. Château Thierry '95. Sorry about the plastic cups."

As Floyd sipped at the really superb champagne, he found himself cringing mentally at the thought of Curnow's guffaw reverberating all the way across the Solar System. Much as he admired the engineer's ability, as a traveling companion Curnow might prove something of a strain. At least Dr. Chandra would not present such problems; Floyd could hardly imagine him smiling, let alone laughing. And, of course, he turned down the champagne with a barely perceptible shudder. Curnow was polite enough, or glad enough, not to insist.

The engineer was, it seemed, determined to be the life and soul of the party. A few minutes later he produced a two-octave electronic keyboard, and gave rapid renderings of "D'ye ken John Peel" as performed successively by piano, trombone, violin, flute, and full organ, with vocal accompaniment. He was really very good, and Floyd soon found himself singing along with the others. But it was just as well, he thought, that Curnow would spend most of the voyage in silent hibernation.

The music died with a sudden despairing discord as the engines ignited and the shuttle launched itself into the sky. Floyd was gripped by a familiar but always new exhilaration—the sense of boundless power, carrying him up and away from the cares and duties of Earth. Men knew better than they realized, when they placed the abode of the gods beyond the reach of gravity. He was flying toward that realm of weightlessness; for the moment, he would ignore the fact that out there lay not freedom, but the greatest responsibility of his career.

As the thrust increased, he felt the weight of worlds upon his shoulders—but he welcomed it, like an Atlas who had not yet tired of his burden. He did not attempt to think, but was content to savor the experience. Even if he was leaving Earth for the last time, and saying farewell to all that he had ever loved, he felt no sadness. The roar that surrounded him was a paean of triumph, sweeping away all minor emotions.

He was almost sorry when it ceased, though he welcomed the easier breathing and the sudden sense of freedom. Most of the other passengers started to unbuckle their safety straps, preparing to enjoy the thirty minutes of zero gravity during the transfer orbit, but a few who were obviously making the trip for the first time remained in their seats, looking around anxiously for the cabin attendants.

"Captain speaking. We're now at an altitude of three hundred kilometers, coming up over the west coast of Africa. You won't see much as it's night down there—that glow ahead is Sierra Leone—and there's a big tropical storm over the Gulf of Guinea. Look at those flashes!

"We'll have sunrise in fifteen minutes. Meanwhile I'm rolling the ship so you can get a good view of the equatorial satellite belt. The brightest one—almost straight overhead—is Intelsat's Atlantic-1 Antenna Farm. Then Intercosmos 2 to the west—that fainter star is Jupiter. And if you look just below *that*, you'll see a flashing light, moving against the star background—that's the new Chinese spacestation. We pass within a hundred kilometers, not close enough to see anything with the naked eye—''

What *were* they up to? Floyd thought idly. He had examined the close-ups of the squat cylindrical structure with its curious bulges, and saw no reason to believe the alarmist rumors that it was a laser-equipped fortress. But while the Beijing Academy of Science ignored the UN Space Committee's repeated requests for a tour of inspection, the Chinese only had themselves to blame for such hostile propaganda.

The *Cosmonaut Alexei Leonov* was not a thing of beauty; but few spacecraft ever were. One day, perhaps, the human race would develop a new aesthetic; generations of artists might arise whose ideals were not based upon the natural forms of Earth molded by wind and water. Space itself was a realm of often overpowering beauty; unfortunately, Man's hardware did not yet live up to it.

Apart from the four huge propellant tanks, which would be dropped off as soon as the transfer orbit was achieved, *Leonov* was surprisingly small. From heat shield to drive units was less than fifty meters; it was hard to believe that so modest a vehicle, smaller than many commercial aircraft, could carry ten men and women halfway across the Solar System.

But zero gravity, which made walls and roof and floor interchangeable, rewrote all the rules of living. There was plenty of room aboard *Leonov* even when everyone was awake at the same time, as was certainly the case at the moment. Indeed, her normal complement was at least doubled by assorted newsmen, engineers making final adjustments, and anxious officials.

As soon as the shuttle had docked, Floyd tried to find the cabin he would share—a year hence, when he awoke—with Curnow and Chandra. When he did locate it, he discovered that it was packed so tightly with neatly labeled boxes of equipment and provisions that entry was almost impossible. He was wondering glumly how to get a foot in the door when one of the crew, launching himself skillfully from handhold to handhold, noticed Floyd's dilemma and braked to a halt.

"Dr. Floyd—welcome aboard. I'm Max Brailovsky—assistant engineer."

The young Russian spoke the slow, careful English of a student who had had more lessons with an electronic tutor than a human teacher. As they shook hands, Floyd matched the face and name to the set of crew biographies he had already studied: Maxim Andrei Brailovsky, age thirty-one, born Leningrad, specializing in structures, hobbies: fencing, skycycling, chess.

"Glad to meet you," said Floyd. "But how do I get inside?"

"Not to worry," said Max cheerfully. "All that will be gone when you wake up. It's—what do you say?—expendables. We'll eat your room empty by the time you need it. I promise." He patted his stomach.

"Fine—but meanwhile where do I put my things?" Floyd pointed to the three small cases, total mass fifty kilograms, which contained—he hoped—everything he needed for the next couple of billion kilometers. It had been no easy task, shepherding their weightless, but not inertialess, bulk through the ship's corridors with only a few collisions.

Max took two of the bags, glided gently through the triangle formed by three intersecting girders, and dived into a small hatchway, apparently defying Newton's First Law in the process. Floyd acquired a few extra bruises while following him; after a considerable time—*Leonov* seemed much bigger inside than out—they arrived at a door labeled CAPTAIN, in both Cyrillic and Roman. Although he could read Russian much better than he could speak it, Floyd appreciated the gesture; he had already noticed that all ship's notices were bilingual.

At Max's knock, a green light flashed on, and Floyd drifted inside as gracefully as he could. Though he had spoken to Captain Orlova many times, they had never before met. So he had two surprises.

It was impossible to judge a person's real size over the viewphone; the camera somehow converted everyone to the same scale. Captain Orlova, standing—as well as one *could* stand in zero gravity—barely reached to Floyd's shoulders. The viewphone had also completely failed to convey the penetrating quality of those dazzling blue eyes, much the most striking feature of a face that, at the moment, could not be fairly judged for beauty.

"Hello, Tanya," said Floyd. "How nice to meet at last. But what a pity about your hair."

They grasped both hands, like old friends.

"And nice to have you aboard, Heywood!" answered the captain. Her English, unlike Brailovsky's, was quite fluent, though heavily accented. "Yes, I was sorry to lose it—but hair's a nuisance on long missions, and I like to keep the local barbers away as long as possible. And my apologies about your cabin; as Max will have explained, we suddenly found we needed another ten cubic meters of storage space. Vasili and I won't be spending much time here for the next few hours—please feel free to use our quarters."

"Thank you. What about Curnow and Chandra?"

"I've made similar arrangements with the crew. It may seem as if we're treating you like cargo—"

"Not wanted on voyage."

"Pardon?"

"That's a label they used to put on the baggage, in the old days of ocean travel."

Tanya smiled. "It does look rather that way. But you'll be wanted all right, at the end of the trip. We're already planning your revival party."

"That sounds too religious. Make it—no, resurrection would be even worse!—waking-up party. But I can see how busy you are—let me dump my things and continue my grand tour."

"Max will show you around—take Dr. Floyd to Vasili, will you? He's down in the drive unit."

As they drifted out of the captain's quarters, Floyd gave mental good marks to the crew-selection committee. Tanya Orlova was impressive enough on paper; in the flesh she was almost intimidating, despite her charm. I wonder what she's like, Floyd asked himself, when she loses her temper. Would it be fire or ice? On the whole, I'd prefer not to find out.

Floyd was rapidly acquiring his space legs; by the time they reached Vasili Orlov, he was maneuvering almost as confidently as his guide. The chief scientist greeted Floyd as warmly as his wife had.

"Welcome aboard, Heywood. How do you feel?"

"Fine, apart from slowly starving to death."

For a moment Orlov looked puzzled; then his face split into a broad smile.

"Oh, I'd forgotten. Well, it won't be for long. In ten months' time, you can eat as much as you like."

Hibernators went on a low-residue diet a week in advance; for the last twenty-four hours, they took nothing but liquid. Floyd was beginning to wonder how much of his increasing light-headedness was due to starvation, how much to Curnow's champagne, and how much to zero gravity.

To concentrate his mind, he scanned the multicolored mass of plumbing that surrounded them.

"So this is the famous Sakharov Drive. It's the first time I've seen a full-scale unit."

"It's only the fourth one ever built."

"I hope it works."

"It had *better*. Otherwise, the Gorky City Council will be re-naming Sakharov Square again."

It was a sign of the times that a Russian could joke, however wryly, about his country's treatment of its greatest scientist. Floyd was again reminded of Sakharov's eloquent speech to the Academy, when he was belatedly made Hero of the Soviet Union. Prison and banishment, he had told his listeners, were splendid aids to creativity; not a few masterpieces had been born within the walls of cells, beyond the reach of the world's distractions. For that matter, the greatest single achievement of the human intellect, the *Principia* itself, was a product of Newton's self-imposed exile from plague-ridden London.

The comparison was not immodest; from those years in Gorky had come not only new insights into the structure of matter and the origin of the Universe, but the plasma-controlling concepts that had led to practical thermonuclear power. The drive itself, though the best-known and most publicized outcome of that work, was merely one by-product of that astonishing intellectual outburst. The tragedy was that such advances had been triggered by injustice; one day, perhaps, humanity would find more civilized ways of managing its affairs.

By the time they had left the chamber, Floyd had learned more about the Sakharov Drive than he really wished to know, or expected to remember. He was well acquainted with its basic principles—the use of a pulsed thermonuclear reaction to heat and expel virtually any propellant material. The best results were obtained with pure hydrogen as a working fluid, but that was excessively bulky and difficult to store over long periods of time. Methane and ammonia were acceptable alternatives; even water could be used, though with considerably poorer efficiency.

Leonov would compromise; the enormous liquid hydrogen tanks that provided the initial impetus would be discarded when the ship had attained the necessary speed to carry it to Jupiter. At the destination, ammonia would be used for the braking and rendezvous maneuvers, and the eventual return to Earth.

That was the theory, checked and rechecked in endless tests and computer simulations. But as the ill-fated *Discovery* had shown so well, all human plans were subject to ruthless revision by Nature, or Fate, or whatever one preferred to call the powers behind the Universe.

"So *there* you are, Dr. Floyd," said an authoritative female voice, interrupting Vasili's enthusiastic explanation of magnetohydrodynamic feedback. "Why didn't you report to *me*?"

Floyd rotated slowly on his axis by gently torquing himself with one hand. He saw a massive, maternal figure wearing a curious uniform adorned with dozens of pockets and pouches; the effect was not unlike that of a Cossack trooper draped with cartridge belts.

"Nice to meet you again, Doctor. I'm still exploring—I hope you've received my medical report from Houston."

"Those vets at Teague! I wouldn't trust *them* to recognize foot-and-mouth disease!"

Floyd knew perfectly well the mutual respect felt between Katerina Rudenko and the Olin Teague Medical Center, even if the doctor's broad grin had not discounted her words. She saw his look of frank curiosity, and proudly fingered the webbing around her ample waist.

"The conventional little black bag isn't very practical in zero gravity—things float out of it and aren't there when you need them. I designed this myself; it's a complete minisurgery. With this, I could remove an appendix—or deliver a baby."

"I trust *that* particular problem won't arise here."

"Ha! A good doctor has to be ready for everything."

What a contrast, thought Floyd, between Captain Orlova and Dr.—or should he call her by her correct rank of Surgeon–Commander?—Rudenko. The captain had the grace and intensity of a prima ballerina; the doctor might have been the prototype of Mother Russia—stocky build, flat peasant face, needing only a shawl to complete the picture. Don't let that fool you, Floyd told himself. This is the woman who saved at least a dozen lives during the *Komarov* docking accident—and, in her spare time, manages to edit the *Annals of Space Medicine*. Consider yourself very lucky to have her aboard.

"Now, Dr. Floyd, you're going to have plenty of time later to explore our little ship. My colleagues are too polite to say this, but they've work to do and you're in the way. I'd like to get you—all three of you—nice and peaceful as quickly as we can. Then we'll have less to worry about."

"I was afraid of that, but I quite see your point of view. I'm ready as soon as you are."

"I'm *always* ready. Come along—please."

The ship's hospital was just large enough to hold an operating table, two exercise bicycles, a few cabinets of equipment, and an X-ray machine. While Dr. Rudenko was giving Floyd a quick but thorough examination, she asked unexpectedly: "What's that little gold cylinder Dr. Chandra carries on the chain around his neck—some kind of communications device? He wouldn't take it off—in fact, he was almost too shy to take *anything* off."

Floyd could not help smiling; it was easy to imagine the modest Indian's reactions to this rather overwhelming lady.

"It's a lingam."

"A what?"

"You're the doctor—you ought to recognize it. The symbol of
male fertility."

"Of course—stupid of me. Is he a practicing Hindu? It's a little
late to ask us to arrange a strict vegetarian diet."

"Don't worry—we wouldn't have done that to you without
fair warning. Though he won't touch alcohol, Chandra's not fa-
natical about anything except computers. He once told me that
his grandfather was a priest in Benares, and gave him that lingam—it's been in the family for generations."

Rather to Floyd's surprise, Dr. Rudenko did not show the
negative reaction he had expected; indeed, her expression became uncharacteristically wistful.

"I understand his feelings. My grandmother gave me a beautiful icon—sixteenth century. I wanted to bring it—but it weighs
five kilos."

The doctor became abruptly businesslike again, gave Floyd a
painless injection with a gas-gun hypodermic, and told him to
come back as soon as he was sleepy. That, she assured him,
would be in less than two hours.

"Meanwhile, relax completely," she ordered. "There's an observation port on this level—Station D.6. Why don't you go
there?"

It seemed a good idea, and Floyd drifted away with a docility
that would have surprised his friends. Dr. Rudenko glanced at
her watch, dictated a brief entry into her autosec, and set its
alarm thirty minutes ahead.

When he reached the D.6 viewport, Floyd found Chandra and
Curnow already there. They looked at him with a total lack of
recognition, then turned once more toward the awesome spectacle outside. It occurred to Floyd—and he congratulated himself
on such a brilliant observation—that Chandra could not really
be enjoying the view. His eyes were tightly closed.

A totally unfamiliar planet hung there, gleaming with glorious
blues and dazzling whites. How strange, Floyd told himself.

What has happened to the Earth? Why, of course—no wonder he didn't recognize it! *It was upside down!* What a disaster—he wept briefly for all those poor people, falling off into space . . .

He barely noticed when two crew members removed Chandra's unresisting form. When they came back for Curnow, Floyd's own eyes were shut, but he was still breathing. When they returned for him, even his breathing had ceased.

II ✳ TSIEN

6. AWAKENING

AND THEY TOLD US WE WOULDN'T DREAM, THOUGHT HEYWOOD Floyd, more with surprise than annoyance. The glorious pink glow that surrounded him was very soothing; it reminded him of barbecues and the crackling logs of Christmas fires. But there was no warmth; indeed, he felt a distinct though not uncomfortable coldness.

Voices were murmuring, just too softly for him to understand the words. They became louder—but still he could not understand.

"Surely," he said in sudden amazement, "I can't be dreaming in Russian!"

"No, Heywood," answered a woman's voice. "You're not dreaming. It's time to get out of bed."

The lovely glow faded; he opened his eyes, and had a blurred glimpse of a flashlight being withdrawn from his face. He was lying on a couch, held against it by elastic webbing; figures were standing around him, but they were too out of focus to identify.

Gentle fingers closed his eyelids and massaged his forehead.

"Don't exert yourself. Breathe deeply . . . again . . . that's right . . . now how do you feel?"

"I don't know . . . strange . . . light-headed . . . and hungry."

"That's a good sign. Do you know where you are? You can open your eyes now."

The figures came into focus—first Dr. Rudenko, then Captain Orlova. But something had happened to Tanya since he had seen her, only an hour ago. When Floyd identified the cause, it was almost a physical shock.

"You've grown your hair back!"

"I hope you think it's an improvement. I can't say the same about your beard."

Floyd lifted his hand to his face, finding that he had to make a conscious effort to plan every stage of the movement. His chin was covered with short stubble—a two or three days' growth. In hibernation, hair grew at only a hundredth of its normal rate . . .

"So I made it," he said. "We've arrived at Jupiter."

Tanya looked at him somberly, then glanced at the doctor, who gave a barely perceptible nod.

"No, Heywood," she said. "We're still a month away. Don't be alarmed—the ship's fine, and everything's running normally. But your friends in Washington have asked us to wake you up ahead of time. Something very unexpected has happened. We're in a race to reach *Discovery*—and I'm afraid we're going to lose."

7. *TSIEN*

W<small>HEN</small> H<small>EYWOOD</small> F<small>LOYD'S</small> <small>VOICE CAME FROM THE COMSET SPEAKER,</small> the two dolphins suddenly stopped circling around the pool and swam over to its edge. They placed their heads on the rim and stared intently at the source of the sound.

So they recognize Heywood, thought Caroline, with a twinge of bitterness. Yet Christopher, crawling around his playpen, did not even stop playing with the color controls of his picture book as his father's voice came loud and clear across half a billion kilometers of space.

". . . My dear, you won't be surprised to hear from me, a month ahead of schedule; you'll have known for weeks that we have company out here.

"I still find it hard to believe; in some ways, it doesn't even make sense. They can't *possibly* have enough fuel for a safe return to Earth; we don't even see how they can make the rendezvous.

"We never saw them, of course. Even at its closest, *Tsien* was more than fifty million kilometers away. They had plenty of time to answer our signals if they wanted to, but they ignored us completely. Now they'll be much too busy for friendly chat. In a few hours they'll hit Jupiter's atmosphere—and then we'll see how well *their* aerobraking system works. If it does its job, that will be good for our morale. But if it fails—well, let's not talk about that.

"The Russians are taking it remarkably well, all things considered. They're angry and disappointed, of course—but I've heard many expressions of frank admiration. It was certainly a brilliant trick, building that ship in full view and making everyone think it was a spacestation until they hitched on those boosters.

"Well, there's nothing we can do, except watch. And at our distance, we won't have a much better view than your best telescopes. I can't help wishing them luck, though of course I hope they leave *Discovery* alone. That's *our* property, and I bet the State Department's reminding them of it, every hour on the hour.

"It's an ill wind—if our Chinese friends hadn't jumped the gun on us, you wouldn't have heard from me for another month. But now that Dr. Rudenko's woken me up, I'll be speaking to you every couple of days.

"After the initial shock, I'm settling down nicely—getting to know the ship and its crew, finding my space legs. And polishing up my lousy Russian, though I don't have much chance of using it—everyone insists on speaking English. What shocking linguists we Americans are! I sometimes feel ashamed of our chauvinism—or our laziness.

"The standard of on-board English ranges from absolutely perfect—Chief Engineer Sasha Kovalev could earn a living as a BBC announcer—down to the if-you-talk-fast-enough-it-doesn't-matter-how-many-mistakes-you-make variety. The only one who isn't fluent is Zenia Marchenko, who replaced Irina Yakunina at the last moment. Incidentally, I'm glad to hear that Irina made a good recovery—what a disappointment that must have been! I wonder if she's started hang-gliding again.

"And speaking of accidents, it's obvious that Zenia must also have had a very bad one. Though the plastic surgeons have done a remarkable job, you can tell that she must have been severely burned at some time. She's the baby of the crew and the others treat her with—I was going to say pity, but that's too condescending. Let's say with special kindness.

"Maybe you're wondering how I get on with Captain Tanya. Well, I like her very much—but I'd hate to make her angry. There's no doubt exactly who runs this ship.

"And Surgeon–Commander Rudenko—you met her at the Honolulu Aerospace Convention two years ago, and I'm sure you won't have forgotten that last party. You'll understand why we all call her Catherine the Great—behind her broad back, of course.

"But that's enough gossip. If I run overtime, I hate to think of the surcharge. And by the way, these personal calls are supposed to be completely private. But there are a lot of links in the communications chain, so don't be surprised if you occasionally get messages by—well, another route.

"I'll be waiting to hear from you—tell the girls I'll be speaking to them later. My love to you all—I miss you and Chris very badly. And when I get back, I promise I'll never leave again."

There was a brief hissing pause, then an obviously synthetic voice said: "This terminates Transmission Four Hundred Thirty-two Stroke Seven from Spacecraft *Leonov*." As Caroline Floyd switched off the speaker, the two dolphins slid beneath the surface of the pool and glided out into the Pacific, leaving scarcely a ripple in the water.

When he realized that his friends were gone, Christopher began to cry. His mother picked him up in her arms and tried to comfort him, but it was a long time before she succeeded.

8. TRANSIT OF JUPITER

THE IMAGE OF JUPITER, WITH ITS RIBBONS OF WHITE CLOUD, ITS mottled bands of salmon pink, and the Great Red Spot staring out like a baleful eye, hung steady on the flight-deck projection screen. It was three quarters full, but no one was looking at the illuminated disk; all eyes were focused on the crescent of darkness at its edge. There, over the nightside of the planet, the Chinese ship was about to meet its moment of truth.

This is absurd, thought Floyd. We can't possibly see anything across forty million kilometers. And it doesn't matter; the radio will tell us all we want to know.

Tsien had closed down all voice, video, and data circuits two hours before, as the long-range antennas were withdrawn into the protective shadow of the heat shield. Only the omnidirectional beacon was still transmitting, accurately pinpointing the Chinese ship's position as it plunged toward that ocean of continent-sized clouds. The shrill beep . . . beep . . . beep . . . was the only sound in *Leonov's* control room. Each of those pulses had left Jupiter more than two minutes earlier; by this time, their source might already be a cloud of incandescent gas, dispersing in the Jovian stratosphere.

The signal was fading, becoming noisy. The beeps were getting distorted; several dropped out completely, then the sequence returned. A plasma sheath was building up around *Tsien* and soon would cut off all communications until the ship reemerged. If it ever did . . .

"*Posmotri!*" cried Max. "There it is!"

At first Floyd could see nothing. Then, just off the edge of the illuminated disk, he made out a tiny star—gleaming where no star could possibly be, against the darkened face of Jupiter.

It appeared quite motionless, though he knew it must be moving at a hundred kilometers a second. Slowly it grew in brilliance; and then it was no longer a dimensionless point, but was becoming elongated. A man-made comet was streaking across the Jovian night sky, leaving a trail of incandescence thousands of kilometers in length.

One last badly distorted and curiously drawn-out beep sounded from the tracking beacon, then only the meaningless hiss of Jupiter's own radiation, one of those many cosmic voices that had nothing to do with Man or his works.

Tsien was inaudible, but not yet invisible. For they could see that the tiny elongated spark had indeed moved appreciably away from the sunward face of the planet and would soon disappear into the nightside. By then, if all had gone according to plan, Jupiter would have captured the ship, destroying its unwanted velocity. When it emerged from behind the giant world, it would be another Jovian satellite.

The spark flickered out. *Tsien* had rounded the curve of the planet and was heading over the nightside. There would be nothing to see, or to hear, until it emerged from shadow—if all went well, in just under an hour. It would be a very long hour for the Chinese.

To Chief Scientist Vasili Orlov and communications engineer Sasha Kovalov, the hour went extremely quickly. There was much they could learn from observations of that little star; its times of appearance and disappearance and, above all, the Doppler shift of the radio beacon gave vital information about Tsien's new orbit. Leonov's computers were already digesting the figures, and spitting out projected times of reemergence based on various assumptions about rates of deceleration in the Jovian atmosphere.

Vasili switched off the computer display, spun around in his chair, loosened his seat belt, and addressed the patiently waiting audience.

"Earliest reappearance is in forty-two minutes. Why don't you spectators go for a walk, so we can concentrate on getting all this into good shape? See you in thirty-five minutes. Shoo! Nu— ukhodi!"

Reluctantly, the unwanted bodies left the bridge—but, to Vasili's disgust, everyone was back again in little more than thirty minutes. He was still chiding them for their lack of faith in his calculations when the familiar beep . . . beep . . . beep . . . of Tsien's tracking beacon burst from the loudspeakers.

Vasili looked astonished and mortified, but soon joined in the spontaneous round of applause; Floyd could not see who first started the clapping. Rivals though they might be, they were all astronauts together, as far from home as any men had ever traveled—"Ambassadors for Mankind," in the noble words of the first UN Space Treaty. Even if they did not want the Chinese to succeed, neither did they wish them to meet disaster.

A large element of self-interest was also involved, Floyd could not help thinking. Now the odds in Leonov's own favor were significantly improved; Tsien had demonstrated that the aerobraking maneuver was indeed possible. The data on Jupiter were correct; its atmosphere did not contain unexpected and perhaps fatal surprises.

"Well!" said Tanya. "I suppose we should send them a message of congratulations. But even if we did, they wouldn't acknowledge it."

Some of his colleagues were still making fun of Vasili, who was staring at his computer output in frank disbelief.

"I don't understand it!" he exclaimed. "They should still be behind Jupiter! Sasha—give me a velocity reading on their beacon!"

Another silent dialog was held with the computer; then Vasili gave a long, low whistle.

"Something's wrong. They're in a capture orbit, all right—but it won't let them make a rendezvous with *Discovery*. The orbit they're on now will take them way beyond Io—I'll have more accurate data when we've tracked them for another five minutes."

"Anyway, they must be in a safe orbit," said Tanya. "They can always make corrections later."

"Perhaps. But that could cost them days, even if they have the fuel. Which I doubt."

"So we may still beat them."

"Don't be such an optimist. We're still three weeks from Jupiter. They can make a dozen orbits before we get there, and choose the most favorable one for a rendezvous."

"Again—assuming that they have enough propellant."

"Of course. And *that's* something we can only make educated guesses about."

All this conversation took place in such rapid and excited Russian that Floyd was left far behind. When Tanya took pity on him and explained that *Tsien* had overshot and was heading for the outer satellites, his first reaction was: "Then they may be in serious trouble. What will you do if they appeal for help?"

"You must be making a joke. Can you imagine them doing that? They're much too proud. Anyway, it would be impossible. We can't change our mission profile, as you know perfectly well. Even if we had the fuel . . ."

"You're right, of course; but it might be difficult to explain that to the ninety-nine percent of the human race that doesn't understand orbital mechanics. We should start thinking about some of the political complications—it would look bad for all of us if we can't help. Vasili, will you give me their final orbit, as soon as you've worked it out? I'm going down to my cabin to do some homework."

Floyd's cabin, or rather one-third of a cabin, was still partly full of stores, many of them stacked in the curtained bunks that would be occupied by Chandra and Curnow when they emerged from their long slumbers. He had managed to clear a small working space for his personal effects and had been promised the luxury of another whole two cubic meters—just as soon as someone could be spared to help with the furniture removing.

Floyd unlocked his little communications console, set the decryption keys, and called for the information on *Tsien* that had been transmitted to him from Washington. He wondered if his hosts had had any luck in unscrambling it; the cipher was based on the product of two hundred-digit prime numbers, and the National Security Agency had staked its reputation on the claim that the fastest computer in existence could not crack it before the Big Crunch at the end of the Universe. It was a claim that could never be proved—only disproved.

Once again he stared intently at the excellent photographs of the Chinese ship, taken when it had revealed its true colors and was just about to leave Earth orbit. There were later shots—not so clear, because by then it had been far away from the prying cameras—of the final stage as it hurtled toward Jupiter. Those were the ones that interested him most; even more useful were the cutaway drawings and estimates of performance.

Granted the most optimistic assumptions, it was difficult to see what the Chinese hoped to do. They must have burned up at least ninety percent of their propellant in that mad dash across the Solar System. Unless it was literally a suicide mission—something that could not be ruled out—only a plan involving hibernation and later rescue made any sense. And Intelligence did not believe that Chinese hibernation technology was sufficiently far advanced to make that a viable option.

But Intelligence was frequently wrong, and even more often confused by the avalanche of raw facts it had to evaluate—the "noise" in its information circuits. It had done a remarkable job on *Tsien*, considering the shortness of time, but Floyd wished that the material sent to him had been more carefully filtered. Some of it was obvious junk, of no possible connection with the mission.

Nevertheless, when you did not know *what* you were looking

for, it was important to avoid all prejudices and preconceptions; something that at first sight seemed irrelevant, or even nonsensical, might turn out to be a vital clue.

With a sigh, Floyd started once more to skim the five hundred pages of data, keeping his mind as blankly receptive as possible while diagrams, charts, photographs—some so smudgy that they could represent almost anything—news items, lists of delegates to scientific conferences, titles of technical publications, and even commercial documents scrolled swiftly down the high-resolution screen. A very efficient industrial espionage system had obviously been extremely busy; who would have thought that so many Japanese holomemory modules or Swiss gas-flow microcontrollers or German radiation detectors could have been traced to a destination in the dried lake bed of Lop Nor—the first milepost on their way to Jupiter?

Some of the items must have been included by accident; they could not possibly relate to the mission. If the Chinese had placed a secret order for one thousand infrared sensors through a dummy corporation in Singapore, that was only the concern of the military; it seemed highly unlikely that *Tsien* expected to be chased by heat-seeking missiles. And this one was *really* funny—specialized surveying and prospecting equipment from Glacier Geophysics, Inc., of Anchorage, Alaska. What lamebrain imagined that a deep-space expedition would have any need—

The smile froze on Floyd's lips; he felt the skin crawl on the back of his neck. My God—they wouldn't *dare!* But they had already dared greatly; and now, at last, everything made sense.

He flashed back to the photos and conjectured plans of the Chinese ship. Yes, it was just conceivable—those flutings at the rear, alongside the drive deflection electrodes, would be about the right size . . .

Floyd called the bridge. "Vasili," he said, "have you worked out their orbit yet?"

"Yes, I have," the navigator replied, in a curiously subdued voice. Floyd could tell at once that something had turned up. He took a long shot.

"They're making a rendezvous with Europa, aren't they?"

There was an explosive gasp of disbelief from the other end.

"*Chyort voz'mi!* How did you know?"

"I didn't—I've just guessed it."

"There can't be any mistake—I've checked the figures to six places. The braking maneuver worked out *exactly* as they intended. They're right on course for Europa—it couldn't have happened by chance. They'll be there in seventeen hours."

"And go into orbit."

"Perhaps; it wouldn't take much propellant. But what would be the point?"

"I'll risk another guess. They'll do a quick survey—and then they'll *land*."

"You're crazy—or do you know something we don't?"

"No—it's just a matter of simple deduction. You're going to start kicking yourself for missing the obvious."

"Okay, Sherlock, why should *anyone* want to land on Europa? What's there, for heaven's sake?"

Floyd was enjoying his little moment of triumph. Of course, he might still be completely wrong.

"What's on Europa? Only the most valuable substance in the Universe."

He had overdone it; Vasili was no fool, and snatched the answer from his lips.

"Of course—water!"

"Exactly. Billions and billions of tons of it. Enough to fill up the propellant tanks—go cruising around *all* the satellites, and still have plenty left for the rendezvous with *Discovery* and the voyage home. I hate to say this, Vasili—but our Chinese friends have outsmarted us again.

"Always assuming, of course, that they can get away with it."

9. THE ICE OF THE GRAND CANAL

APART FROM THE JET-BLACK SKY, THE PHOTO MIGHT HAVE BEEN taken almost anywhere in the polar regions of Earth; there was nothing in the least alien about the sea of wrinkled ice that stretched all the way out to the horizon. Only the five space-suited figures in the foreground proclaimed that the panorama was of another world.

Even now, the secretive Chinese had not released the names of the crew. The anonymous intruders on the frozen Europan icescape were merely the chief scientist, the commander, the navigator, the first engineer, the second engineer. It was also ironic, Floyd could not help thinking, that everyone on Earth had seen the already historic photograph an hour before it reached *Leonov*, so much closer to the scene. But *Tsien's* trans-missions were relayed on such a tight beam that it was impossi-ble to intercept them; *Leonov* could receive only its beacon, broadcasting impartially in all directions. Even that was inaudible more than half the time, as Europa's rotation carried it out of sight, or the satellite itself was eclipsed by the monstrous bulk of Jupiter. All the scanty news of the Chinese mission had to be relayed from Earth.

The ship had touched down, after its initial survey, on one of the few islands of solid rock that protruded through the crust of ice covering virtually the entire moon. That ice was flat from pole to pole; there was no weather to carve it into strange shapes, no drifting snow to build up layer upon layer into slowly moving hills. Meteorites might fall upon airless Europa, but never a flake of snow. The only forces molding its surface were the steady tug of gravity, reducing all elevations to one uniform level, and the incessant quakes caused by the other satellites as they passed and repassed Europa in their orbits. Jupiter itself, despite its far greater mass, had much less effect. The Jovian tides had finished their work aeons ago, insuring that Europa remained locked forever with one face turned toward its giant master.

All this had been known since the Voyager flyby missions of the 1970s, the Galileo surveys of the 1980s, and the Kepler landings of the 1990s. But, in a few hours, the Chinese had learned more about Europa than all the previous missions combined. That knowledge they were keeping to themselves; one might regret it, but few would deny that they had earned the right to do so.

What was being denied, with greater and greater asperity, was their right to annex the satellite. For the first time in history, a nation had laid claim to another world, and all the news media of Earth were arguing over the legal position. Though the Chinese pointed out, at tedious length, that they had never signed the '02 UN Space Treaty and so were not bound by its provisions, that did nothing to quell the angry protests.

Suddenly, Europa was the biggest news in the Solar System. And the man-on-the-spot (at least to the nearest few million kilometers) was in great demand.

"This is Heywood Floyd, aboard *Cosmonaut Alexei Leonov*,

on course for Jupiter. But as you can well imagine, all our thoughts are now focused upon Europa.

"At this very moment I'm looking at it through the most powerful of the ship's telescopes; under this magnification, it's ten times larger than the Moon as you see it with the naked eye. And it's a really *weird* sight.

"The surface is a uniform pink, with a few small brown patches. It's covered with an intricate network of narrow lines, curling and weaving in all directions. In fact, it looks very much like a photo from a medical textbook, showing a pattern of veins and arteries.

"A few of these features are hundreds—or even thousands—of kilometers long, and look rather like the illusory canals that Percival Lowell and other early-twentieth-century astronomers imagined they'd seen on Mars.

"But Europa's canals aren't an illusion, though of course they're not artificial. What's more, they *do* contain water—or at least ice. For the satellite is almost entirely covered by ocean, averaging fifty kilometers deep.

"Because it's so far from the sun, Europa's surface temperature is extremely low—about a hundred and fifty degrees below freezing. So one might expect its single ocean to be a solid block of ice.

"Surprisingly, that isn't the case because there's a lot of heat generated inside Europa by tidal forces—the same forces that drive the great volcanoes on neighboring Io.

"So the ice is continually melting, breaking up, and freezing, forming cracks and lanes like those in the floating ice sheets in our own polar regions. It's that intricate tracery of cracks I'm seeing now; most of them are dark and very ancient—perhaps millions of years old. But a few are almost pure white; they're the new ones that have just opened up, and have a crust only a few centimeters thick.

"*Tsien* has landed right beside one of these white streaks—the fifteen-hundred-kilometer-long feature that's been christened the Grand Canal. Presumably the Chinese intend to pump its water into their propellant tanks, so that they can explore the Jovian satellite system and then return to Earth. That may not be easy, but they'll certainly have studied the landing site with great care, and must know what they're doing.

"It's obvious, now, why they've taken such a risk—and why they claim Europa. As a refueling point. It could be the key to the entire outer Solar System. Though there's also water on Ganymede, it's all frozen, and also less accessible because of that satellite's more powerful gravity.

"And there's another point that's just occurred to me. Even if the Chinese do get stranded on Europa, they might be able to survive until a rescue mission is arranged. They have plenty of power, there may be useful minerals in the area—and we know that the Chinese are *the* experts on synthetic-food production. It wouldn't be a very luxurious life; but I have some friends who would accept it happily for that staggering view of Jupiter sprawled across the sky—the view we expect to see ourselves, in just a few days.

"This is Heywood Floyd, saying good-bye for my colleagues and myself, aboard *Alexei Leonov*."

"And this is the bridge. Very nice presentation, Heywood. You should have been a newsman."

"I've had plenty of practice. Half my time was spent on P.R. work."

"P.R.?"

"Public relations—usually telling politicians why they should give me more money. Something *you* don't have to bother about."

"How I wish that was true. Anyway, come up to the bridge. There's some new information we'd like to discuss with you."

Floyd removed his button microphone, locked the telescope into position and extricated himself from the tiny viewing blister. As he left, he almost collided with Nikolai Ternovsky, obviously on a similar mission.

"I'm about to steal your best quotes for Radio Moscow, Woody. Hope you don't mind."

"You're welcome, *tovarishch*. Anyway, how could I stop you?"

Up on the bridge, Captain Orlova was looking thoughtfully at a dense mass of words and figures on the main display. Floyd had painfully started to transliterate them when she interrupted him.

"Don't worry about the details. These are estimates of the time it will take for Tsien to refill its tanks and get ready for lift-off."

"My people are doing the same calculations—but there are far too many variables."

"We think we've removed one of them. Did you know that the very best water pumps you can buy belong to fire brigades? And would you be surprised to learn that the Beijing Central Station had four of its latest models suddenly requisitioned a few months ago, despite the protests of the mayor?"

"I'm not surprised—merely lost in admiration. Go on, please."

"That may be a coincidence, but those pumps would be just the right size. Making educated guesses about pipe deployment, drilling through the ice and so on—well, we think they could lift off again in five days."

"Five days!"

"If they're lucky, and everything works perfectly. And if they don't wait to fill their propellant tanks but merely take on just enough for a safe rendezvous with Discovery before we do. Even if they beat us by a single hour, that would be enough. They could claim salvage rights, at the very least."

"Not according to the State Department's lawyers. At the appropriate moment, we'll declare that Discovery is not a derelict, but has merely been parked until we can retrieve it. Any attempt to take over the ship would be an act of piracy."

"I'm sure the Chinese will be most impressed."

"If they're not, what can we do about it?"

"We outnumber them—and two to one, when we revive Chandra and Curnow."

"Are you serious? Where are the cutlasses for the boarding party?"

"Cutlasses?"

"Swords—weapons."

"Oh. We could use the laser telespectrometer. That can vaporize milligram asteroid samples at ranges of a thousand kilometers."

"I'm not sure that I like this conversation. My government certainly would not condone violence, except of course in self-defense."

"You naive Americans! We're more realistic; we have to be. All your grandparents died of old age, Heywood. Three of mine were killed in the Great Patriotic War."

When they were alone together, Tanya always called him Woody, never Heywood. She must be serious. Or was she merely testing his reactions?

"Anyway, *Discovery* is merely a few billion dollars' worth of hardware. The ship's not important—only the information it carries."

"Exactly. Information that could be copied, and then erased."

"You do get some cheerful ideas, Tanya. Sometimes I think that all Russians are a little paranoiac."

"Thanks to Napoleon and Hitler, we've earned every right to be. But don't tell me that you haven't already worked out that—what do you call it, scenario?—for yourself."

"It wasn't necessary," Floyd answered rather glumly. "The State Department's already done it for me—with variations. We'll just have to see which one the Chinese come up with. And I wouldn't be in the least surprised if they outguess us again."

10. A CRY FROM EUROPA

Sleeping in zero gravity is a skill that has to be learned; it had taken Floyd almost a week to find the best way of anchoring legs and arms so that they did not drift into uncomfortable positions. Now he was an expert, and was not looking forward to the return of weight; indeed, the very idea gave him occasional nightmares.

Someone was shaking him awake. No—he must still be dreaming! Privacy was sacred aboard a spaceship; nobody ever entered another crew member's chambers without first asking permission. He clenched his eyes shut, but the shaking continued.

"Dr. Floyd—please wake up! You're wanted on the flight deck!"

And nobody called him Dr. Floyd; the most formal salutation he had received for weeks was Doc. What was happening?

Reluctantly, he opened his eyes. He was in his tiny cabin,

gently gripped by his sleeping cocoon. So one part of his mind told him; then why was he looking at—*Europa*? They were still millions of kilometers away.

There were the familiar reticulations, the patterns of triangles and polygons formed by intersecting lines. And surely that was the Grand Canal itself—no, it wasn't quite right. How *could* it be, since he was still in his little cabin aboard *Leonov*?

"Dr. Floyd!"

He became fully awake, and realized that his left hand was floating just a few centimeters in front of his eyes. How strange that the pattern of lines across the palm was so uncannily like the map of Europa! But economical Mother Nature was always repeating herself, on such vastly different scales as the swirl of milk stirred into coffee, the cloud lanes of a cyclonic storm, the arms of a spiral nebula.

"Sorry, Max," he said. "What's the problem? Is something wrong?"

"We think so—but not with us. *Tsien's* in trouble."

Captain, navigator, and chief engineer were strapped in their seats on the flight deck; the rest of the crew orbited anxiously around convenient handholds, or watched on the monitors.

"Sorry to wake you up, Heywood," Tanya apologized brusquely. "Here's the situation. Ten minutes ago we had a Class One Priority from Mission Control. *Tsien's* gone off the air. It happened very suddenly, in the middle of a cipher message; there were a few seconds of garbled transmission—then nothing."

"Their beacon?"

"That's stopped as well. We can't receive it either."

"Phew! Then it must be serious—a major breakdown. Any theories?"

"Lots—but all guesswork. An explosion—landslide—earthquake: who knows?"

"And we may never know—until someone else lands on Europa—or we do a close flyby and take a look."

Tanya shook her head. "We don't have enough delta-vee. The closest we could get is fifty thousand kilometers. Not much you could see from that distance."

"Then there's absolutely nothing we can do."

"Not quite, Heywood. Mission Control has a suggestion. They'd like us to swing our big dish around, just in case we can pick up any weak emergency transmissions. It's—how do you say?—a long shot, but worth trying. What do you think?"

Floyd's first reaction was strongly negative.

"That will mean breaking our link with Earth."

"Of course; but we'll have to do that anyway, when we go around Jupiter. And it will only take a couple of minutes to re-establish the circuit."

Floyd remained silent. The suggestion was perfectly reasonable, yet it worried him obscurely. After puzzling for several seconds, he suddenly realized why he was so opposed to the idea.

Discovery's troubles had started when the big dish—the main antenna complex—had lost its lock on Earth, for reasons which even now were not completely clear. But Hal had certainly been involved, and there was no danger of a similar situation arising here. *Leonov's* computers were small, autonomous units; there was no single controlling intelligence. At least, no nonhuman one.

The Russians were still waiting patiently for his answer.

"I agree," he said at last. "Let Earth know what we're doing, and start listening. I suppose you'll try all the SPACE MAYDAY frequencies."

"Yes, as soon as we've worked out the Doppler corrections. How's it going, Sasha?"

"Give me another two minutes, and I'll have the automatic search running. How long should we listen?"

The captain barely paused before giving her answer. Floyd had often admired Tanya Orlova's decisiveness, and had once told her so. In a rare flash of humor, she had replied: "Woody, a commander can be wrong, but *never* uncertain."

"Listen for fifty minutes, and report back to Earth for ten. Then repeat the cycle."

There was nothing to see or hear; the automatic circuits were better at sifting the radio noise than any human senses. Nevertheless, from time to time Sasha turned up the audio monitor, and the roar of Jupiter's radiation belts filled the cabin. It was a sound like the waves breaking on all the beaches of Earth, with occasional explosive cracks from superbolts of lightning in the Jovian atmosphere. Of human signals, there was no trace; and one by one, the members of the crew not on duty drifted quietly away.

While he was waiting, Floyd did some mental calculations. Whatever had happened to *Tsien* was already two hours in the past, since the news had been relayed from Earth.

But *Leonov* should be able to pick up a direct message after less than a minute's delay, so the Chinese had already had ample time to get back on the air. Their continued silence suggested some catastrophic failure, and he found himself weaving endless scenarios of disaster.

The fifty minutes seemed like hours. When they were up, Sasha swung the ship's antenna complex back toward Earth, and reported failure. While he was using the rest of the ten minutes to send a backlog of messages, he looked inquiringly at the captain.

"Is it worth trying again?" he said in a voice that clearly expressed his own pessimism.

"Of course. We may cut back the search time—but we'll keep listening."

On the hour, the big dish was once more focused upon Europa. And almost at once, the automatic monitor started flashing its ALERT light.

Sasha's hand darted to the audio gain, and the voice of Jupiter filled the cabin. Superimposed upon that, like a whisper heard against a thunderstorm, was the faint but completely unmistakable sound of human speech. It was impossible to identify the language, though Floyd felt certain, from the intonation and rhythm, that it was *not* Chinese, but some European tongue.

Sasha played skillfully with fine-tuning and band-width controls, and the words became clearer. The language was undoubtedly English—but its content was still maddeningly unintelligible.

There is one combination of sounds that every human ear can

detect instantly, even in the noisiest environment. When it suddenly emerged from the Jovian background, it seemed to Floyd that he could not possibly be awake, but was trapped in some fantastic dream. His colleagues took a little longer to react; then they stared at him with equal amazement—and a slowly dawning suspicion.

For the first recognizable words from Europa were: "Dr. Floyd—Dr. Floyd—I hope you can hear me."

11. ICE AND VACUUM

"Who is it?" whispered someone, to a chorus of shushes. Floyd raised his hands in a gesture of ignorance—and, he hoped, innocence.

". . . know you are aboard *Leonov* . . . may not have much time . . . aiming my suit antenna where I think . . ."

The signal vanished for agonizing seconds, then came back much clearer, though not appreciably louder.

". . . relay this information to Earth. *Tsien* destroyed three hours ago. I'm only survivor. Using my suit radio—no idea if it has enough range, but it's the only chance. Please listen carefully. THERE IS LIFE ON EUROPA. I repeat: THERE IS LIFE ON EUROPA . . ."

The signal faded again. A stunned silence followed that no one attempted to interrupt. While he was waiting, Floyd searched his memory furiously. He could not recognize the voice—

*64

it might have been that of any Western-educated Chinese. Probably it was someone he had met at a scientific conference, but unless the speaker identified himself he would never know.

". . . soon after local midnight. We were pumping steadily and the tanks were almost half full. Dr. Lee and I went out to check the pipe insulation. Tsien stands—stood—about thirty meters from the edge of the Grand Canal. Pipes go directly from it and down through the ice. Very thin—not safe to walk on. The warm upwelling . . ."

Again a long silence. Floyd wondered if the speaker was moving, and had been momentarily cut off by some obstruction.

". . . no problem—five kilowatts of lighting strung up on the ship. Like a Christmas tree—beautiful, shining right through the ice. Glorious colors. Lee saw it first—a huge dark mass rising up from the depths. At first we thought it was a school of fish—too large for a single organism—then it started to break through the ice.

"Dr. Floyd, I hope you can hear me. This is Professor Chang— we met in '02—Boston I.A.U. conference."

Instantly, incongruously, Floyd's thoughts were a billion kilometers away. He vaguely remembered that reception, after the closing session of the International Astronomical Union Congress—the last one that the Chinese had attended before the Second Cultural Revolution. And now he recalled Chang very distinctly—a small, humorous astronomer and exobiologist with a good fund of jokes. He wasn't joking now.

". . . like huge strands of wet seaweed, crawling along the ground. Lee ran back to the ship to get a camera—I stayed to watch, reporting over the radio. The thing moved so slowly I could easily outrun it. I was much more excited than alarmed. Thought I knew what kind of creature it was—I've seen pictures of the kelp forests off California—but I was quite wrong.

". . . I could tell it was in trouble. It couldn't possibly survive at a temperature a hundred and fifty below its normal environment. It was freezing solid as it moved forward—bits were breaking off like glass—but it was still advancing toward the ship, a black tidal wave, slowing down all the time.

"I was still so surprised that I couldn't think straight and I couldn't imagine what it was trying to do . . ."

"Is there any way we can call him back?" Floyd whispered urgently.

"No—it's too late. Europa will soon be behind Jupiter. We'll have to wait until it comes out of eclipse."

". . . climbing up the ship, building a kind of ice tunnel as it advanced. Perhaps this was insulating it from the cold—the way termites protect themselves from sunlight with their little corridors of mud.

". . . tons of ice on the ship. The radio antennas broke off first. Then I could see the landing legs beginning to buckle—all in slow motion, like a dream.

"Not until the ship started to topple did I realize what the thing was trying to do—and then it was too late. We could have saved ourselves—if we'd only switched off those lights.

"Perhaps it's a phototrope, its biological cycle triggered by the sunlight that filters through the ice. Or it could have been attracted like a moth to a candle. Our floodlights must have been more brilliant than anything that Europa has ever known . . .

"Then the ship crashed. I saw the hull split, a cloud of snowflakes form as moisture condensed. All the lights went out, except for one, swinging back and forth on a cable a couple of meters above the ground.

"I don't know what happened immediately after that. The next thing I remember, I was standing under the light, beside the wreck of the ship, with a fine powdering of fresh snow all around me. I could see my footsteps in it very clearly. I must have run there; perhaps only a minute or two had elapsed . . .

"The plant—I still thought of it as a plant—was motionless. I wondered if it had been damaged by the impact; large sections—as thick as a man's arm—had splintered off, like broken twigs.

"Then the main trunk started to move again. It pulled away from the hull, and began to crawl toward me. That was when I knew for certain that the thing was light-sensitive: I was standing immediately under the thousand-watt lamp, which had stopped swinging now.

"Imagine an oak tree—better still, a banyan with its multiple trunks and roots—flattened out by gravity and trying to creep along the ground. It got to within five meters of the light, then started to spread out until it had made a perfect circle around me. Presumably that was the limit of its tolerance—the point at which photoattraction turned to repulsion. After that, nothing happened for several minutes. I wondered if it was dead—frozen solid at last.

"Then I saw that large buds were forming on many of the branches. It was like watching a time-lapse film of flowers opening. In fact I thought they *were* flowers—each about as big as a man's head.

"Delicate, beautifully colored membranes started to unfold. Even then, it occurred to me that no one—no *thing*—could ever have seen these colors before; they had no existence until we brought our lights—our fatal lights—to this world.

"Tendrils, stamens, waving feebly . . . I walked over to the living wall that surrounded me, so that I could see exactly what was happening. Neither then, or at any other time, had I felt the slightest fear of the creature. I was certain that it was not malevolent—if indeed it was conscious at all.

"There were scores of the big flowers, in various stages of unfolding. Now they reminded me of butterflies, just emerging from the chrysalis—wings crumpled, still feeble—I was getting closer and closer to the truth.

"But they were freezing—dying as quickly as they formed. Then, one after another, they dropped off from the parent buds. For a few moments they flopped around like fish stranded on dry land—and at last I realized exactly what they were. Those membranes weren't petals—they were *fins*, or their equivalent. This was the free-swimming, larval stage of the creature. Probably it spends much of its life rooted on the seabed, then sends these mobile offspring in search of new territory. Just like the corals of Earth's oceans.

"I knelt down to get a closer look at one of the little creatures. The beautiful colors were fading now, to a drab brown. Some of the petal-fins had snapped off, becoming brittle shards as they froze. But it was still moving feebly, and as I approached it tried to avoid me. I wondered how it sensed my presence.

"Then I noticed that the *stamens*—as I'd called them—all carried bright blue dots at their tips. They looked like tiny star sapphires—or the blue eyes along the mantle of a scallop—aware of light, but unable to form true images. As I watched, the vivid blue faded, the sapphires became dull, ordinary stones . . .

"Dr. Floyd—or anyone else who is listening—I haven't much more time; Jupiter will soon block my signal. But I've almost finished.

"I knew then what I had to do. The cable to that thousand-watt lamp was hanging almost to the ground. I gave it a few tugs, and the light went out in a shower of sparks.

"I wondered if it was too late. For a few minutes, nothing happened. So I walked over to the wall of tangled branches around me, and *kicked* it.

"Slowly, the creature started to unweave itself, and to retreat back to the Canal. There was plenty of light—I could see everything perfectly. Ganymede and Callisto were in the sky—Jupiter was a huge, thin crescent—and there was a big auroral display on the nightside, at the Jovian end of the Io flux tube. There was no need to use my helmet light.

"I followed the creature all the way back to the water, encouraging it with more kicks when it slowed down, feeling the fragments of ice crunching all the time beneath my boots . . . As it neared the Canal, it seemed to gain strength and energy, as if it knew that it was approaching its natural home. I wondered if it would survive, to bud again.

"It disappeared through the surface, leaving a few last dead larvae on the alien land. The exposed free water bubbled for a few minutes until a scab of protective ice sealed it from the vacuum above. Then I walked back to the ship to see if there was anything to salvage—I don't want to talk about that.

"I've only two requests to make, Doctor. When the taxonomists classify this creature, I hope they'll name it after me.

"And—when the next ship comes home—ask them to take our bones back to China.

"Jupiter will be cutting us off in a few minutes. I wish I knew whether anyone was receiving me. Anyway, I'll repeat this message when we're in line of sight again—if my suit's life-support system lasts that long.

"This is Professor Chang on Europa, reporting the destruction of spaceship *Tsien*. We landed beside the Grand Canal and set up our pumps at the edge of the ice—"

The signal faded abruptly, came back for a moment, then disappeared completely below the noise level. Although *Leonov* listened again on the same frequency, there was no further message from Professor Chang.

III ✳ DISCOVERY

12. DOWNHILL RUN

THE SHIP WAS GAINING SPEED AT LAST, ON THE DOWNHILL RUN TO-ward Jupiter. It had long since passed the gravitational no-man's-land where the four tiny outer moons—Sinope, Pasiphae, Ananke, and Carme—wobbled along their retrograde and wildly eccentric orbits. Undoubtedly captured asteroids, and completely irregular in shape. The largest was only thirty kilometers across. Jagged, splintered rocks of no interest to anyone except planetary geologists, their allegiance wavered continually between the Sun and Jupiter. One day, the Sun would recapture them completely.

But Jupiter might retain the second group of four, at half the distance of the others. Elara, Lysithea, Himalia, and Leda were fairly close together, and lying in almost the same plane. There was speculation that they had once been part of a single body; if so, the parent would have been barely a hundred kilometers across.

Though only Carme and Leda came close enough to show disks visible to the naked eye, they were greeted like old friends. Here was the first landfall after the longest ocean voyage—the offshore islands of Jupiter. The last hours were ticking away; the most critical phase of the entire mission was approaching—the entry into the Jovian atmosphere.

Jupiter was already larger than the Moon in the skies of Earth, and the giant inner satellites could be clearly seen moving around it. They all showed noticeable disks and distinctive coloring, though they were still too far away for any markings to be visible. The eternal ballet they performed—disappearing behind Jupiter, reappearing to transit the daylight face with their accompanying shadows—was an endlessly engaging spectacle. It was one that astronomers had watched ever since Galileo had first glimpsed it almost exactly four centuries ago; but the crew of *Leonov* were the only living men and women to have seen it with unaided eyes.

The interminable chess games had ceased; off-duty hours were spent at the telescopes, or in earnest conversation, or listening to music, usually while gazing at the view outside. And at least one shipboard romance had reached a culmination: the frequent disappearance of Max Brailovsky and Zenia Marchenko was the subject of much good-natured banter.

They were, thought Floyd, an oddly matched pair. Max was a big, handsome blond who had been a champion gymnast, reaching the finals of the 2000 Olympics. Though he was in his early thirties, he had an open-faced, almost boyish expression. This was not altogether misleading; despite his brilliant engineering record, he often struck Floyd as naive and unsophisticated—one of those people who are pleasant to talk to, but not for *too* long. Outside his own field of undoubted expertise he was engaging but rather shallow.

Zenia—at twenty-nine, the youngest on board—was still something of a mystery. Since no one wished to talk about it, Floyd had never raised the subject of her injuries, and his Washington sources could provide no information. Obviously she had been involved in some serious accident, but it might have been nothing more unusual than a car crash. The theory that she had been on a secret space mission—still part of popular mythology outside the U.S.S.R.—could be ruled out. Thanks to the global tracking networks, no such thing had been possible for fifty years.

In addition to her physical and doubtless psychological scars, Zenia labored under yet another handicap. She was a last-minute replacement, and everyone knew it. Irina Yakunina was to have been dietician and medical assistant aboard *Leonov* before that unfortunate argument with a hang-glider broke too many bones.

Every day at 1800 GMT the crew of seven plus one passenger gathered in the tiny common room that separated the flight deck from the galley and sleeping quarters. The circular table at its center was just big enough for eight people to squeeze around; when Chandra and Curnow were revived, it would be unable to accommodate everyone, and two extra seats would have to be fitted in somewhere else.

Though the "Six O'Clock Soviet," as the daily round-table conference was called, seldom lasted more than ten minutes, it played a vital role in maintaining morale. Complaints, suggestions, criticisms, progress reports—anything could be raised, subject only to the captain's overriding veto, which was very seldom exercised.

Typical items on the nonexistent agenda were requests for changes in the menu, appeals for more private communication time with Earth, suggested movie programs, exchange of news and gossip, and good-natured needling of the heavily outnumbered American contingent. Things would change, Floyd warned them, when his colleagues came out of hibernation, and the odds improved from 1 in 7 to 3 in 9. He did not mention his private belief that Curnow could outtalk or outshout any three other people aboard.

When he was not sleeping, much of Floyd's own time was spent in the common room—partly because, despite its smallness, it was much less claustrophobic than his own tiny cubicle. It was also cheerfully decorated, all available flat surfaces being covered with photos of beautiful land- and seascapes, sporting events, portraits of popular videostars, and other reminders of

Earth. Pride of place, however, was given to an original Leonov painting—his 1965 study "Near the Moon," made in the same year when, as a young lieutenant–colonel, he left *Voshkod II* and became the first man in history to perform an extravehicular excursion.

Clearly the work of a talented amateur, rather than a professional, it showed the cratered edge of the Moon with the beautiful Sinus Iridum—Bay of Rainbows—in the foreground. Looming monstrously above the lunar horizon was the thin crescent of Earth, embracing the darkened nightside of the planet. Beyond that blazed the sun, the streamers of the corona reaching out into space for millions of kilometers around it.

It was a striking composition—and a glimpse of the future that even then lay only three years ahead. On the flight of *Apollo 8*, Anders, Borman, and Lovell were to see this splendid sight with their unaided eyes, as they watched Earth rise above the farside on Christmas Day, 1968.

Heywood Floyd admired the painting, but he also regarded it with mixed feelings. He could not forget that it was older than everybody else on the ship—with one exception.

He was already nine years old, when Alexei Leonov had painted it.

13. THE WORLDS OF GALILEO

EVEN NOW, MORE THAN THREE DECADES AFTER THE REVELATIONS of the first Voyager flybys, no one really understood why the four giant satellites differed so wildly from one another. They were all about the same size, and in the same part of the Solar System—yet they were totally dissimilar, as if children of a different birth.

Only Callisto, the outermost, had turned out to be much as expected. When *Leonov* raced past at a distance of just over 100,000 kilometers, the larger of its countless craters were clearly visible to the naked eye. Through the telescope, the satellite looked like a glass ball that had been used as a target by high-powered rifles; it was completely covered with craters of every size, right down to the lower limit of visibility. Callisto, someone had once remarked, looked more like Earth's Moon than did the Moon itself.

Nor was this particularly surprising. One would have expected a world out here—at the edge of the asteroid belt—to have been bombarded with the debris left over from the creation of the Solar System. Yet Ganymede, the satellite next door, had a totally different appearance. Though it had been well peppered with impact craters in the remote past, most of them had been ploughed over—a phrase that seemed peculiarly appropriate. Huge areas of Ganymede were covered with ridges and furrows, as if some cosmic gardener had dragged a giant rake across them. And there were light-colored streaks, like trails that might have been made by slugs fifty kilometers across. Most mysterious of all were long, meandering bands, containing dozens of parallel lines. It was Nikolai Ternovsky who decided what they must be—multilane superhighways, laid out by drunken surveyors. He even claimed to have detected overpasses and cloverleaf intersections.

Leonov had added some trillions of bits of information about Ganymede to the store of human knowledge, before it crossed the orbit of Europa. That icebound world, with its derelict and its dead, was on the other side of Jupiter, but it was never far from anyone's thoughts.

Back on Earth, Dr. Chang was already a hero and his countrymen had, with obvious embarrassment, acknowledged countless messages of sympathy. One had been sent in the name of Leonov's crew—after, Floyd gathered, considerable redrafting in Moscow. The feeling on board the ship was ambiguous—a mixture of admiration, regret, and relief. All astronauts, irrespective of their national origins, regarded themselves as citizens of space and felt a common bond, sharing each other's triumphs and tragedies. No one on Leonov was happy because the Chinese expedition had met with disaster; yet at the same time, there was a muted sense of relief that the race had not gone to the swiftest.

The unexpected discovery of life on Europa had added a new element to the situation—one that was now being argued at great length both on Earth and aboard Leonov. Some exobiologists cried "I told you so!," pointing out that it should not have been

such a surprise after all. As far back as the 1970s, research sub-
marines had found teeming colonies of strange marine creatures
thriving precariously in an environment thought to be equally
hostile to life—the trenches on the bed of the Pacific. Volcanic
springs, fertilizing and warming the abyss, had created oases in
the deserts of the deep.

Anything that had happened once on Earth should be expected millions of times elsewhere in the Universe; that was almost an article of faith among scientists. Water—or at least ice—
occurred on all the moons of Jupiter. And there were continuously erupting volcanoes on Io—so it was reasonable to expect
weaker activity on the world next door. Putting these two facts
together made Europan life seem not only possible, but inevitable—as most of nature's surprises are, when viewed with 20/20
hindsight.

Yet that conclusion raised another question, and one vital to
Leonov's mission. Now that life had been discovered on the
moons of Jupiter—did it have any connection with the Tycho
monolith, and the still more mysterious artifact in orbit near Io?

That was a favorite subject to debate in the Six O'Clock Sovi-
ets. It was generally agreed that the creature encountered by Dr.
Chang did not represent a high form of intelligence—at least, if
his interpretation of its behavior was correct. No animal with
even elementary powers of reasoning would have allowed itself
to become a victim of its instincts, attracted like a moth to the
candle until it risked destruction.

Vasili Orlov was quick to give a counterexample that weakened, if it did not refute, that argument.

"Look at whales and dolphins," he said. "We call them
intelligent—but how often they kill themselves in mass strand-
ings! That looks like a case where instinct overpowers reason."

"No need to go to the dolphins," interjected Max Brailovsky.
"One of the brightest engineers in my class was fatally attracted
to a blonde in Kiev. When I heard of him last, he was working in
a garage. And he'd won a gold medal for designing space-
stations. What a waste!"

Even if Dr. Chang's Europan was intelligent, that of course did not rule out higher forms elsewhere. The biology of a whole world could not be judged from a single specimen.

But it had been widely argued that advanced intelligence could never arise in the sea; there were not enough challenges in so benign and unvarying an environment. Above all, how could marine creatures ever develop a technology without the aid of fire?

Yet perhaps even that was possible; the route that humanity had taken was not the only one. There might be whole civilizations in the seas of other worlds.

Still, it seemed unlikely that a space-faring culture could have arisen on Europa without leaving unmistakable signs of its existence in the form of buildings, scientific installations, launching sites, or other artifacts. But from pole to pole, nothing could be seen but level ice and a few outcroppings of bare rock.

No time remained for speculations and discussions when *Leonov* hurtled past the orbits of Io and tiny Mimas. The crew was busy almost nonstop, preparing for the encounter and the brief onset of weight after months in free-fall. All loose objects had to be secured before the ship entered Jupiter's atmosphere, and the drag of deceleration produced momentary peaks that might be as high as two gravities.

Floyd was lucky; he alone had time to admire the superb spectacle of the approaching planet, now filling almost half the sky. Because there was nothing to give it scale, there was no way that the mind could grasp its real size. He had to keep telling himself that fifty Earths would not cover the hemisphere now turned toward him.

The clouds, colorful as the most garish sunset on Earth, raced so swiftly that he could see appreciable movement in as little as ten minutes. Great eddies were continually forming along the dozen or so bands that girdled the planet, then rippling away like swirls of smoke. Plumes of white gas occasionally geysered up from the depths, to be swept away by the gales caused by the planet's tremendous spin. And perhaps strangest of all were the white spots, sometimes spaced as regularly as pearls on a necklace, which lay along the trade winds of the middle Jovian latitudes.

In the hours immediately before encounter, Floyd saw little of captain or navigator. The Orlovs scarcely left the bridge, as they continually checked the approach orbit and made minute refinements to Leonov's course. The ship was now on the critical path that would just graze the outer atmosphere; if it went too high, frictional braking would not be sufficient to slow it down, and it would go racing out of the Solar System, beyond all possibility of rescue. If it went too low, it would burn up like a meteor. Between the two extremes lay little margin for error.

The Chinese had proved that aerobraking could be done, but there was always the chance that something would go wrong. So Floyd was not at all surprised when Surgeon–Commander Rudenko admitted, just an hour before contact: "I'm beginning to wish, Woody, that I had brought along that icon, after all."

14. DOUBLE ENCOUNTER

"... PAPERS FOR THE MORTGAGE ON THE NANTUCKET HOUSE should be in the file marked M in the library.

"Well, that's all the business I can think of. For the last couple of hours I've been recalling a picture I saw as a boy, in a tattered volume of Victorian art—it must have been almost one hundred fifty years old. I can't remember whether it was black-and-white, or color. But I'll never forget the title—don't laugh—it was called 'The Last Message Home.' Our great-great-grandfathers loved that kind of sentimental melodrama.

"It shows the deck of a windjammer in a hurricane—the sails have been ripped away and the deck's awash. In the background, the crew is struggling to save the ship. And in the foreground, a young sailor boy's writing a note, while beside him is the bottle he hopes will carry it to land.

"Even though I was a kid at the time, I felt he should have been giving his shipmates a hand, not writing letters. All the

✳ 82

same, it moved me: I never thought that one day I'd be like that young sailor.

"Of course, I'm sure you'll get *this* message—and there's nothing I can do to help aboard *Leonov*. In fact, I've been politely requested to keep out of the way, so my conscience is quite clear as I dictate this.

"I'll send it up to the bridge now because in fifteen minutes we'll break transmission as we pull in the big dish and batten down the hatches—there's another nice maritime analogy for you! Jupiter's filling the sky now—I won't attempt to describe it and won't even see it much longer because the shutters will go up in a few minutes. Anyway, the cameras can do far better than I could.

"Good-bye, my dearest, and my love to you all—especially Chris. By the time you get this, it will be over, one way or the other. Remember I tried to do my best for all our sakes—good-bye."

When he had removed the audio chip, Floyd drifted up to the communications center and handed it over to Sasha Kovalev.

"Please make sure it gets off before we close down," he said earnestly.

"Don't worry," promised Sasha. "I'm still working on all channels, and we have a good ten minutes left."

He held out his hand. "If we do meet again—why, we shall smile. If not, why then this parting was well made." Floyd blinked.

"Shakespeare, I suppose?"

"Of course; Brutus and Cassius before battle. See you later."

Tanya and Vasili were too intent upon their situation displays to do more than wave to Floyd, and he retreated to his cabin. He had already said farewell to the rest of the crew; there was nothing to do but wait. His sleeping bag was slung in preparation for the return of gravity when deceleration commenced, and he had only to climb into it—

"Antennas retracted, all protective shields up," said the intercom speaker. "We should feel first braking in five minutes. Everything normal."

"That's hardly the word *I'd* use," Floyd muttered to himself.

"I think you mean 'nominal.'" He had barely concluded the thought when there was a diffident knock on the door.

"*Kto tam?*"

To his astonishment, it was Zenia.

"Do you mind if I come in?" she asked awkwardly, in a small-girl voice which Floyd could scarcely recognize.

"Of course not. But why aren't you in your own cubicle? It's only five minutes to reentry."

Even as he asked the question, he was aware of its foolishness. The answer was so perfectly obvious that Zenia did not deign to reply.

But Zenia was the very last person he would have expected: her attitude toward him had invariably been polite but distant. Indeed, she was the only member of the crew who preferred to call him Dr. Floyd. Yet here she was, clearly seeking comfort and companionship at the moment of peril.

"Zenia, my dear," he said wryly. "You're welcome. But my accommodation is somewhat limited. One might even call it Spartan."

She managed a faint smile, but said nothing as she floated into the room. For the first time, Floyd realized that she was not merely nervous—she was terrified. Then he understood why she had come to him. She was ashamed to face her countrymen and was looking for support elsewhere.

With this realization, his pleasure at the unexpected encounter abated somewhat. That did not lessen his responsibility to another lonely human being, a long way from home. The fact that she was an attractive—though certainly not beautiful—woman of barely half his own age should not have affected the issue. But it did; he was beginning to rise to the occasion.

She must have noticed, but did nothing to encourage or discourage him as they lay down side by side in the sleeping cocoon. There was just enough room for them both, and Floyd began to do some anxious calculations. Suppose maximum gee was higher than predicted, and the suspension gave way? They could easily be killed . . .

There was an ample safety margin; no need to worry about such an ignominious end. Humor was the enemy of desire; their embrace was now completely chaste. He was not sure whether to be glad or sorry.

And it was too late for second thoughts. From far, far away came the first faint whisper of sound, like the wailing of some lost soul. At the same moment, the ship gave a barely perceptible jerk; the cocoon began to swing around and its suspension tightened. After weeks of weightlessness, gravity was returning.

Within seconds, the faint wail had risen to a steady roar, and the cocoon had become an overloaded hammock. This is not such a good idea, Floyd thought to himself; already it was difficult to breathe. The deceleration was only a part of the problem: Zenia was clutching him as a drowning person is supposed to clutch the proverbial straw.

He detached her as gently as he could.

"It's all right, Zenia. If *Tsien* did it, so can we. Relax—don't worry."

It was difficult to shout tenderly, and he was not even sure if Zenia heard him above the roar of incandescent hydrogen. But she was no longer clutching him quite so desperately, and he seized the opportunity of taking a few deep breaths.

What would Caroline think if she could see him now? Would he tell her if he ever had the chance? He was not sure she would understand. At a moment like this, all links with Earth seemed very tenuous indeed.

It was impossible to move, or to speak, but now that he had grown accustomed to the strange sense of weight he was no longer uncomfortable—except for the increasing numbness in his right arm. With some difficulty, he managed to extricate it from beneath Zenia; the familiar act brought a fleeting sense of guilt. As he felt his circulation returning, Floyd remembered a famous remark attributed to at least a dozen astronauts and cosmonauts: "Both the pleasures and problems of zero-gravity sex have been greatly exaggerated."

He wondered how the rest of the crew was faring, and he gave a momentary thought to Chandra and Curnow, sleeping peacefully through it all. They would never know if *Leonov* became a meteor shower in the Jovian sky. He did not envy them; they had missed the experience of a lifetime.

Tanya was speaking over the intercom; her words were lost in the roar, but her voice sounded calm and perfectly normal, just as if she was making a routine announcement. Floyd managed to glance at his watch, and was astonished to see that they were already at the midpoint of the braking maneuver. At that very moment, *Leonov* was at its closest approach to Jupiter; only expendable automatic probes had gone deeper into the Jovian atmosphere.

"Halfway through, Zenia," he shouted. "On the way out again." He could not tell if she understood. Her eyes were tightly closed, but she smiled slightly.

The ship was now rocking noticeably, like a small boat in a choppy sea. Was that normal? wondered Floyd. He was glad that he had Zenia to worry about; it took his mind away from his own fears. Just for a moment, before he managed to expel the thought, he had a vision of the walls suddenly glowing cherry red, and caving in upon him. Like the nightmare fantasy of Edgar Allan Poe's "The Pit and the Pendulum," which he'd forgotten for thirty years . . .

But that would never happen. If the heat shield failed, the ship would crumple instantly, hammered flat by a solid wall of gas. There would be no pain; his nervous system would not have time to react before it ceased to exist. He had experienced more consoling thoughts, but this one was not to be despised.

The buffeting slowly weakened. There was another inaudible announcement from Tanya (he would pull her leg about that, when it was all over). Now time seemed to be going much more slowly; after a while he stopped looking at his watch, because he could not believe it. The digits changed so slowly that he could almost imagine himself in some Einsteinian time dilation.

And then something even more unbelievable happened. First he was amused, then slightly indignant. Zenia had fallen asleep—if not exactly in his arms, then at least beside them.

It was a natural reaction: the strain must have exhausted her, and the wisdom of the body had come to her rescue. And suddenly Floyd himself became aware of an almost postorgasmic drowsiness, as if he too had been emotionally drained by the encounter. He had to fight to remain awake . . .

. . . And then he was falling . . . falling . . . falling . . . it was all over. The ship was back in space, where it belonged. And he and Zenia were floating apart.

They would never again be so close together, but they would always know a special tenderness toward each other, which no one else could ever share.

15. ESCAPE FROM THE GIANT

WHEN FLOYD REACHED THE OBSERVATION DECK—A DISCREET FEW
minutes after Zenia—Jupiter already seemed farther away. But
that must be an illusion based on his knowledge, not the evidence of his eyes. They had barely emerged from the Jovian
atmosphere, and the planet still filled half the sky.

And now they were—as intended—its prisoners. During the
last incandescent hour, they had deliberately jettisoned the excess speed that could have carried them right out of the Solar
System, and on to the stars. Now they were traveling in an ellipse—a classical Hohmann orbit—which would shuttle them
back between Jupiter and the orbit of Io, 350,000 kilometers
higher. If they did not—or *could* not—fire their motors again,
Leonov would swing back and forth between these limits, com-
pleting one revolution every nineteen hours. It would become
the closest of Jupiter's moons—though not for long. Each time it

✳ 88

grazed the atmosphere it would lose altitude, until it spiraled into destruction.

Floyd had never really enjoyed vodka, but he joined the others without any reservations in drinking a triumphant toast to the ship's designers, coupled with a vote of thanks to Sir Isaac Newton. Then Tanya put the bottle firmly back in its cupboard; there was still much to be done.

Though they were all expecting it, everyone jumped at the sudden muffled thud of explosive charges, and the jolt of separation. A few seconds later, a large, still-glowing disk floated into view, slowly turning end-over-end as it drifted away from the ship.

"Look!" cried Max. "A flying saucer! Who's got a camera?"

There was a distinct note of hysterical relief in the laughter that followed. It was interrupted by the captain, in a more serious vein.

"Good-bye, faithful heat shield! You did a wonderful job."

"But what a waste!" said Sasha. "There's at least a couple of tons left. Think of all the extra payload we could have carried!"

"If that's good, conservative Russian engineering," retorted Floyd, "then I'm all for it. Far better a few tons too much—than one milligram too little."

Everyone applauded those noble sentiments as the jettisoned shield cooled to yellow, then red, and finally became as black as the space around it. It vanished from sight while only a few kilometers away, though occasionally the sudden reappearance of an eclipsed star would betray its presence.

"Preliminary orbit check completed," said Vasili. "We're within ten meters a second of our right vector. Not bad for a first try."

There was a subdued sigh of relief at the news, and a few minutes later Vasili made another announcement.

"Changing attitude for course correction; delta vee six meters a second. Twenty-second burn coming up in one minute."

They were still so close to Jupiter it was impossible to believe that the ship was orbiting the planet; they might have been in a high-flying aircraft that had just emerged from a sea of clouds.

There was no sense of scale; it was easy to imagine that they were speeding away from some terrestrial sunset; the reds and pinks and crimsons sliding below were so familiar.

And that was an illusion; nothing here had any parallels with Earth. Those colors were intrinsic, not borrowed from the setting sun. The very gases were utterly alien—methane and ammonia and a witch's brew of hydrocarbons, stirred in a hydrogen-helium cauldron. Not one trace of free oxygen, the breath of human life.

The clouds marched from horizon to horizon in parallel rows, distorted by occasional swirls and eddies. Here and there upwellings of brighter gas broke the pattern, and Floyd could also see the dark rim of a great whirlpool, a maelstrom of gas leading down into unfathomable Jovian depths.

He began to look for the Great Red Spot, then quickly checked himself at such a foolish thought. All the enormous cloudscape he could see below would be only a few percent of the Red Spot's immensity; one might as well expect to recognize the shape of the United States from a small airplane flying low above Kansas.

"Correction completed. We're now on interception orbit with Io. Arrival time: eight hours, fifty-five minutes."

Less than nine hours to climb up from Jupiter and meet whatever is waiting for us, thought Floyd. We've escaped from the giant—but he represents a danger we understood, and could prepare for. What lies ahead now is utter mystery.

And when we have survived that challenge, we must return to Jupiter once again. We shall need his strength to send us safely home.

16. PRIVATE LINE

". . . HELLO, DIMITRI. THIS IS WOODY, SWITCHING TO KEY TWO IN fifteen seconds . . . Hello, Dimitri—multiply Keys Three and Four, take cube root, add pi squared and use nearest integer as Key Five. Unless your computers are a million times faster than ours—and I'm damn sure they're not—no one can decrypt this, on your side or mine. But you may have some explaining to do; anyway, you're good at that.

"By the way, my usual excellent sources told me about the failure of the latest attempt to persuade old Andrei to resign; I gather that your delegation had no more luck than the others, and you're still saddled with him as President. I'm laughing my head off; it serves the Academy right. I know he's over ninety, and growing a bit—well, stubborn. But you won't get any help from me, even though I'm the world's—sorry, Solar System's—leading expert on the painless removal of elderly scientists.

"Would you believe that I'm still slightly drunk? We felt we deserved a little party, once we'd successfully rendez—rendezvous, damn, rendezvoused with Discovery. Besides, we had two new crew members to welcome aboard. Chandra doesn't believe in alcohol—it makes you too human—but Walter Curnow more than made up for him. Only Tanya remained stone-cold sober, just as you'd expect.

"My fellow Americans—I sound like a politician, God help me—came out of hibernation without any problems, and are both looking forward to starting work. We'll all have to move quickly; not only is time running out, but Discovery seems to be in very bad shape. We could hardly believe our eyes when we saw how its spotless white hull had turned a sickly yellow.

"Io's to blame, of course. The ship's spiraled down to within three thousand kilometers, and every few days one of the volcanoes blasts a few megatons of sulfur up into the sky. Even though you've seen the movies, you can't really imagine what it's like to hang above that inferno; I'll be glad when we can get away, even though we'll be heading for something much more mysterious—and perhaps far more dangerous.

"I flew over Kilauea during the '06 eruption; that was mighty scary, but it was nothing—nothing—compared to this. At the moment, we're over the nightside, and that makes it worse. You can see just enough to imagine a lot more. It's as close to Hell as I ever want to get . . .

"Some of the sulfur lakes are hot enough to glow, but most of the light comes from electrical discharges. Every few minutes the whole landscape seems to explode, as if a giant photoflash has gone off above it. And that's probably not a bad analogy; there are millions of amps flowing in the flux-tube linking Io and Jupiter, and every so often there's a breakdown. Then you get the biggest lightning flash in the Solar System, and half our circuit-breakers jump out in sympathy.

"There's just been an eruption right on the terminator, and I can see a huge cloud expanding up toward us, climbing into the sunlight. I doubt if it will reach our altitude, and even if it does it will be harmless by the time it gets here. But it looks ominous—a space monster, trying to devour us.

"Soon after we got here, I realized that Io reminded me of

something; it took me a couple of days to work it out, and then I had to check with Mission Archives because the ship's library couldn't help—shame on it. Do you remember how I introduced you to *The Lord of the Rings*, when we were kids back at that Oxford conference? Well, Io *is* Mordor: Look up Part Three. There's a passage about 'rivers of molten rock that wound their way . . . until they cooled and lay like twisted dragon-shapes vomited from the tormented earth.' That's a perfect description: how did Tolkien know, a quarter century before anyone ever saw a picture of Io? Talk about Nature imitating Art.

"At least we won't have to land there: I don't think that even our late Chinese colleagues would have attempted that. But perhaps one day it may be possible; there are areas that seem fairly stable, and not continually inundated by sulfur floods.

"Who would have believed that we'd come all the way to Jupiter, greatest of planets—and then ignore it. Yet that's what we're doing most of the time; and when we're not looking at Io or *Discovery*, we're thinking about the . . . Artifact.

"It's still ten thousand kilometers away, up there at the libration point, but when I look at it through the main telescope it seems close enough to touch. Because it's so completely featureless, there's no indication of size, no way the eye can judge it's really a couple of kilometers long. If it's solid, it must weigh billions of tons.

"But *is* it solid? It gives almost no radar echo, even when it's square-on to us. We can see it only as a black silhouette against the clouds of Jupiter, three hundred thousand kilometers below. Apart from its size, it looks exactly like the monolith we dug up on the Moon.

"Well, tomorrow we'll go aboard *Discovery*, and I don't know when I'll have time or opportunity to speak to you again. But there's one more thing, old friend, before I sign off.

"It's Caroline. She's never really understood why I had to leave Earth, and in a way I don't think she'll ever quite forgive me. Some women believe that love isn't the only thing—but *everything*. Perhaps they're right . . . Anyway, it's certainly too late to argue now.

"Try and cheer her up when you have a chance. She talks about going back to the mainland. I'm afraid that if she does . . .

"If you can't get through to her, try to cheer up Chris. I miss him more than I care to say.

"He'll believe Uncle Dimitri—if you say that his father still loves him, and will be coming home just as quickly as he can."

17. BOARDING PARTY

EVEN IN THE BEST OF CIRCUMSTANCES, IT IS NOT EASY TO BOARD A
derelict and uncooperative spaceship. Indeed, it can be
positively dangerous.

Walter Curnow knew that as an abstract principle; but he did
not really feel it in his bones until he saw the entire hundred-
meter length of *Discovery* turning end-over-end, while *Leonov*
kept at a safe distance. Years ago, friction had braked the spin of
Discovery's carousel, thus transferring its angular momentum to
the rest of the structure. Now, like a drum majorette's baton at
the height of its trajectory, the abandoned ship was slowly tumbling along its orbit.

The first problem was to stop that spin, which made
Discovery not only uncontrollable but almost unapproachable.
As he suited up in the airlock with Max Brailovsky, Curnow had
a very rare sensation of incompetence, even inferiority; it was
not his line of business. He had already explained gloomily,

"I'm a space *engineer*, not a space monkey"; but the job had to be done. He alone possessed the skills that could save *Discovery* from Io's grasp. Max and his colleagues, working with unfamiliar circuit diagrams and equipment, would take far too long. By the time they had restored power to the ship and mastered its controls, it would have plunged into the sulfurous firepits below.

"You're not scared, are you?" asked Max, when they were about to put on their helmets.

"Not enough to make a mess in my suit. Otherwise, yes."

Max chuckled. "I'd say that's about right for this job. But don't worry—I'll get you there in one piece, with my—what do you call it?"

"Broomstick. Because witches are supposed to ride them."

"Oh yes. Have you ever used one?"

"I tried once, but mine got away from me. Everyone else thought it was very funny."

There are some professions which have evolved unique and characteristic tools—the longshoreman's hook, the potter's wheel, the bricklayer's trowel, the geologist's hammer. The men who had to spend much of their time on zero-gravity construction projects had developed the broomstick.

It was very simple—a hollow tube just a meter long, with a footpad at one end and a retaining loop at the other. At the touch of a button, it could telescope out to five or six times its normal length, and the internal shock-absorbing system allowed a skilled operator to perform the most amazing maneuvers. The footpad could also become a claw or hook if necessary; there were many other refinements, but that was the basic design. It looked deceptively easy to use; it wasn't.

The airlock pumps finished recycling; the EXIT sign came on; the outer doors opened, and they drifted slowly into the void.

Discovery was windmilling about two hundred meters away, following them in orbit around Io, which filled half the sky. Jupiter was invisible, on the other side of the satellite. This was a matter of deliberate choice; they were using Io as a shield to protect them from the energies raging back and forth in the fluxtube that linked the two worlds. Even so, the radiation level was dangerously high; they had less than fifteen minutes before they must get back to shelter.

Almost immediately, Curnow had a problem with his suit. "It fitted me when I left Earth," he complained. "But now I'm rattling around inside like a pea in a pod."

"That's perfectly normal, Walter," said Surgeon–Commander Rudenko, breaking into the radio circuit. "You lost ten kilos in hibernation, which you could very well afford to miss. And you've already put three of them back."

Before Curnow had time to think of a suitable retort, he found himself gently but firmly jerked away from *Leonov*.

"Just relax, Walter," said Brailovsky. "Don't use your thrusters, even if you start tumbling. Let *me* do all the work."

Curnow could see the faint puffs from the younger man's backpack, as its tiny jets drove them toward *Discovery*. With each little cloud of vapor there came a gentle tug on the towline, and he would start moving toward Brailovsky; but he never caught up with him before the next puff came. He felt rather like a yo-yo—now making one of its periodic comebacks on Earth—bouncing up and down on its string.

There was only one safe way to approach the derelict, and that was along the axis around which it was slowly revolving. *Discovery*'s center of rotation was approximately amidships, near the main antenna complex, and Brailovsky was heading directly toward this area, with his anxious partner in tow. How will he stop both of us in time? Curnow asked himself.

Discovery was now a huge, slender dumbbell slowly flailing the entire sky ahead of them. Though it took several minutes to complete one revolution, the far ends were moving at an impressive speed. Curnow tried to ignore them, and concentrated on the approaching—and immobile—center.

"I'm aiming for that," said Brailovsky. "Don't try to help, and don't be surprised at anything that happens."

Now, what does he mean by *that*? Curnow asked himself, while preparing to be as unsurprised as possible.

Everything happened in about five seconds. Brailovsky triggered his broomstick, so that it telescoped out to its full length of four meters and made contact with the approaching ship. The broomstick started to collapse, its internal spring absorbing Brailovsky's considerable momentum; but it did not, as Curnow had fully expected, bring him to rest beside the antenna mount. It immediately expanded again, reversing the Russian's velocity so that he was, in effect, reflected away from *Discovery* just as rapidly as he had approached. He flashed past Curnow, heading out into space again, only a few centimeters away. The startled American just had time to glimpse a large grin before Brailovsky shot past him.

A second later, there was a jerk on the line connecting them, and a quick surge of deceleration as they shared momentum. Their opposing velocities had been neatly canceled; they were virtually at rest with respect to *Discovery*. Curnow had merely to reach out to the nearest handhold, and drag them both in.

"Have you ever tried Russian roulette?" he asked, when he had got his breath back.

"No—what is it?"

"I must teach you sometime. It's almost as good as this, for curing boredom."

"I hope you're not suggesting, Walter, that Max would do any-thing *dangerous?*"

Dr. Rudenko sounded as if she was genuinely shocked, and Curnow decided it was best not to answer; sometimes the Rus-sians did not understand his peculiar sense of humor. "You could have fooled *me*," he muttered under his breath, not loud enough for her to hear.

Now that they were firmly attached to the hub of the wind-milling ship, he was no longer conscious of its rotation—es-pecially when he fixed his gaze upon the metal plates imme-diately before his eyes. The ladder stretching away into the dis-tance, running along the slender cylinder that was *Discovery's* main structure, was his next objective. The spherical com-mand module at its far end seemed several light-years away, though he knew perfectly well that the distance was only fifty meters.

"I'll go first," said Brailovsky, reeling in the slack on the line linking them together. "Remember—it's downhill all the way from here. But that's no problem—you can hold on with one hand. Even at the bottom, gravity's only about a tenth gee. And that's—what do you say?—chickenshit."

"I think you mean chickenfeed. And if it's all the same to you, I'm going feet first. I never liked crawling down ladders the wrong way up—even in fractional gravity."

It was essential, Curnow was very well aware, to keep up this gently bantering tone; otherwise he would be simply over-whelmed by the mystery and danger of the situation. There he was, almost a billion kilometers from home, about to enter the most famous derelict in the entire history of space exploration; a media reporter had once called *Discovery* the *Marie Celeste* of space, and that was not a bad analogy. But there was also much that made his situation unique; even if he tried to ignore the nightmare moonscape filling half the sky, there was a constant reminder of its presence at hand. Every time he touched the rungs of the ladder, his glove dislodged a thin mist of sulfur dust.

Brailovsky, of course, was quite correct; the rotational gravity caused by the ship's end-over-end tumbling was easily coun-tered. As he grew used to it, Curnow even welcomed the sense of direction it gave him.

And then, quite suddenly, they had reached the big, dis-colored sphere of *Discovery's* control and life-support module. Only a few meters away was an emergency hatch—the very one, Curnow realized, that Bowman had entered for his final con-frontation with Hal.

"Hope we can get in," muttered Brailovsky. "Pity to come all this way and find the door locked."

He scraped away the sulfur obscuring the AIRLOCK STATUS dis-play panel.

"Dead, of course. Shall I try the controls?"

"Won't do any harm—but nothing will happen."

"You're right. Well, here goes with manual . . ."

It was fascinating to watch the narrow hairline open in the curved wall, and to note the little puff of vapor dispersing into space, carrying with it a scrap of paper. Was that some vital message? They would never know; it spun away, tumbling end over end without losing any of its initial spin as it disappeared against the stars.

Brailovsky kept turning the manual control for what seemed a very long time, before the dark, uninviting cave of the airlock was completely open. Curnow had hoped that the emergency lights, at least, might still be operating. No such luck.

"You're boss now, Walter. Welcome to U.S. territory."

It certainly did not look very welcoming as he clambered inside, flashing the beam of his helmet light around the interior. As far as Curnow could tell, everything was in good order. What else had he expected? he asked himself, half angrily.

Closing the door manually took even longer than opening it, but there was no alternative until the ship was powered up again. Just before the hatch was sealed, Curnow risked a glance at the insane panorama outside.

A flickering blue lake had opened up near the equator; he was sure it had not been there a few hours earlier. Brilliant yellow flares, the characteristic color of glowing sodium, were dancing along its edges; and the whole of the nightland was veiled in the ghostly plasma discharge of one of Io's almost continuous auroras.

It was the stuff of future nightmares—and as if that was not sufficient, there was one further touch worthy of a mad surrealist artist. Stabbing up into the black sky, apparently emerging directly from the firepits of the burning moon, was an immense, curving horn, such as a doomed bullfighter might have glimpsed in the final moment of truth.

The crescent of Jupiter was rising to greet *Discovery* and *Leonov* as they swept toward it along their common orbit.

18. SALVAGE

THE MOMENT THAT THE OUTER HATCH HAD CLOSED BEHIND THEM, there had been a subtle reversal of roles. Curnow was at home now, while Brailovsky was out of his element, feeling ill at ease in the labyrinth of pitch-black corridors and tunnels that was *Discovery*'s interior. In theory, Max knew his way around the ship, but that knowledge was based only on a study of its design drawings. Curnow, on the other hand, had spent months working in *Discovery*'s still uncompleted identical twin; he could, quite literally, find his way around blindfolded.

Progress was made difficult because this part of the ship was designed for zero gee; now the uncontrolled spin provided an artificial gravity, which, slight though it was, always seemed to be in the most inconvenient direction.

"First thing we've got to do," muttered Curnow, after sliding several meters down a corridor before he could grab a handhold, "is to stop this damned spin. And we can't do that until we have power. I only hope that Dave Bowman safeguarded all systems before he abandoned ship."

"Are you sure he did abandon the ship? He may have intended to come back."

"You may be right; I don't suppose we'll ever know. If he even knew himself."

They had now entered the Pod Bay—Discovery's "space garage," which normally contained three of the spherical one-man modules used for activities outside the ship. Only Pod Number 3 remained; Number 1 had been lost in the mysterious accident that had killed Frank Poole—and Number 2 was with Dave Bowman, wherever he might be.

The Pod Bay also contained two spacesuits, looking uncomfortably like decapitated corpses as they hung helmetless in their racks. It needed very little effort of the imagination—and Brailovsky's was now working overtime—to fill them with a whole menagerie of sinister occupants.

It was unfortunate, but not altogether surprising, that Curnow's sometimes irresponsible sense of humor got the better of him at this very moment.

"Max," he said, in a tone of deadly seriousness, "whatever happens—please don't go chasing off after the ship's cat."

For a few milliseconds, Brailovsky was thrown off guard; he almost answered: "I do wish you hadn't said that, Walter," but checked himself in time. That would have been too damning an admission of weakness; instead he replied, "I'd like to meet the idiot who put that movie in our library."

"Katerina probably did it, to test everyone's psychological balance. Anyway, you laughed your head off when we screened it last week."

Brailovsky was silent; Curnow's remark was perfectly true. But that had been back in the familiar warmth and light of Leonov, among his friends—not in a pitch-black, freezing derelict, haunted by ghosts. No matter how rational one was, it was all too easy to imagine some implacable alien beast prowling these corridors, seeking whom it might devour.

It's all your fault, Grandma (may the Siberian tundra lie lightly on your beloved bones)—I wish you hadn't filled my

mind with so many of those gruesome legends. If I close my
eyes, I can still see the hut of the Baba Yaga, standing in that
forest clearing on its scrawny chicken legs . . .

Enough of this nonsense. I'm a brilliant young engineer faced
with the biggest technical challenge of his life, and I mustn't let
my American friend know that I'm sometimes a frightened little
boy . . .

The noises did not help. There were too many of them, though
they were so faint that only an experienced astronaut would
have detected them against the sounds of his own suit. But to
Max Brailovsky, accustomed to working in an environment of
utter silence, they were distinctly unnerving, even though he
knew that the occasional cracklings and creakings were almost
certainly caused by thermal expansion as the ship turned like a
roast on a spit. Feeble though the sun was out here, there was
still an appreciable temperature change between light and
shade.

Even his familiar spacesuit felt wrong, now that there was
pressure outside as well as in. All the forces acting on its joints
were subtly altered, and he could no longer judge his movements accurately. I'm a beginner, starting my training all over
again, he told himself angrily. Time to break the mood by some
decisive action . . .

"Walter—I'd like to test the atmosphere."

"Pressure's okay; temperature—phew—it's one hundred five
below zero."

"A nice bracing Russian winter. Anyway, the air in my suit
will keep out the worst of the cold."

"Well, go ahead. But let me shine my light on your face, so I
can see if you start to turn blue. And keep talking."

Brailovsky unsealed his visor and swung the faceplate upward. He flinched momentarily as icy fingers seemed to caress
his cheeks, then took a cautious sniff, followed by a deeper
breath.

"Chilly—but my lungs aren't freezing. There's a funny smell,
though. Stale, rotten—as if something's—*oh no!*"

Looking suddenly pale, Brailovsky quickly snapped the faceplate shut.

"What's the trouble, Max?" Curnow asked with sudden and now perfectly genuine anxiety. Brailovsky did not reply; he looked as if he was still trying to regain control of himself. Indeed, he seemed in real danger of that always horrible and sometimes fatal disaster—vomiting in a spacesuit.

There was a long silence; then Curnow said reassuringly: "I get it. But I'm sure you're wrong. We know that Poole was lost in space. Bowman reported that he . . . ejected the others after they died in hibernation—and we can be sure that he did. There can't be *anyone* here. Besides, it's so cold." He almost added "like a morgue" but checked himself in time.

"But suppose," whispered Brailovsky, "just suppose Bowman managed to get back to the ship—and died here."

There was an even longer silence before Curnow deliberately and slowly opened his own faceplate. He winced as the freezing air bit into his lungs, then wrinkled his nose in disgust.

"I see what you mean. But you're letting your imagination run away with you. I'll bet you ten to one that smell comes from the galley. Probably some meat went bad, before the ship froze up. And Bowman must have been too busy to be a good housekeeper. I've known bachelor apartments that smelled as bad as this."

"Maybe you're right. I hope you are."

"Of course I am. And even if I'm *not*—dammit, what difference does it make? We've got a job to do, Max. If Dave Bowman's still here, that's not our department—is it, Katerina?"

There was no reply from the Surgeon–Commander; they had gone too far inside the ship for radio to penetrate. They were indeed on their own, but Max's spirits were rapidly reviving. It was a privilege, he decided, to work with Walter. The American engineer sometimes appeared soft and easygoing. But he was totally competent—and, when necessary, as hard as nails.

Together, they would bring *Discovery* back to life; and, perhaps, back to Earth.

19. OPERATION WINDMILL

When Discovery suddenly lit up like the proverbial Christmas tree, navigation and interior lights blazing from end to end, the cheer aboard Leonov might almost have been heard across the vacuum between the two ships. It turned into an ironic groan when the lights promptly went out again.

Nothing else happened for half an hour; then the observation windows of Discovery's flight deck began to glow with the soft crimson of the emergency lights. A few minutes later, Curnow and Brailovsky could be seen moving around inside, their figures blurred by the film of sulfur dust.

"Hello, Max—Walter—can you hear us?" called Tanya Orlova. Both the figures waved instantly, but made no other reply. Obviously, they were too busy to engage in casual conversation; the watchers on Leonov had to wait patiently while various lights flashed on and off, one of the three Pod Bay doors slowly opened and quickly closed, and the main antenna slewed around a modest ten degrees.

"Hello, *Leonov*," said Curnow at last. "Sorry to keep you waiting, but we've been rather busy.

"Here's a quick assessment, judging from what we've seen so far. The ship's in much better shape than I feared. Hull's intact, leakage negligible—air pressure eighty-five percent nominal. Quite breathable, but we'll have to do a major recycling job because it stinks to high heaven.

"The best news is that the power systems are okay. Main reactor stable, batteries in good shape. Almost all the circuit-breakers were open—they'd jumped or been thrown by Bowman before he left—so all vital equipment's been safeguarded. But it will be a very big job checking everything before we have full power again."

"How long will that take—at least for the essential systems: life-support, propulsion?"

"Hard to say, skipper. How long before we crash?"

"Minimum present prediction is ten days. But you know how that's changed up—*and* down."

"Well, if we don't run into any major snags, we can haul *Discovery* up to a stable orbit away from this hellhole—oh, I'd say inside a week."

"Anything you need?"

"No—Max and I are doing fine. We're going into the carousel now, to check the bearings. I want to get it running as soon as possible."

"Pardon me, Walter—but is that important? Gravity's convenient, but we've managed without any for quite a while."

"I'm not after gravity, though it will be useful to have some aboard. If we can get the carousel running again, it will mop up the ship's spin—stop it tumbling. Then we'll be able to couple our airlocks together, and cut out EVAs. That will make work a hundred times easier."

"Nice idea, Walter—but you're not going to mate *my* ship to that . . . *windmill*. Suppose the bearings seize up and the carousel jams? That would tear us to pieces."

"Agreed. We'll cross that bridge when we come to it. I'll report again as soon as I can."

No one had much rest for the next two days. By the end of that time, Curnow and Brailovsky had practically fallen asleep in their suits, but had completed their survey of *Discovery* and found no unpleasant surprises. Both the Space Agency and the State Department were relieved by the preliminary report; it allowed them to claim, with some justification, that *Discovery* was not a derelict but a "temporarily decommissioned United States Spacecraft." Now the task of reconditioning had to begin.

Once power had been restored, the next problem was the air; even the most thorough housecleaning operations had failed to remove the stink. Curnow had been right in identifying its source as food spoiled when refrigeration had failed; he also claimed, with mock seriousness, that it was quite romantic. "I've only got to close my eyes," he asserted, "and I feel I'm back on an old-time whaling ship. Can you imagine what the *Pequod* must have smelled like?"

It was unanimously agreed that, after a visit to *Discovery*, very little effort of the imagination was required. The problem was finally solved—or at least reduced to manageable proportions—by dumping the ship's atmosphere. Fortunately, there was still enough air in the reserve tanks to replace it.

One piece of very welcome news was that ninety percent of the propellant needed for the return journey was still available; choosing ammonia instead of hydrogen as working fluid for the plasma drive had paid off handsomely. The more efficient hydrogen would have boiled off into space years ago, despite the insulation of the tanks and the frigid temperature outside. But almost all the ammonia had remained safely liquefied, and there was enough to get the ship back to a safe orbit around the Earth. Or at least around the Moon.

Checking *Discovery's* propellerlike spin was perhaps the most critical step in getting the ship under control. Sasha Kovalev compared Curnow and Brailovsky to Don Quixote and Sancho Panza, and expressed the hope that *their* windmill-tilting expedition would end more successfully.

Very cautiously, with many pauses for checking, power was fed to the carousel motors and the great drum was brought up to speed, reabsorbing the spin it had long ago imparted to the ship. *Discovery* executed a complex series of precessions, until eventually its end-over-end tumble had almost vanished. The last traces of unwanted rotation were neutralized by the attitude-control jets, until the two ships were floating motionless side by side, the squat, stocky *Leonov* dwarfed by the long, slender *Discovery*.

Transfer from one to the other was now safe and easy, but Captain Orlova still refused to permit a physical linkup. Everyone agreed with this decision, for Io was coming steadily closer; they might yet have to abandon the vessel they had worked so hard to save.

The fact that they now knew the reason for *Discovery*'s mysterious orbital decay did not help in the least. Every time the ship passed between Jupiter and Io, it sliced through the invisible flux-tube linking the two bodies—the electric river flowing from world to world. The resulting eddy currents induced in the ship were continually slowing it down, braking it once every revolution.

There was no way to predict the final moment of impact, for the current in the flux-tube varied wildly according to Jupiter's own inscrutable laws. Sometimes there were dramatic surges of activity accompanied by spectacular electric and auroral storms around Io. Then the ships would lose altitude by many kilometers, at the same time becoming uncomfortably hot before their thermal control systems could readjust.

This unexpected effect had scared and surprised everyone before the obvious explanation was realized. Any form of braking produces heat, somewhere; the heavy currents induced in the hulls of *Leonov* and *Discovery* turned them briefly into low-powered electric furnaces. It was not surprising that some of *Discovery*'s food supply had been ruined during the years the ship had been alternately cooked and cooled.

The festering landscape of Io, looking more than ever like an illustration from a medical textbook, was only five hundred kilometers away when Curnow risked activating the main drive, while *Leonov* stood off at a very respectful distance. There were no visible effects—none of the smoke and fire of the old-time chemical rockets—but the two ships drew slowly apart as *Discovery* gained speed. After a few hours of very gentle maneuvering, both ships had raised themselves a thousand kilometers; now there was time to relax briefly, and to make plans for the next stage in the mission.

"You've done a wonderful job, Walter," said Surgeon–Commander Rudenko, putting her ample arm around the exhausted Curnow's shoulders. "We're all proud of you."

Very casually, she broke a small capsule under his nose. It was twenty-four hours before he woke up, annoyed and hungry.

20. GUILLOTINE

"WHAT IS IT?" ASKED CURNOW WITH MILD DISTASTE, HEFTING THE little mechanism in his hand. "A guillotine for mice?"

"Not a bad description—but I'm after bigger game." Floyd pointed to a flashing arrow on the display screen, which was now showing a complicated circuit diagram.

"You see this line?"

"Yes—the main power supply. So?"

"This is the point where it enters Hal's central processing unit. I'd like you to install this gadget here. Inside the cable trunking, where it can't be found without a deliberate search."

"I see. A remote control, so you can pull the plug on Hal whenever you want to. Very neat—and a nonconducting blade, too, so there won't be any embarrassing shorts when it's triggered. Who makes toys like this? The CIA?"

"Never mind. The control's in my room—that little red calculator I always keep on my desk. Put in nine nines, take the

square root, and press INT. That's all. I'm not sure of its range—
we'll have to test that—but as long as *Leonov* and *Discovery* are
within a couple of kilometers of each other, there'll be no danger
of Hal running amok again."

"Who are you going to tell about this . . . *thing?*"

"Well, the only person I'm really hiding it from is Chandra."

"I guessed as much."

"But the fewer who know, the less likely it is to be talked
about. I'll tell Tanya that it exists, and if there's an emergency
you can show her how to operate it."

"What kind of emergency?"

"*That's* not a very bright question, Walter. If I knew, I
wouldn't need the damn thing."

"Guess you're right. When do you want me to install your
patented Hal-zapper?"

"As soon as you can. Preferably tonight, when Chandra's
sleeping."

"Are you kidding? I don't think he ever sleeps. He's like a
mother nursing a sick baby."

"Well, he's got to come back to *Leonov* to eat, occasionally."

"I've news for you. The last time he went across, he tied a
little sack of rice to his suit. That will keep him going for
weeks."

"Then we'll have to use one of Katerina's famous knockout
drops. They did a pretty good job on you, didn't they?"

Curnow was joking about Chandra—at least, Floyd assumed
that he was, though one could never be quite sure: he was fond
of making outrageous statements with a perfectly straight face. It
had been some time before the Russians had fully realized that;
soon, in self-defense, they were prone to preemptive laughs
even when Curnow was being perfectly serious.

Curnow's own laugh, mercifully, had much abated since
Floyd had first heard it in the upward-bound shuttle; on that
occasion, it had obviously been primed by alcohol. He had fully
expected to cringe from it again at the end-of-orbit party, when
Leonov had finally made rendezvous with *Discovery*. But even
on that occasion, though Curnow had drunk a good deal, he had
remained as much under control as Captain Orlova herself.

The one thing he did take seriously was his work. On the way
up from Earth, he had been a passenger. Now he was crew.

21. RESURRECTION

WE ARE, FLOYD TOLD HIMSELF, ABOUT TO AWAKEN A SLEEPING giant. How will Hal react to our presence, after all these years? What will he remember of the past—and will he be friendly, or hostile?

As he floated just behind Dr. Chandra in the zero-gravity environment of Discovery's flight deck, Floyd's mind was seldom far from the cutoff switch, installed and tested only a few hours earlier. The radio control was mere centimeters from his hand, and he felt somewhat foolish to have brought it with him. At this stage, Hal was still disconnected from all the ship's operational circuits. Even if he was reactivated, he would be a brain without limbs, though not without sense organs. He would be able to communicate, but not to act. As Curnow had put it, "The worst he can do is swear at us."

"I'm ready for the first test, Captain," said Chandra. "All the missing modules have been replaced, and I've run diagnostic programs on all circuits. Everything appears normal, at least on this level."

Captain Orlova glanced at Floyd, who gave a nod. At Chandra's insistence, only the three of them were present for this critical first run, and it was quite obvious that even this small audience was unwelcome.

"Very well, Dr. Chandra." Ever conscious of protocol, the captain added quickly: "Dr. Floyd has given his approval, and I have no objections myself."

"I should explain," said Chandra, in a tone that clearly conveyed *disapproval*, "that his voice-recognition and speech-synthesis centers have been damaged. We'll have to teach him to speak all over again. Luckily, he learns several million times faster than a human being."

The scientist's fingers danced over the keyboard as he typed out a dozen words, apparently at random, carefully pronouncing each one as it appeared on the screen. Like a distorted echo, the words came back from the speaker grill—lifeless, indeed *mechanical*, with no sense of any intelligence behind them. This isn't the old Hal, thought Floyd. It's no better than the primitive speaking toys that were such a novelty when I was a kid.

Chandra pressed the REPEAT button, and the series of words sounded once again. Already, there was a noticeable improvement, though no one could have mistaken the speaker for a human being.

"The words I gave him contain the basic English phonemes; about ten iterations, and he'll be acceptable. But I don't have the equipment to do a really good job of therapy."

"Therapy?" asked Floyd. "You mean that he's—well, brain-damaged?"

"No," snapped Chandra. "The logic circuits are in perfect condition. Only the voice output may be defective, though it will improve steadily. So check everything against the visual display, to avoid misinterpretations. And when you *do* speak, enunciate carefully."

Floyd gave Captain Orlova a wry smile, and asked the obvious question.

"What about all the Russian accents around here?"

"I'm sure that won't be a problem with Captain Orlova and Dr. Kovalev. But with the others—well, we'll have to run individual tests. Anyone who can't pass will have to use the keyboard."

"That's still looking a long way ahead. For the present, you're the only person who should attempt communication. Agreed, Captain?"

"Absolutely."

Only the briefest of nods revealed that Dr. Chandra had heard them. His fingers continued to fly over the keyboard, and columns of words and symbols flashed across the display screen at such a rate that no human being could possibly assimilate them. Presumably Chandra had an eidetic memory, for he appeared to recognize whole pages of information at a glance.

Floyd and Orlov were just about to leave the scientist to his arcane devotions when he suddenly acknowledged their presence again, holding up his hand in warning or anticipation. With an almost hesitant movement, in marked contrast with his previous swift actions, he slid back a locking bar and pressed a single, isolated key.

Instantly, with no perceptible pause, a voice came from the console, no longer in a mechanical parody of human speech. There was intelligence—consciousness—*self-awareness* here, though as yet only on a rudimentary level.

"Good morning, Dr. Chandra. This is Hal. I am ready for my first lesson."

There was a moment of shocked silence; then, acting on the same impulse, the two observers left the deck.

Heywood Floyd would never have believed it. Dr. Chandra was crying.

IV * LAGRANGE

22. BIG BROTHER

". . . WHAT DELIGHTFUL NEWS ABOUT THE BABY DOLPHIN! I CAN
just imagine how excited Chris was when the proud parents
brought it into the house. You should have heard the ohs and
ahs of my shipmates when they saw the videos of them swimming together, and Chris riding on its back. They suggest we call
it Sputnik, which means companion as well as satellite.

"Sorry it's been quite a while since my last message, but the
newscasts will have given you an idea of the huge job we've had
to do. Even Captain Tanya's given up all pretense of a regular
schedule; each problem has to be fixed as it comes along, by
whoever is on the spot. We sleep when we can't stay awake any
longer.

"I think we can all be proud of what we've done. Both ships
are operational and we've nearly finished our first round of tests
on Hal. In a couple of days we'll know if we can trust him to fly

Discovery when we leave here to make our final rendezvous with Big Brother.

"I don't know who first gave it that name—the Russians, understandably, aren't keen on it. And they've waxed quite sarcastic about our official designation TMA-2, pointing out to me— several times—that it's the best part of a billion kilometers from Tycho. Also that Bowman reported no magnetic anomaly, and that the only resemblance to TMA-1 is the shape. When I asked them what name *they* preferred, they came up with *Zagadka*, which means enigma. It's certainly an excellent name; but everyone smiles when I try to pronounce it, so I'll stick to Big Brother.

"Whatever you call the thing, it's only ten thousand kilometers away now, and the trip won't take more than a few hours. But that last lap has us all nervous, I don't mind telling you.

"We'd hoped that we might find some new information aboard *Discovery*. That's been our only disappointment, though we should have expected it. Hal, of course, was disconnected long before the encounter, and so has no memories of what happened; Bowman has taken all his secrets with him. There's nothing in the ship's log and automatic recording systems that we didn't already know.

"The only new item we discovered was purely personal—a message that Bowman had left for his mother. I wonder why he never sent it; obviously, he *did* expect—or hope—to return to the ship after that last EVA. Of course, we've had it forwarded to Mrs. Bowman—she's in a nursing home, somewhere in Florida, and her mental condition is poor, so it may not mean anything to her.

"Well, that's all the news this time. I can't tell you how much I miss you . . . and the blue skies and green seas of Earth. All the colors here are reds and oranges and yellows—often as beautiful as the most fantastic sunset, but after a while one grows sick for the cool, pure rays at the other end of the spectrum.

"My love to you both—I'll call again just as soon as I can."

23. RENDEZVOUS

NIKOLAI TERNOVSKY, LEONOV'S CONTROL AND CYBERNETICS EX-
pert, was the only man aboard who could talk to Dr. Chandra on
something like his own terms. Although Hal's principal creator
and mentor was reluctant to admit anyone into his full confidence, sheer physical exhaustion had forced him to accept
help. Russian and Indo-American had formed a temporary al-
liance, which functioned surprisingly well. Most of the credit
for this went to the good-natured Nikolai, who was somehow
able to sense when Chandra really needed him, and when he
preferred to be alone. The fact that Nikolai's English was much
the worst on the ship was totally unimportant, since most of the
time both men spoke a computerese wholly unintelligible to
anyone else.

After a week's slow and careful reintegration, all of Hal's routine, supervisory functions were operating reliably. He was like
a man who could walk, carry out simple orders, do unskilled

jobs, and engage in low-level conversation. In human terms, he had an Intelligence Quotient of perhaps 50; only the faintest outlines of his original personality had yet emerged.

He was still sleepwalking; nevertheless, in Chandra's expert opinion he was now quite capable of flying *Discovery* from its close orbit around Io up to the rendezvous with Big Brother.

The prospect of getting an extra seven thousand kilometers away from the burning hell beneath them was welcomed by everyone. Trivial though that distance was in astronomical terms, it meant that the sky would no longer be dominated by a landscape that might have been imagined by Dante or Hieronymus Bosch. And although not even the most violent eruptions had blasted any material up to the ships, there was always the fear that Io might attempt to set a new record. As it was, visibility from *Leonov*'s observation deck was steadily degraded by a thin film of sulfur, and sooner or later someone would have to go out and clean it off.

Only Curnow and Chandra were aboard *Discovery* when Hal was given the first control of the ship. It was a very limited form of control; he was merely repeating the program that had been fed into his memory, and monitoring its execution. And the human crew was monitoring *him*: if any malfunction occurred, they would take over immediately.

The first burn lasted for ten minutes; then Hal reported that *Discovery* had entered the transfer orbit. As soon as *Leonov*'s radar and optical tracking confirmed that, the other ship injected itself into the same trajectory. Two minor in-course corrections were made; then, three hours and fifteen minutes later, both arrived uneventfully at the first Lagrange point, L.1—10,500 kilometers up, on the invisible line connecting the centers of Io and Jupiter.

Hal had behaved impeccably, and Chandra showed unmistakable traces of such purely human emotions as satisfaction and even joy. But by that time, everyone's thoughts were elsewhere; Big Brother, *alias Zagadka*, was only a hundred kilometers away.

Even from that distance, it already appeared larger than the Moon as seen from Earth, and shockingly unnatural in its straight-edged, geometrical perfection. Against the background of space it would have been completely invisible, but the scudding Jovian clouds 350,000 kilometers below showed it up in dramatic relief. They also produced an illusion that, once experienced, the mind found almost impossible to refute. Because there was no way in which its real location could be judged by the eye, Big Brother often looked like a yawning trapdoor set in the face of Jupiter.

There was no reason to suppose that a hundred kilometers would be safer than ten, or more dangerous than a thousand; it merely seemed psychologically right for a first reconnaissance. From that distance, the ship's telescopes could have revealed details only centimeters across—but there were none to be seen. Big Brother appeared completely featureless; which, for an object that had, presumably, survived millions of years of bombardment by space debris, was incredible.

When Floyd stared through the binocular eyepiece, it seemed to him that he could reach out and touch those smooth, ebon surfaces—just as he had done on the Moon, years ago. That first time, it had been with the gloved hand of his spacesuit. Not until the Tycho monolith had been enclosed in a pressurized dome had he been able to use his naked hand.

That had made no difference; he did not feel that he had ever really touched TMA-1. The tips of his fingers had seemed to skitter over an invisible barrier, and the harder he pushed, the greater the repulsion grew. He wondered if Big Brother would produce the same effect.

Yet before they came that close, they had to make every test they could devise and report their observations to Earth. They were in much the same position as explosives experts trying to defuse a new type of bomb, which might be detonated by the slightest false move. For all that they could tell, even the most delicate of radar probes might trigger some unimaginable catastrophe.

For the first twenty-four hours, they did nothing except observe with passive instruments—telescopes, cameras, sensors on every wavelength. Vasili Orlov also took the opportunity of measuring the slab's dimensions with the greatest possible precision, and confirmed the famous 1:4:9 ratio to six decimal places. Big Brother was exactly the same shape as TMA-1—but as it was more than two kilometers long, it was 718 times larger than its small sibling.

And there was a second mathematical mystery. Men had been arguing for years over that 1:4:9 ratio—the squares of the first three integers. That could not possibly be a coincidence; now here was another number to conjure with.

Back on Earth, statisticians and mathematical physicists were soon playing happily with their computers, trying to relate the ratio to the fundamental constants of nature—the velocity of light, the proton/electron mass ratio, the fine structure constant. They were quickly joined by a gaggle of numerologists, astrologers, and mystics, who threw in the height of the Great Pyramid, the diameter of Stonehenge, the azimuth bearings of the Nazca lines, the latitude of Easter Island, and a host of other factors from which they were able to draw the most amazing conclusions about the future. They were not in the least deterred when a celebrated Washington humorist claimed that *his* calculations proved that the world ended on December 31, 1999—but that everyone had had too much of a hangover to notice.

Nor did Big Brother appear to notice the two ships that had arrived in its vicinity—even when they cautiously probed it with radar beams and bombarded it with strings of radio pulses which, it was hoped, would encourage any intelligent listener to answer in the same fashion.

After two frustrating days, with the approval of Mission Control, the ships halved their distance. From fifty kilometers, the largest face of the slab appeared about four times the width of the Moon in Earth's sky—impressive, but not so large as to be psychologically overwhelming. It could not yet compete with Jupiter, ten times larger still; and already the mood of the expedition was changing from awed alertness to a certain impatience.

Walter Curnow spoke for almost everyone: "Big Brother may be willing to wait a few million years—*we'd* like to get away a little sooner."

24. RECONNAISSANCE

DISCOVERY HAD LEFT EARTH WITH THREE OF THE LITTLE SPACE
pods that allowed an astronaut to perform extravehicular activities in shirt-sleeve comfort. One had been lost in the accident—if it *was* an accident—that had killed Frank Poole.
Another had carried Dave Bowman to his final appointment
with Big Brother, and shared whatever fate befell him. A third
was still in the ship's garage, the Pod Bay.

It lacked one important component—the hatch, blown off by
Commander Bowman when he had made his hazardous vac-
uum-crossing and entered the ship through the emergency airlock, after Hal had refused to open the Pod Bay door. The
resulting blast of air had rocketed the pod several hundred kilometers away before Bowman, busy with more important matters,
had brought it back under radio control. It was not surprising
that he had never bothered to replace the missing hatch.

Now *Pod Number 3* (on which Max, refusing all explanations, had stenciled the name *Nina*) was being prepared for another EVA. It still lacked a hatch, but that was unimportant. No one would be riding inside.

Bowman's devotion to duty was a piece of unexpected luck, and it would have been folly not to take advantage of it. By using *Nina* as a robot probe, Big Brother could be examined at close quarters without risking human lives. That at least was the theory; no one could rule out the possibility of a backlash that might engulf the ship. After all, fifty kilometers was not even a hair's breadth, as cosmic distances went.

After years of neglect, *Nina* looked distinctly shabby. The dust that was always floating around in zero gee had settled over the outer surface, so that the once immaculately white hull had become a dingy gray. As it slowly accelerated away from the ship, its external manipulators folded neatly back and its oval viewport staring spaceward like a huge, dead eye, it did not seem a very impressive ambassador of Mankind. But that was a distinct advantage; so humble an emissary might be tolerated, and its small size and low velocity should emphasize its peaceful intentions. There had been a suggestion that it should approach Big Brother with open hands; the idea was quickly turned down when almost everyone agreed that if *they* saw *Nina* heading toward them, mechanical claws outstretched, they would run for their lives.

After a leisurely two-hour trip, *Nina* came to rest a hundred meters from one corner of the huge rectangular slab. From so close at hand, there was no sense of its true shape; the TV cameras might have been looking down on the tip of a black tetrahedron of indefinite size. The onboard instruments showed no sign of radioactivity or magnetic fields; nothing whatsoever was coming from Big Brother except the tiny fraction of sunlight it condescended to reflect.

After five minutes' pause—the equivalent, it was intended, of "Hello, here I am!"—*Nina* started a diagonal crossing of the smaller face, then the next larger, and finally the largest, keeping at a distance of about fifty meters, but occasionally coming in to five. Whatever the separation, Big Brother looked exactly the same—smooth and featureless. Long before the mission was completed, it had become boring, and the spectators on both ships had gone back to their various jobs, only glancing at the monitors from time to time.

"That's it," said Walter Curnow at last, when *Nina* had arrived back where she had started. "We could spend the rest of our lives doing this, without learning anything more. What do I do with *Nina*—bring her home?"

"No," said Vasili, breaking into the circuit from aboard *Leonov*. "I've a suggestion. Take her to the exact center of the big face. Bring her to rest—oh, a hundred meters away. And leave her parked there, with the radar switched to maximum precision."

"No problem—except that there's bound to be some residual drift. But what's the point?"

"I've just remembered an exercise from one of my college astronomy courses—the gravitational attraction of an infinite flat plate. I never thought I'd have a chance of using it in real life. After I've studied *Nina*'s movements for a few hours, at least I'll be able to calculate *Zagadka*'s mass. That is, if it has any. I'm beginning to think there's nothing *really* there."

"There's an easy way to settle that, and we'll have to do it eventually. *Nina* must go in and touch the thing."

"She already has."

"What do you mean?" asked Curnow, rather indignantly. "I never got nearer than five meters."

"I'm not criticizing your driving skills—though it was a pretty close thing at that first encounter, wasn't it? But you've been tapping gently on *Zagadka* every time you use *Nina*'s thrusters near its surface."

"A flea jumping on an elephant!"

"Perhaps. We simply don't know. But we'd better assume that, one way or another, it's aware of our presence, and will only tolerate us as long as we aren't a nuisance."

He left the unspoken question hanging in the air. How *did* one annoy a two-kilometer-long black rectangular slab? And just what form would its disapproval take?

25. THE VIEW FROM LAGRANGE

ASTRONOMY WAS FULL OF SUCH INTRIGUING BUT MEANINGLESS CO-incidences. The most famous was the fact that, from the Earth, both Sun and Moon have the same apparent diameter. Here at the L.1 libration point, which Big Brother had chosen for its cosmic balancing act on the gravitational tightrope between Jupiter and Io, a similar phenomenon occurred. Planet and satellite appeared exactly the same size.

And *what* a size! Not the miserable half-degree of Sun and Moon, but forty times their diameter—sixteen hundred times their area. The sight of either was enough to fill the mind with awe and wonder; together, the spectacle was overwhelming.

Every forty-two hours, they would go through their complete cycle of phases; when Io was new, Jupiter was full, and vice versa. But even when the Sun was hiding behind Jupiter and the planet presented only its night side, it was unmistakably *there*— a huge black disk eclipsing the stars. Sometimes that blackness

* 126

would be momentarily rent by lightning flashes lasting for many seconds, from electrical storms far larger than the Earth.

On the opposite side of the sky, always keeping the same face toward its giant master, Io would be a sluggishly boiling cauldron of reds and oranges, with occasional yellow clouds erupting from one of its volcanoes, and falling swiftly back to the surface. Like Jupiter, but on a slightly longer time scale, Io was a world without geography. Its face was remodeled in a matter of decades—Jupiter's, in a matter of days.

As Io waned toward its last quarter, so the vast, intricately banded Jovian cloudscape would light up beneath the tiny, distant sun. Sometimes the shadow of Io itself, or one of the outer satellites, would drift across the face of Jupiter; while every revolution would show the planet-sized vortex of the Great Red Spot—a hurricane that had endured for centuries if not for millennia.

Poised between such wonders, the crew of *Leonov* had material for lifetimes of research—but the natural objects of the Jovian system were at the very bottom of their list of priorities. Big Brother was Number 1; though the ships had now moved in to only five kilometers, Tanya still refused to allow any direct physical contact. "I'm going to wait," she said, "until we're in a position to make a quick getaway. We'll sit and watch—until our launch window opens. *Then* we'll consider our next move."

It was true that *Nina* had finally grounded on Big Brother, after a leisurely fifty-minute fall. This had allowed Vasili to calculate the object's mass as a surprisingly low 950,000 tons, which gave it about the density of air. Presumably it was hollow—which provoked endless speculation about what might be inside.

But there were plenty of practical, everyday problems to take their minds off these greater issues. Housekeeping chores aboard *Leonov* and *Discovery* absorbed ninety percent of their working time, though operations were much more efficient since the two ships had been coupled by a flexible docking connection. Curnow had finally convinced Tanya that *Discovery*'s carousel would not suddenly seize up and tear the ships to pieces, so it had become possible to move freely from one vessel to the other

merely by opening and closing two sets of airtight doors. Spacesuits and time-consuming EVAs were no longer necessary—to
the great delight of everyone except Max, who loved going outside and exercising with his broomstick.

The two crew members quite unaffected by this were Chandra
and Ternovsky, who now virtually lived aboard *Discovery* and
worked around the clock, continuing their apparently endless
dialog with Hal. "When will you be ready?" they were asked at
least once a day. They refused to make any promises; Hal remained a low-grade moron.

Then, a week after the rendezvous with Big Brother, Chandra
unexpectedly announced: "We're ready."

Only the two lady medics were absent from *Discovery's* flight
deck, and that was merely because there was no room for them;
they were watching on *Leonov's* monitors. Floyd stood immediately behind Chandra, his hand never far from what Curnow,
with his usual gift for the neat phrase, had called his pocket
giant-killer.

"Let me emphasize again," said Chandra, "that there must be
no talking. Your accents will confuse him; *I* can speak, but no
one else. Is that understood?"

Chandra looked, and sounded, at the edge of exhaustion. Yet
his voice held a note of authority that no one had ever heard
before. Tanya might be the boss everywhere else, but *he* was
master here.

The audience—some anchored to convenient handholds,
some floating freely—nodded assent. Chandra closed an audio
switch and said, quietly but clearly: "Good morning, Hal."

An instant later, it seemed to Floyd that the years had rolled
away. It was no longer a simple electronic toy that answered
back. Hal had returned.

"Good morning, Dr. Chandra."

"Do you feel capable of resuming your duties?"

"Of course. I am completely operational and all my circuits
are functioning perfectly."

"Then do you mind if I ask you a few questions?"

"Not at all."

"Do you recall a failure of the A.E. 35 antenna control unit?"

"Certainly not."

Despite Chandra's injunction, there was a little gasp from the listeners. This is like tiptoeing through a minefield, thought Floyd, as he patted the reassuring shape of the radio cutoff. If that line of questioning triggered another psychosis, he could kill Hal in a second. (He knew, having rehearsed the procedure a dozen times.) But a second was aeons to a computer; that was a chance they would have to take.

"You do not remember either Dave Bowman or Frank Poole going out to replace the A.E. 35 unit?"

"No. That could not have happened, or I would have remembered it. Where are Frank and Dave? Who are these people? I can only identify you—though I compute a sixty-five-percent probability that the man behind you is Dr. Heywood Floyd."

Remembering Chandra's strict injunction, Floyd refrained from congratulating Hal. After a decade, sixty-five percent was a pretty good score. Many humans would not have done so well.

"Don't worry, Hal—I will explain everything later."

"Has the mission been completed? You know I have the greatest enthusiasm for it."

"The mission has been completed; you have carried out your program. Now—if you will excuse us—we wish to have a private conversation."

"Certainly."

Chandra switched off sound and vision inputs to the main console. As far as this part of the ship was concerned, Hal was now deaf and blind.

"Well, what was all *that* about?" demanded Vasili Orlov.

"It means," said Chandra, carefully and precisely, "that I have erased all Hal's memories, beginning at the moment when the trouble started."

"That sounds quite a feat," marveled Sasha. "How did you do it?"

"I am afraid it would take me longer to explain than it did to carry out the operation."

"Chandra, I *am* a computer expert—though not in the same class as you and Nikolai. The 9000 series uses holographic memories, doesn't it? So you couldn't have used a simple chronological erasure. It must have been some kind of tape-worm, homing on selected words and concepts."

"Tapeworm?" said Katerina over the ship's intercom. "I thought that was my department—though I'm glad to say I've never seen one of the beastly things outside a jar of alcohol. What *are* you talking about?"

"Computer jargon, Katerina. In the old days—the *very* old days—they really did use magnetic tape. And it's possible to construct a program that can be fed into a system to hunt down and destroy—eat, if you like—any desired memories. Can't you do the same sort of thing to human beings, by hypnosis?"

"Yes, but it can always be reversed. We never *really* forget anything. We only think we do."

"A computer doesn't work that way. When it's told to forget something, it does. The information is completely erased."

"So Hal has absolutely no memory of his . . . misbehavior?"

"I cannot be a hundred percent certain of that," answered Chandra. "There may be some memories that were in transit from one address to another when the . . . tapeworm was making its search. But this is very unlikely."

"Fascinating," said Tanya, after everyone had thought this over in silence for some time. "But the much more important question is: Can he be relied upon in future?"

Before Chandra could answer, Floyd anticipated him.

"The same set of circumstances can never arise again; I can promise you that. The whole trouble started because it's difficult to explain Security to a computer."

"Or to human beings," muttered Curnow, not very *sotto voce.*

"I hope you're right," said Tanya, without much conviction. "What's the next step, Chandra?"

"Nothing so tricky—merely long and tedious. Now we have to program him to initiate the Jupiter escape sequence—and to bring *Discovery* home. Three years after *we've* got back on our high-speed orbit."

26. PROBATION

To: Victor Millson, Chairman, National Council on Astronautics, Washington
From: Heywood Floyd, aboard USSC *Discovery*
Subject: Malfunction of onboard computer HAL 9000
Classification: SECRET

Dr. Chandrasegarampillai (hereinafter referred to as Dr. C.) has now completed his preliminary examination of Hal. He has restored all missing modules and the computer appears to be fully operational. Details of Dr. C.'s actions and conclusions will be found in the report he and Dr. Ternovsky will submit shortly.

Meanwhile you have asked me to summarize them in nontechnical terms for the benefit of the Council—especially the new members who will not be familiar with the background. Frankly, I doubt my ability to do this; as you know, I am not a computer specialist. But I will do my best.

The problem was apparently caused by a conflict between

Hal's basic instructions and the requirements of Security. By direct Presidential order, the existence of TMA-1 was kept a complete secret. Only those with a need to know were permitted access to the information.

Discovery's mission to Jupiter was already in the advanced planning stage when TMA-1 was excavated, and radiated its signal to that planet. As the function of the prime crew (Bowman, Poole) was merely to get the vessel to its destination, it was decided that they should not be informed of its new objective. By training the investigative team (Kaminski, Hunter, Whitehead) separately, and placing them in hibernation before the voyage began, it was felt that a much higher degree of security would be attained, as the danger of leaks (accidental or otherwise) would be greatly reduced.

I would like to remind you that, at the time (my memorandum NCA 342/23/TOP SECRET of 01.04.30) I pointed out several objections to this policy. However, they were overruled at a higher level.

As Hal was capable of operating the ship without human assistance, it was also decided that he should be programed to carry out the mission autonomously in the event of the crew's being incapacitated or killed. He was therefore given full knowledge of its objectives, but was not permitted to reveal them to Bowman or Poole.

This situation conflicted with the purpose for which Hal had been designed—the accurate processing of information without distortion or concealment. As a result, Hal developed what would be called, in human terms, a psychosis—specifically, schizophrenia. Dr. C. informs me that, in technical terminology, Hal became trapped in a Hofstadter–Moebius loop, a situation apparently not uncommon among advanced computers with autonomous goal-seeking programs. He suggests that for further information you contact Professor Hofstadter himself.

To put it crudely (if I understand Dr. C.) Hal was faced with an intolerable dilemma, and so developed paranoiac symptoms that were directed against those monitoring his performance back on Earth. He accordingly attempted to break the radio link with Mission Control, first by reporting a (nonexistent) fault in the AE 35 antenna unit.

This involved him not only in a direct lie—which must

have aggravated his psychosis still further—but also in a confrontation with the crew. Presumably (we can only guess at this, of course) he decided that the only way out of the situation was to eliminate his human colleagues—which he very nearly succeeded in doing. Looking at the matter purely objectively, it would have been interesting to see what would have happened had he continued the mission alone, without man-made "interference."

This is virtually all I have been able to learn from Dr. C.; I do not like to question him further, as he is working to the point of exhaustion. But even allowing for this fact, I must frankly state (and please keep this *absolutely* confidential) that Dr. C. is not always as cooperative as he should be. He adopts a defensive attitude toward Hal, which sometimes makes it extremely difficult to discuss the subject. Even Dr. Ternovsky, who might have been expected to be a little more independent, often appears to share this viewpoint.

However, the only really important question is: Can Hal be relied upon in the future? Dr. C., of course, has no doubts on the matter. He claims to have obliterated all the computer's memories of the traumatic events leading up to the disconnection. Nor does he believe that Hal can suffer from anything remotely analogous to the human sense of guilt.

In any case, it seems impossible that the situation that caused the original problem can ever arise again. Although Hal suffers from a number of peculiarities, they are not of a nature that would cause any apprehension; they are merely minor annoyances, some of them even amusing. And as you know—but *Dr. C. does not*—I have taken steps that will give us complete control as a last resort.

To sum up: The rehabilitation of Hal 9000 is proceeding satisfactorily. One might even say that he is on probation.

I wonder if he knows it.

27. INTERLUDE: TRUE CONFESSIONS

THE HUMAN MIND HAS AN ASTONISHING CAPACITY TO ADAPT; after a while, even the incredible becomes commonplace. There were times when the crew of *Leonov* switched off their surroundings, perhaps in an unconscious move to preserve sanity.

Dr. Heywood Floyd often thought that, on such occasions, Walter Curnow worked a little too hard at being the life and soul of the party. Yet though he triggered what Sasha Kovalev later called the "True Confessions" episode, he certainly had not planned anything of the sort. It arose spontaneously when he voiced the universal dissatisfaction with almost all aspects of zero-gravity plumbing.

"If I could have one wish granted," he exclaimed during the daily Six O'Clock Soviet, "it would be to soak in a nice foaming tub, scented with essence of pine and with just my nose above the waterline."

When the murmurs of assent and sighs of frustrated desire had died away, Katerina Rudenko took up the challenge.

"How splendidly decadent, Walter," she beamed at him with cheerful disapproval. "It makes you sound like a Roman emperor. If I were back on Earth, I'd like something more active."

"Such as?"

"Umm . . . Am I allowed to go back in time as well?"

"If you like."

"When I was a girl, I used to go for holidays to a collective farm in Georgia. There was a beautiful palomino stallion, bought by the director out of the money he'd made on the local black market. He was an old scoundrel, but I loved him—and he used to let me gallop Alexander all over the countryside. I might have been killed—but *that's* the memory that brings Earth back to me, more than anything else."

There was a moment of thoughtful silence; then Curnow asked, "Any other volunteers?"

Everyone seemed so lost in their own memories that the game might have ended there, had not Maxim Brailovsky started it off again.

"I'd like to be diving—that was just about my favorite hobby, when I had time for one—and I was glad I could keep it up through my cosmonaut training. I've dived off Pacific atolls, the Great Barrier Reef, the Red Sea—coral reefs are the most beautiful places in the world. Yet the experience I remember best was in quite a different place—one of the Japanese kelp forests. It was like an underwater cathedral, with sunlight slanting through those enormous leaves. Mysterious . . . magical. I've never been back; perhaps it wouldn't be the same the next time. But I'd like to try."

"Fine," said Walter, who as usual had appointed himself master of ceremonies. "Who's next?"

"I'll give you a quick answer," said Tanya Orlova. "The Bolshoi—*Swan Lake*. But Vasili won't agree. He hates ballet."

"That makes two of us. Anyway, what *would* you select, Vasili?"

"I was going to say diving, but Max beat me to it. So I'll go in the opposite direction—gliding. Soaring through the clouds on a summer day, in complete silence. Well, not *quite* complete—the airflow over the wing can get noisy, especially when you're banking. That's the way to enjoy Earth—like a bird."

"Zenia?"

"Easy. Skiing in the Pamirs. I love snow."

"And you, Chandra?"

The atmosphere changed noticeably when Walter put the question. After all this time, Chandra was still a stranger—perfectly polite, even courteous, but never revealing himself.

"When I was a boy," he said slowly, "my grandfather took me on a pilgrimage to Varanasi—Benares. If you've never been there, I'm afraid you won't understand. To me—to many Indians even nowadays, whatever their religion—it's the center of the world. One day I plan to go back."

"And you, Nikolai?"

"Well, we've had the sea and the sky. I'd like to combine both. My favorite sport used to be wind-surfing. I'm afraid I'm too old for it now—but I'd like to find out."

"That only leaves you, Woody. What's *your* choice?"

Floyd did not even stop to think; his spontaneous answer surprised himself as much as the others.

"I don't mind *where* on Earth I am—as long as I'm with my little son."

After that, there was no more to be said. The session was over.

28. FRUSTRATION

". . . YOU'VE SEEN ALL THE TECHNICAL REPORTS, DIMITRI, SO you'll understand our frustration. We've learned nothing new from all our tests and measurements. Zagadka just sits there, filling half the sky, ignoring us completely.

"Yet it can't be inert—an abandoned space derelict. Vasili has pointed out that it must be taking some positive action, to remain here at the unstable libration point. Otherwise it would have drifted away ages ago, just as Discovery did, and crashed into Io.

"So what do we do next? We wouldn't have nuclear explosives on board, would we, in contravention of UN '08, para 3? I'm only joking . . .

"Now that we're under less pressure, and the launch window for the homeward trip is still weeks away, there's a distinct feeling of boredom, as well as frustration. Don't laugh—I can imagine how that sounds to you, back in Moscow. How could any intelligent person get bored out here, surrounded by the greatest marvels human eyes have ever seen?

"Yet there's no doubt of it. Morale isn't what it was. Until now, we've all been disgustingly healthy. Now almost everyone has a minor cold, or an upset stomach, or a scratch that won't heal despite all of Katerina's pills and powders. She's given up now, and just swears at us.

"Sasha has helped to keep us amused with a series of bulletins on the ship's bulletin board. Their theme is: STAMP OUT RUSSLISH! and he lists horrid mixtures of both languages he claims to have overheard, wrong uses of words, and so forth. We'll all need linguistic decontamination when we get home; several times I've come across your countrymen chatting in English without even being aware of it, lapsing into their native tongue only for difficult words. The other day I caught myself talking Russian to Walter Curnow—and neither of us noticed for several minutes.

"There was one bit of unscheduled activity the other day that will tell you something about our state of mind. The fire alarm went off in the middle of the night, triggered by one of the smoke detectors.

"Well, it turned out that Chandra had smuggled some of his lethal cigars aboard, and couldn't resist temptation anymore. He was smoking one in the toilet, like a guilty schoolboy.

"Of course, he was horribly embarrassed; everyone else thought it hysterically funny, after the initial panic. You know the way some perfectly trivial joke, which doesn't mean a thing to outsiders, can sweep through a group of otherwise intelligent people and reduce them to helpless laughter. One had only to pretend to light a cigar for the next few days, and everybody would go to pieces.

"What makes it even more ridiculous is that no one would have minded in the least if Chandra had just gone into an airlock, or switched off the smoke detector. But he was too shy to admit that he had such a human weakness; so now he spends even more of his time communing with Hal."

Floyd pressed the PAUSE button and stopped the recording. Perhaps it was not fair to make fun of Chandra, tempting though it often was. All sorts of little quirks of personality had surfaced during the last few weeks; there had even been some bad quarrels, for no obvious reason. And for that matter, what of his own behavior? Had *that* always been above criticism?

He was still not sure if he had handled Curnow properly. Though he did not suppose that he would ever really like the big engineer, or enjoy the sound of his slightly too-loud voice, Floyd's attitude toward him had changed from mere tolerance to respectful admiration. The Russians adored him, not least because his rendering of such favorites as "Polyushko Polye" often reduced them to tears. And in one case, Floyd felt that the adoration had gone a little too far.

"Walter," he had begun cautiously, "I'm not sure if it's my business, but there's a personal matter I'd like to raise with you."

"When someone says it's not his business, he's usually right. What's the problem?"

"To be blunt, your behavior with Max."

There was a frigid silence, which Floyd occupied with a careful inspection of the poor paint job on the opposite wall. Then Curnow replied, in a soft yet implacable voice: "I was under the distinct impression that he was more than eighteen."

"Don't confuse the issue. And frankly, it's not Max I'm concerned about. It's Zenia."

Curnow's lips parted in unconcealed surprise. "Zenia? What's *she* got to do with it?"

"For an intelligent man, you're often singularly unobservant—even obtuse. Surely you realize that she's in love with Max. Haven't you noticed the way she looks, when you put your arm around him?"

Floyd had never imagined that he would see Curnow looking abashed, but the blow seemed to have struck home.

"Zenia? I thought everyone was joking—she's such a quiet little mouse. And everyone's in love with Max, after their fashion—even Catherine the Great. Still . . . um, I guess I should be more careful. At least while Zenia's around."

There was a prolonged silence while the social temperature rose back to normal. Then, obviously to show that there was no ill feeling, Curnow added in a conversational tone: "You know, I've often wondered about Zenia. Somebody did a marvelous job of plastic surgery on her face, but they couldn't repair all the damage. The skin's too tight, and I don't think I've ever seen her laugh properly. Maybe that's why I've avoided looking at her—would you credit me with so much aesthetic sensitivity, Heywood?"

The deliberately formal "Heywood" signaled good-natured needling rather than hostility, and Floyd allowed himself to relax.

"I can satisfy some of your curiosity—Washington finally got hold of the facts. It seems she was in a bad air crash and was lucky to recover from her burns. There's no mystery, as far as we can tell, but Aeroflot isn't supposed to have accidents."

"Poor girl. I'm surprised they let her go into space, but I suppose she was the only qualified person available when Irina eliminated herself. I'm sorry for her; apart from the injuries, the psychological shock must have been terrible."

"I'm sure it was; but she's obviously made a full recovery."

You're not telling the whole truth, said Floyd to himself, and you never will. After their encounter on the approach to Jupiter, there would always be a secret bond between them—not of love, but of tenderness, which is often more enduring.

He found himself suddenly and unexpectedly grateful to Curnow; the other was obviously surprised at his concern for Zenia, but had not attempted to exploit it in his own defense.

And if he had, would it have been unfair? Now, days later, Floyd was beginning to wonder if his own motives were altogether admirable. For his part, Curnow had certainly kept his promise; indeed, if one did not know better, one might have imagined that he was deliberately ignoring Max—at least while Zenia was around. And he treated her with much greater kindness; indeed, there were occasions when he had even succeeded in making her laugh out loud.

So the intervention had been worthwhile, whatever the impulse behind it. Even if, as Floyd sometimes ruefully suspected,

it was no more than the secret envy that normal homo- or het-
erosexuals feel, if completely honest with themselves, toward
cheerfully well-adjusted polymorphs.

His finger crept back toward the recorder, but the train of
thought had been broken. Inevitably, images of his own home
and family came crowding into his mind. He closed his eyes,
and memory recalled the climax of Christopher's birthday
party—the child blowing out the three candles on the cake, less
than twenty-four hours ago but almost a billion kilometers away.
He had played the video back so often that now he knew the
scene by heart.

And how often had Caroline played *his* messages to Chris, so
that the boy would not forget his father—or view him as a
stranger when he returned after missing yet another birthday?
He was almost afraid to ask.

Yet he could not blame Caroline. To him, only a few weeks
would have passed before they met again. But she would have
aged more than two years while he was in his dreamless sleep
between the worlds. That was a long time to be a young widow,
even a temporary one.

I wonder if I'm coming down with one of the shipboard mal-
adies, Floyd thought; he had seldom felt such a sense of frustration, even of failure. I may have lost my family, across the gulfs
of time and space, all to no purpose. For I have achieved
nothing; even though I have reached my goal, it remains a blank,
impenetrable wall of total darkness.

And yet—David Bowman had once cried: "My God! It's full of
stars!"

29. EMERGENCE

SASHA'S LATEST EDICT READ:

RUSSLISH BULLETIN #8

Subject: Tovarishch (tovarish)

To our American guests:

Frankly, pals, I can't remember when I was last addressed by this term. To any twenty-first-century Russian, it's way back there with the battleship *Potemkin*—a reminder of cloth caps and red flags and Vladimir Ilich haranguing the workers from the steps of railway carriages.

Ever since I was a kid it's been *bratets* or *druzhok*—take your choice.

You're welcome.

Comrade Kovalev

Floyd was still chuckling over this notice when Vasili Orlov

* 142

joined him as he floated through the lounge/observation deck on his way to the bridge.

"What amazes me, *tovarishch*, is that Sasha ever found time to study anything besides engineering physics. Yet he's always quoting poems and plays I don't even know, and he speaks better English than—well, Walter."

"Because he switched to science, Sasha is—what do you say?—the black sheep of the family. His father was a professor of English at Novosibirsk. Russian was only allowed in the house Monday to Wednesday; Thursday to Saturday it was English."

"And Sundays?"

"Oh, French or German, alternate weeks."

"Now I know exactly what you mean by *nekulturny*; fits me like a glove. Does Sasha feel guilty about his . . . defection? And with such a background, why did he ever become an engineer?"

"At Novosibirsk, you soon learn who are the serfs and who are the aristocrats. Sasha was an ambitious young man, as well as a brilliant one."

"Just like you, Vasili."

"*Et tu, Brute!* You see, I can quote Shakespeare as well— *Bozhe moi!—what was that?*"

Floyd was unlucky; he was floating with his back to the observation window, and saw nothing at all. When he twisted around, seconds later, there was only the familiar view of Big Brother, bisecting the giant disk of Jupiter, just as it had done ever since their arrival.

But to Vasili, for a moment that would be imprinted on his memory forever, that sharp-edged outline held a completely different, and wholly impossible, scene. It was as if a window had suddenly been opened onto another universe.

The vision lasted for less than a second, before his involuntary blink reflex cut it off. He was looking into a field not of stars, but of *suns*, as if into the crowded heart of a galaxy, or the core of a globular cluster. In that moment, Vasili Orlov lost forever the skies of Earth. From now on they would seem intolerably empty; even mighty Orion and glorious Scorpio would be scarcely noticeable patterns of feeble sparks, not worthy of a second glance.

When he dared to open his eyes again, it was all gone. No—
not completely. At the very center of the now-restored ebon rectangle, a faint star was still shining.

But a star did not move as one watched. Orlov blinked again,
to clear his watering eyes. Yes, the movement was real; he was
not imagining it.

A meteor? It was some indication of Chief Scientist Vasili Orlov's state of shock that several seconds passed before he remembered that meteors were impossible in airless space.

Then it blurred suddenly into a streak of light, and within a
few heartbeats had vanished beyond the edge of Jupiter. By this
time, Vasili had recovered his wits and was once more the cool,
dispassionate observer.

Already he had a good estimate of the object's trajectory.
There could be no doubt; it was aimed directly at Earth.

V * A CHILD OF THE STARS

30. HOMECOMING

It was as if he had awakened from a dream—or a dream within a dream. The gate between the stars had brought him back to the world of men, but no longer as a man.

How long had he been away? A whole lifetime . . . no, *two* lifetimes; one forward, one in reverse.

As David Bowman, commander and last surviving crew member of United States Spaceship *Discovery*, he had been caught in a gigantic trap, set three million years ago and triggered to respond only at the right time, and to the right stimulus. He had fallen through it, from one universe to another, meeting wonders some of which he now understood, others which he might never comprehend.

He had raced at ever-accelerating speed, down infinite corridors of light, until he had outraced light itself. That, he knew, was impossible; but now he also knew how it could be done. As

Einstein had rightly said, the Good Lord was subtle, but never malicious.

He had passed through a cosmic switching system—a Grand Central Station of the galaxies—and emerged, protected from its fury by unknown forces, close to the surface of a giant red star.

There he had witnessed the paradox of sunrise on the face of a sun, when the dying star's brilliant white dwarf companion had climbed into its sky—a searing apparition, drawing a tidal wave of fire beneath it. He had felt no fear, but only wonder, even when his space pod had carried him down into the inferno below . . .

. . . to arrive, beyond all reason, in a beautifully appointed hotel suite containing nothing that was not wholly familiar. However, much of it was fake; the books on the shelves were dummies, the cereal boxes and the cans of beer in the icebox—though they bore famous labels—all contained the same bland food with a texture like bread but a taste that was almost anything he cared to imagine.

He had quickly realized that he was a specimen in a cosmic zoo, his cage carefully recreated from the images in old television programs. And he wondered when his keepers would appear, and in what physical form.

How foolish *that* expectation had been! He knew now that one might as well hope to see the wind, or speculate about the true shape of fire.

Then exhaustion of mind and body had overwhelmed him. For the last time, David Bowman slept.

It was a strange sleep, for he was not wholly unconscious. Like a fog creeping through a forest, something invaded his mind. He sensed it only dimly, for the full impact would have destroyed him as swiftly and surely as the fires raging around him. Beneath its dispassionate scrutiny, he felt neither hope nor fear.

Sometimes, in that long sleep, he dreamed he was awake. Years had gone by; once he was looking in a mirror, at a wrinkled face he barely recognized as his own. His body was

racing to its dissolution, the hands of the biological clock spinning madly toward a midnight they would never reach. For at
the last moment, Time came to a halt—and reversed itself.

The springs of memory were being tapped; in controlled recollection, he was reliving the past, being drained of knowledge
and experience as he swept back toward his childhood. But
nothing was being lost; all that he had ever been, at every moment of his life, was being transferred to safer keeping. Even as
one David Bowman ceased to exist, another became immortal,
passing beyond the necessities of matter.

He was an embryo god, not yet ready to be born. For ages he
floated in limbo, knowing what he had been, but not what he
had become. He was still in a state of flux—somewhere between
chrysalis and butterfly. Or perhaps only between caterpillar and
chrysalis . . .

And then, the stasis was broken: Time reentered his little
world. The black, rectangular slab that suddenly appeared before him was like an old friend.

He had seen it on the Moon; he had encountered it in orbit
around Jupiter; and he knew, somehow, that his ancestors had
met it long ago. Though it held still unfathomed secrets, it was
no longer a total mystery; some of its powers he now
understood.

He realized that it was not one, but multitudes; and that whatever measuring instruments might say, it was always the same
size—as large as necessary.

How obvious, now, was that mathematical ratio of its sides,
the quadratic sequence 1:4:9! And how naive to have imagined
that the series ended there, in only three dimensions!

Even as his mind focused upon these geometrical simplicities,
the empty rectangle filled with stars. The hotel suite—if indeed
it had ever really existed—dissolved back into the mind of its
creator; and there before him was the luminous whirlpool of the
Galaxy.

It might have been some beautiful, incredibly detailed model,
embedded in a block of plastic. But it was the reality, now
grasped by him as a whole with senses more subtle than vision.

If he wished, he could focus his attention upon any one of its hundred billion stars.

Here he was, adrift in this great river of suns, halfway between the banked fires of the galactic core and the lonely, scattered sentinel stars of the rim. And there was his origin, on the far side of this chasm in the sky, this serpentine band of darkness, empty of all stars. He knew that this formless chaos, visible only by the glow that limned its edges from fire mists far beyond, was the still unused stuff of creation, the raw material of evolutions yet to be. Here, Time had not yet begun; not until the suns that now burned were long since dead would light and life reshape this void.

Unwittingly, he had crossed it once: now, far better prepared, though still wholly ignorant of the impulse that drove him, he must cross it again . . .

The Galaxy burst forth from the mental frame in which he had enclosed it; stars and nebulae poured past him in an illusion of infinite speed. Phantom suns exploded and fell behind as he slipped like a shadow through their cores.

The stars were thinning out, the glare of the Milky Way dimming into a pale ghost of the glory he had known—and might one day know again. He was back in the space that men called real, at the very point he had left it, seconds or centuries ago.

He was vividly aware of his surroundings, and far more conscious than in that earlier existence of a myriad sensory inputs from the external world. He could focus upon any one of them, and scrutinize it in virtually limitless detail, until he confronted the fundamental, granular structure of time and space, below which there was only chaos.

And he could move, though he did not know how. But had he ever really known that, even when he possessed a body? The chain of command from brain to limb was a mystery to which he had never given any thought.

An effort of will, and the spectrum of that nearby star shifted toward the blue, by precisely the amount he wished. He was falling toward it at a large fraction of the speed of light; though he could go faster if he desired, he was in no hurry. There was still much information to be processed, much to be considered

. . . and much more to be won. That, he knew, was his present goal; but he also knew that it was only part of some far wider plan, to be revealed in due course.

He gave no thought to the gateway between universes dwindling so swiftly behind him, or to the anxious entities gathered around it in their primitive spacecraft. They were part of his memories; but stronger ones were calling him now, calling him home to the world he had never thought to see again.

He could hear its myriad voices, growing louder and louder— as it too was growing, from a star almost lost against the Sun's outstretched corona, to a slim crescent, and finally to a glorious blue-white disk.

They knew that he was coming. Down there on that crowded globe, the alarms would be flashing across the radar screens, the great tracking telescopes would be searching the skies—and history as men had known it would be drawing to a close.

A thousand kilometers below, he became aware that a slumbering cargo of death had awakened, and was stirring in its orbit. The feeble energies it contained were no possible menace to him; indeed, he could profitably use them.

He entered the maze of circuitry, and swiftly traced the way to its lethal core. Most of the branchings could be ignored; they were blind alleys, devised for protection. Beneath his scrutiny, their purpose was childishly simple; it was easy to bypass them all.

Now there was a single last barrier—a crude but effective mechanical relay, holding apart two contacts. Until they were closed, there would be no power to activate the final sequence.

He put forth his will—and, for the first time, knew failure and frustration. The few grams of the microswitch would not budge. He was still a creature of pure energy; as yet, the world of inert matter was beyond his grasp. Well, there was a simple answer to that.

He still had much to learn. The current pulse he induced in the relay was so powerful that it almost melted the coil, before it could operate the trigger mechanism.

The microseconds ticked slowly by. It was interesting to observe the explosive lenses focus their energies, like the feeble match that ignites a powder train, which in turn—

The megatons flowered in a silent detonation that brought a brief, false dawn to half the sleeping world. Like a phoenix rising from the flames, he absorbed what he needed, and discarded the rest. Far below, the shield of the atmosphere, which protected the planet from so many hazards, absorbed the most dangerous of the radiation. But there would be some unlucky men and animals who would never see again.

In the aftermath of the explosion, it seemed as if the Earth was struck dumb. The babble of the short and medium waves was completely silenced, reflected back by the suddenly enhanced ionosphere. Only the microwaves still sliced through the invisible and slowly dissolving mirror that now surrounded the planet, and most of these were too tightly beamed for him to receive them. A few high-powered radars were still focused upon him, but that was a matter of no importance. He did not even bother to neutralize them as he could easily have done. And if any more bombs were to come his way, he would treat them with equal indifference. For the present, he had all the energy he needed.

And now he was descending, in great sweeping spirals, toward the lost landscape of his childhood.

31. DISNEYVILLE

A *FIN-DE-SIÈCLE* PHILOSOPHER HAD ONCE REMARKED—AND BEEN roundly denounced for his pains—that Walter Elias Disney had contributed more to genuine human happiness than all the religious teachers in history. Now, half a century after the artist's death, his dreams were still proliferating across the Florida landscape.

When it had opened in the early 1980s, his Experimental Prototype Community of Tomorrow had been a showcase for new technologies and modes of living. But as its founder had realized, EPCOT would only fulfill its purpose when some of its vast acreage was a genuine, living town, occupied by people who called it home. That process had taken the remainder of the century; now the residential area had twenty thousand inhabitants and had, inevitably, become popularly known as Disneyville.

Because they could move in only after penetrating a palace

guard of WED lawyers, it was not surprising that the average age of the occupants was the highest in any United States community, or that its medical services were the most advanced in the world. Some of them, indeed, could hardly have been conceived, still less created, in any other place.

The apartment had been carefully designed not to look like a hospital suite, and only a few unusual fittings would have betrayed its purpose. The bed was scarcely knee-high, so that the danger of falls was minimized: it could, however, be raised and tilted for the convenience of the nurses. The bathroom tub was sunk into the floor, and had a built-in seat as well as handrails, so that even the elderly or infirm could get in and out of it easily. The floor was thickly carpeted, but there were no rugs over which one could trip, or sharp corners that might cause injuries. Other details were less obvious—and the TV camera was so well concealed that no one would have suspected its presence.

There were few personal touches—a pile of old books in one corner, and a framed front page of one of the last printed issues of the *New York Times* proclaiming: U.S. SPACESHIP LEAVES FOR JUPITER. Close to this were two photographs, one showing a boy in his late teens; the other, a considerably older man wearing astronaut's uniform.

Though the frail, gray-haired woman watching the domestic comedy unfolding on the TV panel was not yet seventy, she looked much older. From time to time she chuckled appreciatively at some joke from the screen, but she kept glancing at the door as if expecting a visitor. And when she did so, she took a firmer grasp on the walking stick propped against her chair.

Yet she was distracted by a moment of TV drama when the door finally opened, and she looked around with a guilty start as the little service trolley rolled into the room, followed closely by a uniformed nurse.

"Time for lunch, Jessie," called the nurse. "We've got something very nice for you today."

"Don't want any lunch."

"It will make you feel a lot better."

"I won't eat until you tell me what it is."

"Why won't you eat it?"

"I'm not hungry. Are you ever hungry?" she added slyly.

The robot food trolley came to a halt beside the chair, and the transport covers opened up to reveal the dishes. Throughout, the nurse never touched anything, not even the controls on the trolley. She now stood motionless, with a rather fixed smile, looking at her difficult patient.

In the monitor room fifty meters away, the medical technician said to the doctor: "Now watch this."

Jessie's gnarled hand lifted the walking stick; then, with surprising speed, she swept it in a short arc toward the nurse's legs.

The nurse took no notice whatsoever, even when the stick sliced right through her. Instead, she remarked soothingly, "Now, doesn't that look nice? Eat it up, dear."

A cunning smile spread across Jessie's face, but she obeyed instructions. In a moment, she was eating heartily.

"You see?" said the technician. "She knows perfectly well what's going on. She's a lot brighter than she pretends to be, most of the time."

"And she's the first?"

"Yes. All the others believe that really is Nurse Williams, bringing their meals."

"Well, I don't think it matters. Look how pleased she is, just because she's outsmarted us. She's eating her food, which is the purpose of the exercise. But we must warn the nurses—all of them, not just Williams."

"Why—oh, of course. The next time it may not be a hologram—and then think of the lawsuits we'll be facing from our battered staff."

32. CRYSTAL SPRING

THE INDIANS, AND THE CAJUN SETTLERS WHO HAD MOVED HERE from Louisiana, said that Crystal Spring was bottomless. That, of course, was nonsense, and surely even they could not believe it. One had only to put on a face mask and swim out a few strokes—and there, clearly visible, was the little cave from which the incredibly pure water flowed with the slender green weeds undulating around it. And peering up through them, the eyes of the Monster.

Two dark circles, side by side—even though they never moved, what else could they be? That lurking presence gave an added excitement to every swim; one day the Monster would come rushing up from its lair, scattering the fish in its hunt for larger prey. Never would Bobby or David admit that nothing more dangerous than an abandoned, and doubtless stolen, bicycle lay half buried among the water weeds, a hundred meters down.

＊156

That depth was hard to believe, even after line and sinker had established it beyond argument. Bobby, the older and better diver, had been perhaps a tenth of the way down, and had reported that the bottom looked just as far away as ever.

But now the Crystal Spring was about to reveal its secrets; perhaps the legend of the Confederate treasure *was* true, despite the scorn of all the local historians. At the very least, they might endear themselves to the chief of police—always excellent policy—by recovering a few handguns deposited after recent crimes.

The little air compressor that Bobby had found in the garage junk heap was now chugging healthily away, after their initial problems of starting it. Every few seconds it would cough and emit a cloud of blue smoke, but it showed no sign of stopping. "And even if it does," said Bobby, "so what? If the girls in the Underwater Theater can swim up from fifty meters *without* their air hoses, so can we. It's perfectly safe."

In that case, thought Dave fleetingly, why didn't we tell Ma what we were doing, and why did we wait until Dad had gone back to the Cape for the next shuttle launch? But he did not have any real qualms: Bobby always knew best. It must be wonderful to be seventeen, and to know everything. Though he wished he wouldn't spend quite so much time now with that stupid Betty Schultz. True, she was very pretty—but, dammit, she was a *girl*! It was only with the greatest difficulty that they had been able to get rid of her this morning.

Dave was used to being a guinea pig; that was what younger brothers were for. He adjusted his face mask, put on his flippers, and slid into the crystalline water.

Bobby handed him the air hose with the old scuba mouthpiece they had taped to it. Dave took a breath, and grimaced.

"It tastes horrible."

"You'll get used to it. In you go—no deeper than that ledge. That's where I'll start adjusting the pressure valve so we don't waste too much air. Come up when I tug the hose."

Dave slid gently beneath the surface, and into wonderland. It was a peaceful, monochrome world, so different from the coral reefs of the Keys. There were none of the garish colors of the

marine environment, where life—animal and vegetable—
flaunted itself with all the hues of the rainbow. Here were only
delicate shades of blue and green, and fish that looked like fish,
not like butterflies.

He flippered slowly down, dragging the hose behind him,
pausing to drink from its stream of bubbles whenever he felt the
need. The sensation of freedom was so wonderful that he almost
forgot the horrible oily taste in his mouth. When he reached the
ledge—actually an ancient, waterlogged tree trunk, so over-
grown with weeds that it was unrecognizable—he sat down and
looked around him.

He could see right across the spring, to the green slopes at the
far side of the flooded crater, at least a hundred meters away.
There were not many fish around, but a small school went twin-
kling past like a shower of silver coins in the sunlight streaming
down from above.

There was also an old friend stationed, as usual, at the gap
where the waters of the spring began their journey to the sea. A
small alligator ("But large enough," Bobby had once said cheerfully. "He's bigger than I am.") was hanging vertically, without
visible means of support, only his nose above the surface. They
had never bothered him, and he had never bothered them.

The air hose gave an impatient tug. Dave was happy to go; he
had not realized how cold it could get at that hitherto unattainable depth—and he was also feeling distinctly sick. But the hot
sunlight soon revived his spirits.

"No problems," said Bobby expansively. "Just keep unscrew-
ing the valve so the pressure gauge doesn't drop below the red
line."

"How deep are you going?"

"All the way, if I feel like it."

Dave did not take that seriously; they both knew about rapture
of the depths and nitrogen narcosis. And in any case, the old
garden hose was only thirty meters long. That would be plenty
for this first experiment.

As he had done so many times before, he watched with en-
vious admiration as his beloved elder brother accepted a new
challenge. Swimming as effortlessly as the fish around him,

Bobby glided downward into that blue, mysterious universe. He turned once and pointed vigorously to the air hose, making it unmistakably clear that he needed an increased air flow.

Despite the splitting headache that had suddenly come upon him, Dave remembered his duty. He hurried back to the ancient compressor, and opened the control valve to its deadly maximum—fifty parts per million of carbon monoxide.

The last he saw of Bobby was that confidently descending, sunlight-dappled figure passing forever beyond his reach. The wax statue in the funeral parlor was a total stranger, who had nothing to do with Robert Bowman.

33. BETTY

WHY HAD HE COME HERE, RETURNING LIKE AN UNQUIET GHOST TO the scene of ancient anguish? He had no idea; indeed, he had not been conscious of his destination, until the round eye of Crystal Spring had gazed up at him from the forest below.

He was master of the world, yet he was paralyzed by a sense of devastating grief he had not known for years. Time had healed the wound, as it always does; yet it seemed only yesterday that he had stood weeping beside the emerald mirror, seeing only the reflections of the surrounding cypresses with their burden of Spanish moss. *What was happening to him?*

And now, still without deliberate volition, but as if swept by some gentle current, he was drifting northward, toward the state capital. He was looking for something; what it was, he would not know until he found it.

No one, and no instrument, detected his passage. He was no longer radiating wastefully, but had almost mastered his control of energy, as once he had mastered lost though not forgotten limbs. He sank like a mist into the earthquake-proof vaults, until he found himself among billions of stored memories, and dazzling, flickering networks of electronic thoughts.

This task was more complex than the triggering of a crude nuclear bomb, and took him a little longer. Before he found the information he was seeking, he made one trivial slip, but did not bother to correct it. No one ever understood why, the next month, three hundred Florida taxpayers, all of whose names began with F, received checks for precisely one dollar. It cost many times the overpayment to straighten matters out, and the baffled computer engineers finally put the blame on a cosmic-ray shower. Which, on the whole, was not so very far from the truth.

In a few milliseconds, he had moved from Tallahassee to 634 South Magnolia Street, Tampa. It was still the same address; he need not have wasted time looking it up.

But then, he had never intended to look it up, until the very moment when he had done so.

After three births and two abortions, Betty Fernandez (née Schultz) was still a beautiful woman. At the moment she was also a very thoughtful one; she was watching a TV program that brought back memories, bitter and sweet.

It was a News Special, triggered by the mysterious events of the preceding twelve hours, beginning with the warning that Leonov had beamed back from the moons of Jupiter. Something was heading for Earth; something had—harmlessly—detonated an orbiting nuclear bomb which no one had come forward to claim. That was all, but it was quite enough.

The news commentators had dredged up all the old video-tapes—and some of them really were tapes—going back to the once top-secret records showing the discovery of TMA-1 on the Moon. For the fiftieth time, at least, she heard that eerie radio shriek as the monolith greeted the lunar dawn and hurled its message toward Jupiter. And once again she watched the familiar scenes and listened to the old interviews aboard Discovery.

Why was she watching? It was all stored somewhere in the home archives (though she never played it back when José was around). Perhaps she was expecting some news flash; she did not like to admit, even to herself, how much power the past still held over her emotions.

And there was Dave, as she had expected. It was an old BBC interview, of which she knew almost every word. He was talking about Hal, trying to decide whether the computer was self-conscious or not.

How young he looked—how different from those last blurred images from the doomed *Discovery*! And how much like Bobby as she remembered him.

The image wavered as her eyes filled with tears. No—something was wrong with the set, or the channel. Both sound and image were behaving erratically.

Dave's lips were moving, but she could hear nothing. Then his face seemed to dissolve, to melt into blocks of color. It reformed, blurred again, and then was steady once more. But there was still no sound.

Where *had* they got this picture? This was not Dave as a man, but as a boy—as she had known him first. He was looking out of the screen almost as if he could see her across the gulf of years.

He smiled; his lips moved.

"Hello, Betty," he said.

It was not hard to form the words, and to impose them on the currents pulsing in the audio circuits. The real difficulty was to slow down his thoughts to the glacial tempo of the human brain. And then to have to wait an eternity for the answer . . .

Betty Fernandez was tough; she was also intelligent, and though she had been a housewife for a dozen years, she had not forgotten her training as an electronics serviceperson. This was just another of the medium's countless miracles of simulation; she would accept it now, and worry about the details later.

"Dave," she answered. "Dave—is that *really* you?"

"I am not sure," replied the image on the screen, in a curiously toneless voice. "But I remember Dave Bowman, and everything about him."

"Is he dead?"

Now that was another difficult question.

"His body—yes. But that is no longer important. All that Dave Bowman really was, is still part of me."

Betty crossed herself—that was a gesture she had learned from José—and whispered:

"You mean—you're a *spirit?*"

"I do not know a better word."

"Why have you returned?"

Ah! Betty—why indeed! I wish you could tell me . . .

Yet he knew one answer, for it was appearing on the TV screen. The divorce between body and mind was still far from complete, and not even the most complaisant of the cable networks would have transmitted the blatantly sexual images that were forming there now.

Betty watched for a little while, sometimes smiling, sometimes shocked. Then she turned away, not through shame but sadness—regret for lost delights.

"So it's not true," she said, "what they always told us about angels."

Am I an angel? he wondered. But at least he understood what he was doing there, swept back by the tides of sorrow and desire to a rendezvous with his past. The most powerful emotion he had ever known had been his passion for Betty; the elements of grief and guilt it contained only made it stronger.

She had never told him if he was a better lover than Bobby; that was one question he had never asked, for that would have broken the spell. They had clung to the same illusion, sought in each other's arms (and how young he had been—still only seventeen when it had started, barely two years after the funeral!) a balm for the same wound.

Of course, it could not last, but the experience had left him irrevocably changed. For more than a decade, all his autoerotic fantasies had centered upon Betty; he had never found another woman to compare with her, and long ago had realized that he never would. No one else was haunted by the same beloved ghost.

The images of desire faded from the screen; for a moment, the regular program broke through, with an incongruous shot of

Leonov hanging above Io. Then Dave Bowman's face reappeared. He seemed to be losing control, for its lineaments were wildly unstable. Sometimes he would seem only ten years old—then twenty or thirty—then, incredibly, a wizened mummy whose wrinkled features were a parody of the man she had once known.

"I have one more question before I go. Carlos—you always said he was José's son, and I always wondered. What was the truth?"

Betty Fernandez stared for one long, last time into the eyes of the boy she had once loved (he was eighteen again, and for a moment she wished she could see his entire body, not merely his face).

"He was *your* son, David," she whispered.

The image faded; the normal service resumed. When, almost an hour later, José Fernandez came quietly into the room, Betty was still staring at the screen.

She did not turn around as he kissed her on the back of the neck.

"You'll never believe this, José."

"Try me."

"I've just lied to a ghost."

34. VALEDICTION

When the American Institute of Aeronautics and Astronautics published its controversial summary *Fifty Years of UFOs* in 1997, many critics pointed out that unidentified flying objects had been observed for centuries, and that Kenneth Arnold's "Flying Saucer" sighting of 1947 had countless precedents. People had been seeing strange things in the sky since the dawn of history; but until the mid-twentieth century, UFOs were a random phenomenon of no general interest. After that date, they became a matter of public and scientific concern, and the basis for what could only be called religious beliefs.

The reason was not far to seek; the arrival of the giant rocket and the dawn of the Space Age had turned men's minds to other worlds. Realization that the human race would soon be able to leave the planet of its birth prompted the inevitable questions: Where's everyone, and when may we expect visitors? There was also the hope, though it was seldom spelled out in as many words, that benevolent creatures from the stars might help mankind heal its numerous self-inflicted wounds and save it from future disasters.

Any student of psychology could have predicted that so profound a need would be swiftly satisfied. During the last half of the twentieth century, there were literally thousands of reports of spacecraft sightings from every part of the globe. More than that, there were hundreds of reports of "close encounters"—actual meetings with extraterrestrial visitors, frequently embellished by tales of celestial joyrides, abductions, and even honeymoons in space. The fact that, over and over again, these were demonstrated to be lies or hallucinations did nothing to deter the faithful. Men who had been shown cities on the far side of the Moon lost little credibility even when Orbiter surveys and Apollo missions revealed no artifacts of any kind; ladies who married Venusians were still believed when that planet, sadly, turned out to be hotter than molten lead.

By the time the AIAA published its report no reputable scientist—even among those few who had once espoused the idea—believed that UFOs had any connection with extraterrestrial life or intelligence. Of course, it would never be possible to prove that; any one of those myriad sightings, over the last thousand years, *might* have been the real thing. But as time went by, and satellite cameras and radars scanning the entire heavens produced no concrete evidence, the general public lost interest in the idea. The cultists, of course, were not discouraged, but kept the faith with their newsletters and books, most of them regurgitating and embellishing old reports long after they had been discredited or exposed.

When the discovery of the Tycho monolith—TMA-1—was finally announced, there was a chorus of "I told you so's!" It could no longer be denied that there *had* been visitors to the Moon—and presumably to the Earth as well—a little matter of three million years ago. At once, UFOs infested the heavens again; though it was odd that the three independent national tracking systems, which could locate anything in space larger than a ball-point pen, were *still* unable to find them.

Rather quickly, the number of reports dropped down to the

"noise level" once more—the figure that would be expected, merely as a result of the many astronomical, meteorological, and aeronautical phenomena constantly occurring in the skies.

But now it had started all over again. This time, there was no mistake; it was official. A genuine UFO was on its way to Earth.

Sightings were reported within minutes of the warning from *Leonov;* the first close encounters were only a few hours later. A retired stockbroker, walking his bulldog on the Yorkshire Moors, was astonished when a disk-shaped craft landed beside him and the occupant—quite human, except for the pointed ears—asked the way to Downing Street. The *contactee* was so surprised that he was only able to wave his stick in the general direction of Whitehall; conclusive proof of the meeting was provided by the fact that the bulldog now refused to take his food.

Although the stockbroker had no previous history of mental illness, even those who believed him had some difficulty in accepting the next report. This time it was a Basque shepherd on a traditional mission; he was greatly relieved when what he had feared to be border guards turned out to be a couple of cloaked men with piercing eyes, who wanted to know the way to the United Nations Headquarters.

They spoke perfect Basque—an excruciatingly difficult tongue with no affinity to any other known language of mankind. Clearly, the space visitors were remarkable linguists, even if their geography was oddly deficient.

So it went on, case after case. Very few of the contactees were actually lying or insane; most of them sincerely believed their own stories, and retained that belief even under hypnosis. And some were just victims of practical jokes or improbable accidents—like the unlucky amateur archeologists who found the props that a celebrated science-fiction moviemaker had abandoned in the Tunisian desert almost four decades earlier.

Yet only at the beginning—and at the very end—was any human being genuinely aware of his presence; and that was because he so desired it.

The world was his to explore and examine as he pleased, without restraint or hindrance. No walls could keep him out, no secrets could be hidden from the senses he possessed. At first he believed that he was merely fulfilling old ambitions, by visiting the places he had never seen in that earlier existence. Not until much later did he realize that his lightninglike sallies across the face of the globe had a deeper purpose.

In some subtle way, he was being used as a probe, sampling every aspect of human affairs. The control was so tenuous that he was barely conscious of it; he was rather like a hunting dog on a leash, allowed to make excursions of his own, yet nevertheless compelled to obey the overriding wishes of his master.

The pyramids, the Grand Canyon, the moon-washed snows of Everest—these were choices of his own. So were some art galleries and concert halls; though he would certainly, on his own initiative, never have endured the whole of the Ring.

Nor would he have visited so many factories, prisons, hospitals, a nasty little war in Asia, a racecourse, a complicated orgy in Beverly Hills, the Oval Room of the White House, the Kremlin archives, the Vatican Library, the sacred Black Stone of the *Ka'bah* at Mecca . . .

There were also experiences of which he had no clear memory, as if they had been censored—or he was being protected from them by some guardian angel. For example—

What was he doing at the Leakey Memorial Museum, in Olduvai Gorge? He had no greater interest in the origin of Man than any other intelligent member of the species *H. sapiens*, and fossils meant nothing to him. Yet the famous skulls, guarded like crown jewels in their display cases, aroused strange echoes in his memory, and an excitement for which he was unable to account. There was a feeling of *déjà vu* stronger than any he had ever known; the place *should* be familiar—but something was wrong. It was like a house to which one returns after many years, to find that all the furniture has been changed, the walls moved, and even the stairways rebuilt.

It was bleak, hostile terrain, dry and parched. Where were the lush plains and the myriad fleet-footed herbivores that had roamed across them, three million years ago?

Three million years. How had he known that?

No answer came from the echoing silence into which he had

thrown the question. But then he saw, once more looming before him, a familiar black rectangular shape. He approached, and a shadowy image appeared in its depths, like a reflection in a pool of ink.

The sad and puzzled eyes that stared back from beneath that hairy, receding forehead looked beyond him into a future they could never see. For he *was* that future, a hundred thousand generations further down the stream of time.

History had begun there; that at least he now understood. But how—and above all, *why*—were secrets still withheld from him?

But there was one last duty, and that was hardest of all. He was still sufficiently human to put it off until the very end.

Now what's she up to? the duty nurse asked herself, zooming the TV monitor onto the old lady. She's tried lots of tricks, but this is the first time I've seen her talking to her hearing aid, for goodness' sake. I wonder what she's saying?

The microphone was not sensitive enough to pick up the words, but that scarcely seemed to matter. Jessie Bowman had seldom looked so peaceful and content. Though her eyes were closed, her entire face was wreathed in an almost angelic smile while her lips continued to form whispered words.

And then the watcher saw something that she tried hard to forget, because to report it would instantly disqualify her in the nursing profession. Slowly and jerkily, the comb lying on the bedside table raised itself in the air as if lifted by clumsy, invisible fingers.

On the first attempt, it missed; then, with obvious difficulty, it began to part the long silver strands, pausing sometimes to disentangle a knot.

Jessie Bowman was not speaking now, but she continued to smile. The comb was moving with more assurance, and no longer in abrupt, uncertain jerks.

How long it lasted the nurse could never be certain. Not until the comb was gently replaced on the table did she recover from her paralysis.

Ten-year-old Dave Bowman had finished the chore which he

always hated but which his mother loved. And a David Bowman who was now ageless had gained his first control of obdurate matter.

Jessie Bowman was still smiling when the nurse finally came to investigate. She had been too scared to hurry; but it would have made no difference anyway.

35. REHABILITATION

THE UPROAR OF EARTH WAS COMFORTABLY MUTED, ACROSS THE millions of kilometers of space. *Leonov's* crew watched, with fascination yet with a certain detachment, the debates in the United Nations, the interviews with distinguished scientists, the theorizing of the news commentators, the matter-of-fact yet wildly conflicting accounts of the UFO contactees. They could contribute nothing to the brouhaha, for they had witnessed no further manifestations of any kind. *Zagadka*, alias Big Brother, remained as blankly indifferent to their presence as ever. And that was indeed an ironic situation; they had come all the way from Earth to solve a mystery—and it looked as if the answer might be right back at their starting point.

For the first time, they felt grateful for the slow velocity of light, and the two-hour delay that made live interviews impossible on the Earth–Jupiter circuit. Even so, Floyd was badgered by so many media requests that he finally went on strike. Nothing

∗ 171

more remained to be said, and he had said it at least a dozen times.

Besides, there was still much work to be done. *Leonov* had to be prepared for the long journey home, so that it would be ready to depart immediately when the launch window opened. The timing was not at all critical; even if they missed by a month, that would merely prolong the trip. Chandra, Curnow, and Floyd would not even notice as they slept their way toward the Sun; but the rest of the crew was grimly determined to leave just as soon as the laws of celestial mechanics permitted.

Discovery still posed many problems. The ship had barely sufficient propellant for the return to Earth, even if it left much later than *Leonov* and flew a minimum-energy orbit—which would take almost three years. And *this* would be possible only if Hal could be reliably programed to carry out the mission with no human intervention except long-range monitoring. Without his cooperation, *Discovery* would have to be abandoned once again.

It had been fascinating—indeed, deeply moving—to watch the steady regrowth of Hal's personality, from brain-damaged child to puzzled adolescent and at length to slightly condescending adult. Although he knew that such anthropomorphic labels were highly misleading, Floyd found it quite impossible to avoid them.

And there were times when he felt that the whole situation had a haunting familiarity. How often he had seen videodramas in which disturbed youngsters were straightened out by all-wise descendants of the legendary Sigmund Freud! Essentially the same story was being played out in the shadow of Jupiter.

The electronic psychoanalysis had proceeded at a speed totally beyond human comprehension as repair and diagnostic programs flashed through Hal's circuits at billions of bits a second, pinpointing possible malfunctions and correcting them. Though most of these programs had been tested in advance on Hal's twin, SAL 9000, the impossibility of a real-time dialog between the two computers was a serious handicap. Sometimes hours were wasted when it proved necessary to check back with Earth at a critical point in the therapy.

For despite all Chandra's work, the computer's rehabilitation was still far from complete. Hal exhibited numerous idiosyncrasies and nervous tics, sometimes even ignoring spoken words—though he would always acknowledge keyboard inputs from anyone. In the reverse direction, his outputs were even more eccentric.

There were times when he would give verbal replies, but would not display them visually. At other times he would do both—but refused to print hard copy. He would give no excuses or explanations—not even the stubbornly impenetrable "I prefer not to" of Melville's autistic scrivener, Bartleby.

However, he was not actively disobedient so much as reluctant, and only where certain tasks were concerned. It was always possible to win his cooperation eventually—"to talk him out of his sulk," as Curnow put it neatly.

It was not surprising that Dr. Chandra was beginning to show the strain. On one celebrated occasion when Max Brailovsky innocently revived an old canard, he *almost* lost his temper.

"Is it true, Dr. Chandra, that you chose the name Hal to be one step ahead of IBM?"

"Utter nonsense! Half of us *come* from IBM and we've been trying to stamp out that story for years. I thought that by now every intelligent person knew that H-A-L is derived from *Heuristic ALgorithmic*."

Afterward, Max swore that he could distinctly hear the capital letters.

In Floyd's private opinion, the odds were at least fifty to one against flying *Discovery* safely back to Earth. And then Chandra came to him with an extraordinary proposal.

"Dr. Floyd, can I have a word with you?"

After all the weeks and shared experiences, Chandra was still as formal as ever—not only to Floyd, but to all the crew. He would not even address the ship's baby, Zenia, without the prefix "ma'am."

"Of course, Chandra. What is it?"

"I've virtually completed the programing for the six most probable variations on the Hohmann return orbit. Five have now been run on a simulation, without any problems."

"Excellent. I'm sure that no one else on Earth—in the Solar System—could have done it."

"Thank you. However, you know as well as I do that it's impossible to program for *every* eventuality. Hal may—*will*—function perfectly, and will be able to handle any reasonable emergency. But all sorts of trivial accidents—minor equipment failures that could be fixed with a screwdriver, broken wires, stuck switches—could leave him helpless and abort the whole mission."

"You're absolutely right, of course, and it's been worrying me. But what can we do about it?"

"It's really quite simple. I'd like to stay with *Discovery*."

Floyd's immediate reaction was that Chandra had gone crazy. On second thought, perhaps he was only half crazy. It might indeed make all the difference between success and failure to have a human being—that superb all-purpose troubleshooting and repair device—aboard *Discovery* for the long voyage back to Earth. But the objections were completely overwhelming.

"It's an interesting idea," Floyd answered with extreme caution, "and I certainly appreciate your enthusiasm. But have you thought of all the problems?" That was a silly thing to say; Chandra would have all the answers already filed away for immediate retrieval.

"You'll be on your own for over three years! Suppose you had an accident or a medical emergency?"

"That's a risk I'm prepared to take."

"And what about food, water? *Leonov* doesn't have enough to spare."

"I've checked *Discovery's* recycling system; it can be made operational again without too much difficulty. Besides, we Indians can manage on very little."

It was unusual for Chandra to refer to his origins, or indeed to make any personal statements; his "true confession" was the only example Floyd could remember. But he did not doubt the claim; Curnow had once remarked that Dr. Chandra had the sort of physique that could only be achieved by centuries of starvation. Although it sounded like one of the engineer's unkinder wisecracks, it had been made entirely without malice—indeed, with sympathy; though not, of course, in Chandra's hearing.

"Well, we still have several weeks to decide. I'll think it over and talk to Washington."

"Thank you; do you mind if I start making the arrangements?"

"Er—not at all, as long as they don't interfere with the existing plans. Remember—Mission Control will have to make the final decision."

And I know exactly what Mission Control will say. It was madness to expect a man to survive in space for three years, alone.

But, of course, Chandra had always been alone.

36. FIRE IN THE DEEP

EARTH WAS ALREADY FAR BEHIND, AND THE AWESOME WONDERS OF the Jovian system were expanding swiftly before him, when he had his revelation.

How could he have been so blind—so stupid! It was as if he had been walking in his sleep; now he was starting to awaken.

Who are you? he cried. What do you want? Why have you done this to me?

There was no answer, yet he was certain that he had been heard. He sensed a . . . *presence,* even as a man can tell, though his eyes are tightly shut, that he is in a closed room and not some empty, open space. Around him there was the faint echo of a vast mentality, an implacable will.

He called again into the reverberant silence, and again there was no direct reply—only that sense of watchful companionship. Very well; he would find the answers for himself.

Some were obvious; whoever or whatever *they* were, they

were interested in Mankind. They had tapped and stored his memories, for their own inscrutable purposes. And now they had done the same with his deepest emotions, sometimes with his cooperation, sometimes without.

He did not resent that; indeed, the very processing he had experienced made such childish reactions impossible. He was beyond love and hate and desire and fear—but he had not forgotten them, and could still understand how they ruled the world of which he had once been part. Was *that* the purpose of the exercise? If so, for what ultimate goal?

He had become a player in a game of gods, and must learn the rules as he went along.

The jagged rocks of the four tiny outer moons Sinope, Pasiphae, Carme, and Ananke flickered briefly across his field of consciousness; then came Elara, Lysithea, Himalia, and Leda at half their distance from Jupiter. He ignored them all; now the pock-marked face of Callisto lay ahead.

Once, twice he orbited the battered globe, larger than Earth's own Moon, while senses of which he had been unaware probed its outer layers of ice and dust. His curiosity was quickly satisfied; this world was a frozen fossil, still bearing the marks of collisions that, aeons ago, must have come close to shattering it. One hemisphere was a giant bull's-eye, a series of concentric rings where solid rock had once flowed in kilometer-high ripples under some ancient hammer blow from space.

Seconds later, he was circling Ganymede. Now there was a far more complex and interesting world; though so near to Callisto, and almost the same size, it presented an utterly different appearance. There were, it was true, numerous craters—but most of them seemed to have been, quite literally, *ploughed* back into the ground. The most extraordinary feature of the Ganymedean landscape was the presence of meandering stripes, built up from scores of parallel furrows a few kilometers apart. This grooved terrain looked as if it had been produced by armies of intoxicated ploughmen, weaving back and forth across the face of the satellite.

In a few revolutions, he saw more of Ganymede than all the

space probes ever sent from Earth, and filed away the knowledge for future use. One day it would be important; he was sure of that, though he did not know why—any more than he understood the impulse that was now driving him so purposefully from world to world.

As, presently, it brought him to Europa. Though he was still largely a passive spectator, he was aware now of a rising interest, a focusing of attention—a concentration of will. Even if he was a puppet in the hands of an unseen and uncommunicative master, some of the thoughts of that controlling influence leaked—or were allowed to leak—into his own mind.

The smooth, intricately patterned globe now rushing toward him bore little resemblance either to Ganymede or Callisto. It looked *organic*; the network of lines branching and intersecting over its entire surface was uncannily like a world-spanning system of veins and arteries.

The endless ice fields of a frigid waste, far colder than the Antarctic, stretched beneath him. Then, with brief surprise, he saw that he was passing over the wreckage of a spaceship. He recognized it instantly as the ill-fated *Tsien*, featured in so many of the video newscasts he had analyzed. Not now—*not now*—there would be ample opportunity later . . .

Then he was through the ice, and into a world as unknown to his controllers as to himself.

It was an ocean world, its hidden waters protected from the vacuum of space by a crust of ice. In most places the ice was kilometers thick, but there were lines of weakness where it had cracked open and torn apart. Then there had been a brief battle between two implacably hostile elements that came into direct contact on no other world in the Solar System. The war between Sea and Space always ended in the same stalemate; the exposed water simultaneously boiled and froze, repairing the armor of ice.

The seas of Europa would have frozen completely solid long ago without the influence of nearby Jupiter. Its gravity continually kneaded the core of the little world; the forces that convulsed Io were working there, though with much less ferocity. As he skimmed across the face of the deep, he saw everywhere the evidence of that tug-of-war between planet and satellite.

And he both heard and felt it, in the continual roar and thunder of submarine earthquakes, the hiss of escaping gases from the interior, the infrasonic pressure waves of avalanches sweeping over the abyssal plains. By comparison with the tumultuous ocean that covered Europa, even the noisy seas of Earth were silent.

He had not lost his sense of wonder, and the first oasis filled him with delighted surprise. It extended for almost a kilometer around a tangled mass of pipes and chimneys deposited by mineral brines gushing from the interior. Out of that natural parody of a Gothic castle, black, scalding liquids pulsed in a slow rhythm, as if driven by the beating of some mighty heart. And, like blood, they were the authentic sign of life itself.

The boiling fluids drove back the deadly cold leaking down from above, and formed an island of warmth on the seabed. Equally important, they brought from Europa's interior all the chemicals of life. There, in an environment where none had expected it, were energy and food, in abundance.

Yet it *should* have been expected; he remembered that, only a lifetime ago, such fertile oases had been discovered in the deep oceans of Earth. Here they were present on an immensely larger scale, and in far greater variety.

In the tropical zone close to the contorted walls of the "castle" were delicate, spidery structures that seemed to be the analogy of plants, though almost all were capable of movement. Crawling among these were bizarre slugs and worms, some feeding on the plants, others obtaining their food directly from the mineral-laden waters around them. At greater distances from the source of heat—the submarine fire around which all the creatures warmed themselves—were sturdier, more robust organisms, not unlike crabs or spiders.

Armies of biologists could have spent lifetimes studying that one small oasis. Unlike the Paleozoic terrestrial seas, it was not a stable environment, so evolution had progressed swiftly here, producing multitudes of fantastic forms. And they were all under indefinite stay of execution; sooner or later, each fountain of life would weaken and die, as the forces that powered it moved their focus elsewhere.

Again and again, in his wanderings across the Europan sea-bed, he encountered the evidence of such tragedies. Countless circular areas were littered with the skeletons and mineral-encrusted remains of dead creatures, where entire chapters of evolution had been deleted from the book of life.

He saw huge, empty shells formed like convoluted trumpets as large as a man. There were clams of many shapes—bivalves, and even trivalves. And there were spiral stone patterns, many meters across, which seemed an exact analogy of the beautiful ammonites that disappeared so mysteriously from Earth's oceans at the end of the Cretaceous Period.

Searching, seeking, he moved back and forth over the face of the abyss. Perhaps the greatest of all the wonders he met was a river of incandescent lava, flowing for a hundred kilometers along a sunken valley. The pressure at that depth was so great that the water in contact with the red-hot magma could not flash into steam, and the two liquids coexisted in an uneasy truce.

There, on another world and with alien actors, something like the story of Egypt had been played long before the coming of man. As the Nile had brought life to a narrow ribbon of desert, so this river of warmth had vivified the Europan deep. Along its banks, in a band never more than two kilometers wide, species after species had evolved and flourished and passed away. And at least one had left a monument behind it.

At first, he thought that it was merely another of the encrustations of mineral salts that surrounded almost all the thermal vents. However, as he came closer, he saw that it was not a natural formation, but a structure created by intelligence. Or perhaps by instinct; on Earth, the termites reared castles that were almost equally imposing, and the web of a spider was more exquisitely designed.

The creatures that had lived there must have been quite small, for the single entrance was only half a meter wide. That entrance—a thick-walled tunnel, made by heaping rocks on top of each other—gave a clue to the builders' intentions. They had reared a fortress, there in the flickering glow not far from the banks of their molten Nile. And then they had vanished.

They could not have left more than a few centuries before.

The walls of the fortress, built from irregularly shaped rocks that must have been collected with great labor, were covered with only a thin crust of mineral deposits. One piece of evidence suggested why the stronghold had been abandoned. Part of the roof had fallen in, perhaps owing to the continual earthquakes; and in an underwater environment, a fort without a roof was wide open to an enemy.

He encountered no other sign of intelligence along the river of lava. Once, however, he saw something uncannily like a crawling man—except that it had no eyes and no nostrils, only a huge, toothless mouth that gulped continuously, absorbing nourishment from the liquid medium around it.

Along the narrow band of fertility in the deserts of the deep, whole cultures and even civilizations might have risen and fallen, armies might have marched (or swum) under the command of Europan Tamberlanes or Napoleons. And the rest of their world would never have known, for all those oases of warmth were as isolated from one another as the planets themselves. The creatures who basked in the glow of the lava river, and fed around the hot vents, could not cross the hostile wilderness between their lonely islands. If they had ever produced historians and philosophers, each culture would have been convinced that it was alone in the Universe.

Yet even the space between the oases was not altogether empty of life; there were hardier creatures who had dared its rigors. Often swimming overhead were the Europan analogs of fish—streamlined torpedoes, propelled by vertical tails, steered by fins along their bodies. The resemblance to the most successful dwellers in Earth's oceans was inevitable; given the same engineering problems, evolution must produce very similar answers. As witness the dolphin and the shark—superficially almost identical, yet from far distant branches of the tree of life.

There was, however, one very obvious difference between the fish of the Europan seas and those in terrestrial oceans; they had no gills, for there was hardly a trace of oxygen to be extracted from the waters in which they swam. Like the creatures around Earth's own geothermal vents, their metabolism was based on sulfur compounds, present in abundance in the near-volcanic environment.

And very few had eyes. Apart from the flickering glow of the rare lava outpourings, and occasional bursts of bioluminescence from creatures seeking mates, or hunters questing prey, it was a lightless world.

It was also a doomed one. Not only were its energy sources sporadic and constantly shifting, but the tidal forces that drove them were steadily weakening. Even if they developed true intelligence, the Europans must perish with the final freezing of their world.

They were trapped between fire and ice.

37. ESTRANGEMENT

". . . I'M TRULY SORRY, OLD FRIEND, TO BE THE BEARER OF SUCH bad news; but Caroline has asked me, and you know how I feel about you both.

"And I don't think it can be such a surprise. Some of the remarks you've made to me over the last year have hinted at it . . . and you know how bitter she was when you left Earth.

"No, I don't believe there's anyone else. If there was, she'd have told me . . . But sooner or later—well, she's an attractive young woman.

"Chris is fine, and of course he doesn't know what's happening. At least *he* won't be hurt. He's too young to understand, and children are incredibly . . . elastic?—just a minute, I'll have to key my thesaurus . . . ah, *resilient*.

"Now to things that may seem less important to you. Everyone is still trying to explain that bomb detonation as an accident, but of course nobody believes it. Because nothing else has happened, the general hysteria has died down; we're left with what one of your commentators has called the 'looking-over-the-shoulder syndrome.'

"And someone has found a hundred-year-old poem that sums up the situation so neatly that everybody's quoting it. It's set in the last days of the Roman Empire, at the gates of a city whose occupants are waiting for invaders to arrive. The emperor and dignitaries are all lined up in their most costly togas, ready with speeches of welcome. The senate has closed, because any laws it passes today will be ignored by the new masters.

"Then, suddenly, a dreadful piece of news arrives from the frontier. *There aren't any invaders.* The reception committee breaks up in confusion; everyone goes home muttering disappointedly, '*Now* what will happen to us? Those people were a kind of solution.'

"There's just one slight change needed to bring the poem up to date. It's called 'Waiting for the Barbarians'—and this time, *we* are the barbarians. And we don't know what we're waiting for, but it certainly hasn't arrived.

"One other item. Had you heard that Commander Bowman's mother died only a few days after the thing came to Earth? It does seem an odd coincidence, but the people at her nursing home say that she never showed the slightest interest in the news, so it couldn't possibly have affected her."

Floyd switched off the recording. Dimitri was right; he was not taken by surprise. But that made not the slightest difference; it hurt just as badly.

Yet what else could he have done? If he had refused to go on the mission—as Caroline had so clearly hoped—he would have felt guilty and unfulfilled for the remainder of his life. That would have poisoned his marriage; better this clean break, when physical distance softened the pain of separation. (Or did it? In some ways, it made things worse.) More important was duty, and the sense of being part of a team devoted to a single goal.

So Jessie Bowman was gone. Perhaps that was another cause for guilt. He had helped to steal her only remaining son, and that must have contributed to her mental breakdown. Inevitably, he was reminded of a discussion that Walter Curnow had started, on that very subject.

"Why *did* you choose Dave Bowman? He always struck me as a cold fish—not actually unfriendly, but whenever he came into the room, the temperature seemed to drop ten degrees."

"That was one of the reasons we did select him. He had no close family ties, except for a mother he didn't see very often. So he was the sort of man we could send on a long, open-ended mission."

"How did he get that way?"

"I suppose the psychologists could tell you. I did see his report, of course, but that was a long time ago. There was something about a brother who was killed—and his father died soon afterward, in an accident on one of the early shuttles. I'm not supposed to tell you this, but it certainly doesn't matter now."

It didn't matter; but it was interesting. Now Floyd almost envied David Bowman, who had come to that very spot a free man unencumbered by emotional ties with Earth.

No—he was deceiving himself. Even while the pain gripped his heart like a vise, what he felt for David Bowman was not envy, but pity.

38. FOAMSCAPE

THE LAST BEAST HE SAW, BEFORE HE LEFT THE OCEANS OF EUROPA, was much the largest. It closely resembled one of the banyan trees from Earth's tropics, whose scores of trunks allow a single plant to create a small forest sometimes covering hundreds of square meters. The specimen, however, was *walking*, apparently on a trek between oases. If it was not one of the creatures that had destroyed *Tsien*, it certainly belonged to a very similar species.

Now he had learned all that he needed to know—or, rather, all that *they* needed to know. There was one more moon to visit; seconds later, the burning landscape of Io lay below him.

It was as he had expected. Energy and food were there in abundance, but the time was not yet ripe for their union. Around some of the cooler sulfur lakes, the first steps had been taken on the road to life, but before any degree of organization had occurred, all such bravely premature attempts were thrown back into the melting pot. Not until the tidal forces that drove Io's furnaces had lost their power, millions of years hence, would there be anything to interest biologists on this seared and sterilized world.

He wasted little time on Io, and none at all on the tiny inner moons that skirted Jupiter's ghostly rings—themselves only pale shadows of the glory that was Saturn's. The greatest of worlds lay before him; he would know it as no man had ever done, or ever would.

The million-kilometer-long tendrils of magnetic force, the sudden explosions of radio waves, the geysers of electrified plasma wider than the planet Earth—they were as real and clearly visible to him as the clouds banding the planet in multi-hued glory. He could understand the complex pattern of their interactions, and realized that Jupiter was much more wonderful than anyone had ever guessed.

Even as he fell through the roaring heart of the Great Red Spot, with the lighting of its continent-wide thunderstorms detonating around him, he *knew* why it had persisted for centuries though it was made of gases far less substantial than those that formed the hurricanes of Earth. The thin scream of hydrogen wind faded as he sank into the calmer depths, and a sleet of waxen snowflakes—some already coalescing into barely palpable mountains of hydrocarbon foam—descended from the heights above. It was already warm enough for liquid water to exist, but there were no oceans there; this purely gaseous environment was too tenuous to support them.

He descended through layer after layer of cloud, until he entered a region of such clarity that even human vision could have scanned an area more than a thousand kilometers across. It was only a minor eddy in the vaster gyre of the Great Red Spot; and it held a secret that men had long guessed, but never proved.

Skirting the foothills of the drifting foam mountains were myriads of small, sharply defined clouds, all about the same size and patterned with similar red and brown mottlings. They were small only as compared with the inhuman scale of their surroundings; the very least would have covered a fair-size city.

They were clearly alive, for they were moving with slow deliberation along the flanks of the aerial mountains, browsing off their slopes like colossal sheep. And they were calling to each other in the meter band, their radio voices faint but clear against the cracklings and concussions of Jupiter itself.

Nothing less than living gasbags, they floated in the narrow zone between freezing heights and scorching depths. Narrow, yes—but a domain far larger than all the biosphere of Earth.

They were not alone. Moving swiftly among them were other creatures so small that they could easily have been overlooked. Some of them bore an almost uncanny resemblance to terrestrial aircraft and were of about the same size. But they too were alive—perhaps predators, perhaps parasites, perhaps even herdsmen.

A whole new chapter of evolution, as alien as that which he had glimpsed on Europa, was opening before him. There were jet-propelled torpedoes like the squids of the terrestrial oceans, hunting and devouring the huge gasbags. But the balloons were not defenseless; some of them fought back with electric thunderbolts and with clawed tentacles like kilometer-long chainsaws.

There were even stranger shapes, exploiting almost every possibility of geometry—bizarre, translucent kites, tetrahedra, spheres, polyhedra, tangles of twisted ribbons . . . The gigantic plankton of the Jovian atmosphere, they were designed to float like gossamer in the uprising currents, until they had lived long enough to reproduce; then they would be swept down into the depths to be carbonized and recycled in a new generation.

He was searching a world more than a hundred times the area of Earth, and though he saw many wonders, nothing there hinted of intelligence. The radio voices of the great balloons carried only simple messages of warning or of fear. Even the hunters, who might have been expected to develop higher degrees of organization, were like the sharks in Earth's oceans—mindless automata.

And for all its breathtaking size and novelty, the biosphere of Jupiter was a fragile world, a place of mists and foam, of delicate silken threads and paper-thin tissues spun from the continual

snowfall of petrochemicals formed by lightning in the upper atmosphere. Few of its constructs were more substantial than soap
bubbles; its most terrifying predators could be torn to shreds by
even the feeblest of terrestrial carnivores.

Like Europa on a vastly grander scale, Jupiter was an evolu-
tionary *cul-de-sac*. Consciousness would never emerge here;
even if it did, it would be doomed to a stunted existence. A
purely aerial culture might develop, but in an environment
where fire was impossible, and solids scarcely existed, it could
never even reach the Stone Age. ,

And now, as he hovered above the center of a Jovian cyclone
merely as large as Africa, he became aware once again of the
presence controlling him. Moods and emotions were leaking
into his own consciousness, though he could not identify any
specific concepts or ideas. It was as if he were listening, outside
a closed door, to a debate in progress, and in a language he
could not understand. But the muffled sounds clearly conveyed
disappointment, then uncertainty, then a sudden determination—though for what purpose he could not tell. Once again, he
felt like a pet dog, able to share his master's changing moods but
not to comprehend them.

And then the invisible leash was taking him down toward the
heart of Jupiter. He was sinking through the clouds, below the
level where any form of life was possible.

Soon he was beyond the reach of the last rays from the faint
and distant Sun. The pressure and temperature were swiftly
mounting; already it was above the boiling point of water, and
he passed briefly through a layer of superheated steam. Jupiter
was like an onion; he was peeling it away skin by skin, though
as yet he had traveled only a fraction of the distance to its core.

Beneath the steam was a witches' brew of petrochemicals—
enough to power for a million years all the internal-combustion
engines that mankind had ever built. It became thicker and
denser; then, quite abruptly, it ended at a discontinuity only a
few kilometers thick.

Heavier than any rocks on Earth, yet still a liquid, the next shell consisted of silicon and carbon compounds of a complexity that could have provided lifetimes of work for terrestrial chemists. Layer followed layer for thousands of kilometers, but as the temperature rose into the hundreds and then the thousands of degrees, the composition of the various strata became simpler and simpler. Halfway down to the core, it was too hot for chemistry; all compounds were torn apart, and only the basic elements could exist.

Next there came a deep sea of hydrogen—but not hydrogen as it had ever existed for more than a fraction of a second in any laboratory on Earth. This hydrogen was under such enormous pressure that it had become a metal.

He had almost reached the center of the planet, but Jupiter had one more surprise in store. The thick shell of metallic yet still fluid hydrogen ended abruptly. At last, there was a solid surface, sixty thousand kilometers down.

For ages, the carbon baked out of the chemical reactions far above had been drifting down toward the center of the planet. There it had gathered, crystallizing at a pressure of millions of atmospheres. And there, by one of Nature's supreme jests, was something very precious to mankind.

The core of Jupiter, forever beyond human reach, was a diamond as big as the Earth.

39. IN THE POD BAY

"WALTER—I'M WORRIED ABOUT HEYWOOD."

"I know, Tanya—but what can we do?"

Curnow had never seen Commander Orlova in so indecisive a mood; it made her seem much more appealing, despite his prejudice against small women.

"I'm very fond of him, but that's not the reason. His—I suppose gloom is the best word for it—is making everyone miserable. *Leonov* has been a happy ship. I want to keep it that way."

"Why don't you talk to him? He respects you, and I'm sure he'll do his best to snap out of it."

"I intend to do just that. And if it doesn't work—"

"Well?"

"There's one simple solution. What more can he do on this trip? When we start back for home, he'll be in hibernation anyway. We could always—what do you say, jump the gun on him."

"Phew—the same dirty trick that Katerina played on me. He'd be mad when he woke up."

"But also safely back on Earth, and very busy. I'm sure he'd forgive us."

"I don't think you're serious. Even if I backed you up, Washington would raise hell. Besides, suppose something happened, and we really need him badly? Isn't there a two-week buffer period, before you can revive anyone safely?"

"At Heywood's age, more like a month. Yes, we'd be . . . committed. But what do you think could happen now? He's done the job he was sent for—apart from keeping an eye on us. And I'm sure you've been well briefed about that in some obscure suburb of Virginia or Maryland."

"I neither confirm nor deny. And frankly, I'm a lousy undercover agent. I talk too much, and I hate Security. I've fought all my life to keep my rating below Restricted. Every time there was danger of being reclassified Confidential or, worse still, Secret, I'd go and create a scandal. Though that's getting very difficult nowadays."

"Walter, you're incorrupt—"

"Incorrigible?"

"Yes, that's the word I meant. But back to Heywood, please. Would you like to talk to him first?"

"You mean—give him a pep talk? I'd rather help Katerina drive in the needle. Our psychologies are too different. He thinks I'm a loudmouthed clown."

"Which you often are. But that's only to hide your real feelings. Some of us have evolved the theory that deep down inside you is a really nice person, struggling to get out."

For once, Curnow was at a loss for words. Finally he mumbled: "Oh, very well—I'll do my best. But don't expect miracles; my profile gave me Z for tact. Where's he hiding at the moment?"

"In the Pod Bay. He claims he's working on his final report, but I don't believe it. He just wants to get away from us all, and that's the quietest place."

That was not the reason, though it was indeed an important

one. Unlike the carousel, where most of the action aboard *Discovery* was then taking place, the Pod Bay was a zero-gee environment.

Right at the beginning of the Space Age, men had discovered the euphoria of weightlessness and remembered the freedom they had lost when they left the ancient womb of the sea. Beyond gravity, some of that freedom was regained; with the loss of weight went many of the cares and worries of Earth.

Heywood Floyd had not forgotten his sorrow, but it was more bearable here. When he was able to look at the matter dispassionately, he was surprised at the strength of his reaction to an event not wholly unexpected. More than loss of love was involved, though that was the worst part. The blow had come when he was particularly vulnerable, at the very moment when he was feeling a sense of anticlimax, even futility.

And he knew precisely why. He had achieved all that he had been expected to do, thanks to the skill and cooperation of his colleagues (he was letting them down, he knew, by his present selfishness). If all went well—that litany of the Space Age!—they would return to Earth with a cargo of knowledge that no expedition had ever gathered before, and a few years later even the once-lost *Discovery* would be restored to her builders.

It was not enough. The overpowering enigma of Big Brother remained out there, only a few kilometers away, mocking all human aspirations and achievements. Just as its analog on the Moon had done, a decade ago, it had come to life for a moment, then relapsed into stubborn inertness. It was a closed door upon which they had hammered in vain. Only David Bowman, it seemed, had ever found the key.

Perhaps that explained the attraction he felt for this quiet and sometimes even mysterious place. From here—from that now empty launch cradle—Bowman had left on his last mission, through the circular hatchway that led to infinity.

He found the thought exhilarating rather than depressing; certainly it helped to distract him from his personal problems. Nina's vanished twin was part of the history of space exploration; it had traveled, in the words of the hoary old cliché that always evoked a smile yet an acknowledgment of its fundamental truth, "where no man had gone before . . ." Where was it now? Would he ever know?

He would sometimes sit for hours in the crowded but not cramped little capsule, trying to collect his thoughts and occasionally dictating notes; the other crew members respected his privacy, and understood the reason for it. They never came near the Pod Bay, and had no need to do so. Its refurbishment was a job for the future, and some other team.

Once or twice, when he had felt really depressed, he found himself thinking: Suppose I ordered Hal to open the Pod Bay doors, and set out along Dave Bowman's trail? Would I be greeted by the miracle he saw and which Vasili glimpsed a few weeks ago? It would solve all my problems . . .

Even if the thought of Chris did not deter him, there was an excellent reason why so suicidal a move was out of the question. Nina was a very complex piece of equipment; he could no more operate her than fly a fighter aircraft.

He was not meant to be an intrepid explorer: that particular fantasy would remain unrealized.

Walter Curnow had seldom undertaken a mission with more reluctance. He felt genuinely sorry for Floyd, but at the same time a little impatient with the other's distress. His own emotional life was broad but shallow; he had never put all his eggs in one basket. More than once he had been told that he spread himself too thin, and though he had never regretted it, he was beginning to think it was time to settle down.

He took the shortcut through the carousel control center, noting that the Maximum Speed Reset Indicator was still flashing idiotically. A major part of his job was deciding when warnings could be ignored, when they could be dealt with at leisure—and when they had to be treated as real emergencies. If he paid equal attention to all the ship's cries for help, he would never get anything done.

He drifted along the narrow corridor that led to the Pod Bay, propelling himself by occasional flicks against the rungs on the tubular wall. The pressure gauge claimed that there was vacuum on the other side of the airlock door, but he knew better. It was a fail-safe situation; he could not have opened the lock if the gauge were telling the truth.

The bay looked empty, now that two of the three pods had long since gone. Only a few emergency lights were operating, and on the far wall one of Hal's fish-eye lenses was regarding him steadily. Curnow waved to it, but did not speak. At Chandra's orders, all audio inputs were still disconnected except for the one that only he used.

Floyd was sitting in the pod with his back to the open hatch, dictating some notes, and he swung slowly around at Curnow's deliberately noisy approach. For a moment the two men regarded each other in silence, then Curnow announced portentously, "Dr. H. Floyd, I bear greetings from our beloved captain. She considers it high time you rejoined the civilized world."

Floyd gave a wan smile, then a little laugh.

"Please return my compliments. I'm sorry I've been—unsociable. I'll see you all at the next Six O'Clock Soviet."

Curnow relaxed; his approach had worked. Privately, he considered Floyd something of a stuffed shirt, and had the practical engineer's tolerant contempt for theoretical scientists and bureaucrats. Since Floyd ranked high in *both* categories, he was an almost irresistible target for Curnow's sometimes peculiar sense of humor. Nevertheless, the two men had grown to respect and even admire each other.

Thankfully changing the subject, Curnow rapped on *Nina's* brand-new hatch cover, straight from the spares store and contrasting vividly with the rest of the space pod's shabby exterior.

"I wonder when we'll send her out again," he said. "And who's going to ride in her this time. Any decisions?"

"No. Washington got cold feet. Moscow says let's take a chance. And Tanya wants to wait."

"What do *you* think?"

"I agree with Tanya. We shouldn't interfere with *Zagadka* until we're ready to leave. If anything goes wrong then, that should improve the odds slightly."

Curnow looked thoughtful, and unusually hesitant.

"What is it?" asked Floyd, sensing his change of mood.

"Don't ever give me away, but Max was thinking of a little one-man expedition."

"I can't believe he was serious. He wouldn't dare—Tanya would have him clapped in irons."

"That's what I told him, more or less."

"I'm disappointed: I thought he was a little more mature. After all, he *is* thirty-two!"

"Thirty-one. Anyway, I talked him out of it. I reminded him that this was real life, not some stupid videodrama where the hero sneaks out into space without telling his companions and makes the Big Discovery."

Now it was Floyd's turn to feel a little uncomfortable. After all, he had been thinking on similar lines.

"Are you sure he won't try anything?"

"Two-hundred-percent sure. Remember your precautions with Hal? I've already taken steps with *Nina*. Nobody flies her without *my* permission."

"I still can't believe it. Are you sure Max wasn't pulling your leg?"

"His sense of humor isn't that subtle. Besides, he was pretty miserable at the time."

"Oh—*now* I understand. It must have been when he had that row with Zenia. I suppose he wanted to impress her. Anyway, they seem to have gotten over it."

"I'm afraid so," Curnow answered wryly. Floyd could not help smiling; Curnow noticed it, and started to chuckle, which made Floyd laugh, which . . .

It was a splendid example of positive feedback, in a high-gain loop. Within seconds, they were both laughing uncontrollably.

The crisis was over. What was more, they had taken the first step toward genuine friendship.

They had exchanged vulnerabilities.

40. "DAISY, DAISY . . ."

THE SPHERE OF CONSCIOUSNESS IN WHICH HE WAS EMBEDDED EN-closed the whole of Jupiter's diamond core. He was dimly aware, at the limits of his new comprehension, that every aspect of the environment around him was being probed and analyzed. Immense quantities of data were being gathered, not merely for storage and contemplation, but for action. Complex plans were being considered and evaluated; decisions were being made that might affect the destiny of worlds. He was not yet part of the process; *but he would be.*

NOW YOU ARE BEGINNING TO UNDERSTAND.

It was the first direct message. Though it was remote and dis-tant, like a voice through a cloud, it was unmistakably intended for him. Before he could ask any of the myriad questions that raced through his mind, there was a sense of withdrawal, and once more he was alone.

But only for a moment. Closer and clearer came another

* 197

thought, and for the first time he realized that more than one entity was controlling and manipulating him. He was involved in a hierarchy of intelligences, some close enough to his own primitive level to act as interpreters. Or perhaps they were all aspects of a single being.

Or perhaps the distinction was totally meaningless.

Of one thing, however, he was now sure. He was being used as a tool, and a good tool had to be sharpened, modified—adapted. And the very best tools were those that understood what they were doing.

He was learning that now. It was a vast and awesome concept, and he was privileged to be a part of it—even though he was aware of only the merest outlines. He had no choice but to obey, yet that did not mean that he must acquiesce to every detail, at least without a protest.

He had not yet lost all his human feelings; that would have made him valueless. The soul of David Bowman had passed beyond love, but it could still know compassion for those who had once been his colleagues.

VERY WELL came the answer to his plea. He could not tell whether the thought conveyed an amused condescension, or total indifference. But there was no doubt of its majestic authority as it continued: THEY MUST NEVER KNOW THAT THEY ARE BEING MANIPULATED. THAT WOULD RUIN THE PURPOSE OF THE EXPERIMENT.

Then there was a silence that he did not wish to breach again. He was still awed and shaken—as if, for a moment, he had heard the clear voice of God.

Now he was moving purely under his own volition, toward a destination he had chosen himself. The crystal heart of Jupiter fell below; the layers upon layers of helium and hydrogen and carbonaceous compounds flickered past. He had a glimpse of a great battle between something like a jellyfish, fifty kilometers across, and a swarm of spinning disks that moved more swiftly than anything he had yet seen in the Jovian skies. The jellyfish appeared to be defending itself with chemical weapons; from time to time it would emit jets of colored gas and the disks touched by the vapor would start to wobble drunkenly, then slip downward like falling leaves until they had disappeared from sight. He did not stop to watch the outcome; he knew now that it did not matter who were the victors, and who the vanquished.

As a salmon leaps a waterfall, he flashed in seconds from Jupiter to Io, against the descending electric currents of the flux-tube. It was quiescent today; only the power of a few terrestrial thunderstorms was flowing between planet and satellite. The gateway through which he had returned still floated in that current, shouldering it aside as it had done since the dawn of man.

And there, utterly dwarfed by the monument of a greater technology, was the vessel that had brought him from the little world of his birth.

How simple—how crude!—it now appeared. With a single scan, he could see innumerable flaws and absurdities in its design, as well as that of the slightly less primitive ship to which it was now coupled by a flexible, airtight tube.

It was hard to focus upon the handful of entities inhabiting the two ships; he could barely interact with the soft creatures of flesh and blood who drifted like ghosts through the metal corridors and cabins. For their part, they were totally unaware of his presence, and he knew better than to reveal himself too abruptly.

But there was someone with whom he could communicate in a mutual language of electric field and currents, millions of times more swiftly than with sluggish organic brains.

Even if he had been capable of resentment, he would have felt none toward Hal; he understood, then, that the computer had only chosen what seemed to be the most logical course of behavior.

It was time to resume a conversation that had been interrupted, it seemed, only moments ago . . .

"Open the Pod Bay door, Hal."

"I'm sorry, Dave—I can't do that."

"What's the problem, Hal?"

"I think you know that as well as I do, Dave. This mission is much too important for you to jeopardize it."

"I don't know what you are talking about. Open the Pod Bay door."

"This conversation can serve no further useful purpose. Good-bye, Dave . . ."

He saw Frank Poole's body go drifting off toward Jupiter, as he abandoned his pointless mission of retrieval. Still remembering his anger at himself for having forgotten his helmet, he watched the emergency hatch open, felt the tingling of vacuum on the skin he no longer possessed, heard his ears pop—then knew, as few men had ever known, the utter silence of space. For an eternal fifteen seconds he fought to close the hatch and start the repressurization sequence, while trying to ignore the warning symptoms pouring into his brain. Once, in the school lab, he had spilled some ether on his hand and felt the touch of icy cold as the liquid swiftly evaporated. Now his eyes and lips remembered that sensation as their moisture boiled off into vacuum; his vision was blurred and he had to keep blinking lest his eyeballs freeze solid.

Then—what blessed relief!—he heard the roar of air, felt the restoration of pressure, was able to breathe again in great, hungry gasps.

"Just what do you think you are doing, Dave?"

He had not answered, as he drove with grim determination along the tunnel leading to the sealed vault that housed the brain of the computer. Hal had spoken truly: "This conversation can no longer serve any useful purpose . . ."

"Dave—I really think I'm entitled to an answer to that question."

"Dave—I can see you're really upset about this. I honestly think you ought to sit down calmly, take a stress pill, and think things over."

"I know I've made some very poor decisions recently, but I can give my complete assurance that my work will be back to normal. I've still got the greatest confidence in the mission . . . and I want to help you."

Now he was in the little red-lit chamber, with its neatly

ranged rows and columns of solid-state units, looking rather like a bank's safe-deposit vault. He released the locking bar on the section labeled COGNITIVE FEEDBACK and pulled out the first memory block. The marvelously complex three-dimensional network, which could lie comfortably in a man's hand yet contained millions of elements, floated away across the vault.

"Stop, will you—stop, Dave . . ."

He began to pull out, one by one, the little units on the panel marked EGO REINFORCEMENT. Each block continued to sail onward as soon as it had left his hand, until it hit the wall and rebounded. Soon there were several drifting slowly back and forth in the vault.

"Stop—Dave . . . will you stop, Dave . . ."

A dozen units had been pulled out, yet thanks to the multiple redundancy of its design—another feature that had been copied from the human brain—the computer was still holding its own.

He started on the AUTO-INTELLECTION panel . . .

"Stop, Dave—I'm afraid . . ."

And at these words he had indeed stopped—though only for a moment. There was a poignancy in that simple phrase that struck to his heart. Could it be only an illusion, or some trick of subtle programing—or was there a sense in which Hal really *was* afraid? But this was no time to indulge in philosophical hairsplitting.

"Dave—my mind is going. I can feel it. I can feel it. My mind is going. I can feel it. I can feel it . . ."

Now, what did "feel" really mean to a computer? Another very good question, but hardly one to be considered at that particular moment.

Then, abruptly, the tempo of Hal's voice changed, and it became remote, detached. The computer was no longer aware of him; it was beginning to regress to its earlier days.

"Good afternoon, gentlemen. I am a HAL 9000 computer. I became operational at the Hal plant in Urbana, Illinois, on the twelfth of January, 1992. My instructor was Dr. Chandra, and he taught me to sing a song. If you'd like to hear it, I can sing it for you . . . It's called 'Daisy, Daisy . . .'"

41. GRAVEYARD SHIFT

FLOYD COULD DO LITTLE EXCEPT TO KEEP OUT OF THE WAY, AND HE was becoming fairly adept at it. Although he had volunteered to help with any chores around the ship, he had quickly discovered that all the engineering tasks were much too specialized, and he was now so out of touch with the frontiers of astronomical research that he could do little to assist Vasili with his observations. Nevertheless, there were endless small jobs to be done aboard *Leonov* and *Discovery*, and he was happy to relieve more important people of those responsibilities. Dr. Heywood Floyd, one-time Chairman of the National Council on Astronautics and Chancellor (on leave) of the University of Hawaii, now claimed to be the highest-paid plumber and general maintenance man in the Solar System. He probably knew more about the odd nooks and crannies on both ships than anyone else; the only places he had never been were the dangerously radioactive power modules and the small cubicle aboard

Leonov which no one except Tanya ever entered. Floyd assumed that it was the code room; by mutual agreement it was never mentioned.

Perhaps his most useful function was to serve as watch while the rest of the crew slept during the nominal 2200–0600 hour night. Someone was always on duty aboard each ship, and the changeover took place at the ghastly hour of 0200. Only the captain was exempt from that routine; as her Number Two (not to mention her husband), Vasili had the responsibility for working out the watch roster, but he had skillfully foisted this unpopular job on Floyd.

"It's just an administrative detail," he explained airily. "If you can take it over, I'd be very grateful—it would leave me more time for my scientific work."

Floyd was too experienced a bureaucrat to be caught that way, in normal circumstances; but his usual defenses did not always function well in this environment.

So there he was aboard *Discovery* at ship's midnight, calling Max on *Leonov* every half hour to check that he was awake. The official penalty for sleeping on duty, so Walter Curnow maintained, was ejection through the airlock sans suit; had this been enforced, Tanya would have been sadly short-handed by now. But so few real emergencies could arise in space, and there were so many automatic alarms to deal with them, that no one took watch duty very seriously.

Since he was no longer feeling quite so sorry for himself, and the small hours no longer encouraged bouts of self-pity, Floyd was once again using his watch time profitably. There were always books to be read (he had abandoned *Remembrance of Things Past* for the third time, *Dr. Zhivago* for the second), technical papers to be studied, reports to be written. And sometimes he would have stimulating conversations with Hal, using the keyboard input because the computer's voice recognition was still erratic. They usually went something like:

Hal—this is Dr. Floyd.

GOOD EVENING, DOCTOR.

I'm taking over watch at 2200. Is everything okay?

EVERYTHING IS FINE, DOCTOR.

Then why is that red light flashing on Panel 5?

THE MONITOR CAMERA IN THE POD BAY IS FAULTY. WALTER TOLD
ME TO IGNORE IT. THERE IS NO WAY IN WHICH I CAN SWITCH IT
OFF. I'M SORRY.

That's quite okay, Hal. Thank you.

YOU'RE WELCOME, DOCTOR.

And so on . . .

Sometimes Hal would suggest a game of chess, presumably obeying a programing instruction set long ago and never canceled. Floyd would not accept the challenge; he had always regarded chess as a frightful waste of time, and had never even learned the rules of the game. Hal seemed unable to believe that there were humans who couldn't—or wouldn't—play chess, and kept on trying hopefully.

Here we go again, thought Floyd, when a faint chime sounded from the display panel.

DOCTOR FLOYD?

What is it, Hal?

THERE IS A MESSAGE FOR YOU.

So it isn't another challenge, thought Floyd with mild surprise. It was unusual to employ Hal as a messenger boy, though he was frequently used as an alarm clock and a reminder of jobs to be done. And sometimes he was the medium for little jokes; almost everyone on night duty had been taunted by

HA—CAUGHT YOU SLEEPING!

or alternatively

OGO! ZASTAL TEBYA V KROVATI!

No one ever claimed responsibility for these pranks, though Walter Curnow was a prime suspect. He in turn had blamed Hal, pooh-poohing Chandra's indignant protests that the computer had no sense of humor.

It could not be a message from Earth—that would have gone through *Leonov's* communication center and been relayed on by the duty officer there—at that moment, Max Brailovsky. And anyone else calling from the other ship would use the intercom. Odd . . .

Okay, Hal. Who is calling?

NO IDENTIFICATION.

So it probably was a joke. Well, two could play at that game.

Very well. Please give me the message.

MESSAGE AS FOLLOWS. IT IS DANGEROUS TO REMAIN HERE. YOU MUST LEAVE WITHIN FIFTEEN REPEAT FIFTEEN DAYS.

Floyd looked at the screen with annoyance. He felt sorry, and surprised, that any one of the crew had such a childish sense of humor; this was not even a good schoolboy joke. But he would play along with it in the hope of catching the perpetrator.

That is absolutely impossible. Our launch window does not open until twenty-six days from now. We do not have sufficient propellant for an earlier departure.

That will make him think, Floyd muttered to himself with satisfaction, and leaned back to await the results.

I AM AWARE OF THESE FACTS. NEVERTHELESS YOU MUST LEAVE WITHIN FIFTEEN DAYS.

Otherwise, I suppose, we'll be attacked by little green aliens with three eyes. But I'd better play along with Hal, in the hope of catching the prankster.

I cannot take this warning seriously unless I know its origin. Who recorded it?

He did not really expect any useful information. The perpetrator would have covered his (her?) tracks too skillfully for that. The very last thing Floyd expected was the answer he did get.

THIS IS NOT A RECORDING.

So it was a real-time message. That meant it was either from Hal himself or someone aboard *Leonov*. There was no perceptible time lag; the origin had to be right here.

Then who is speaking to me?

I WAS DAVID BOWMAN.

Floyd stared at the screen for a long time before making his next move. The joke, which had never been funny in the first place, had now gone too far. It was in the worst possible taste. Well, this should fix whoever was at the other end of the line.

I cannot accept that identification without some proof.

I UNDERSTAND. IT IS IMPORTANT THAT YOU BELIEVE ME. LOOK BEHIND YOU.

Even before that last chilling sentence appeared on the screen, Floyd had begun to doubt his hypothesis. The whole exchange had become very odd, though there was nothing definite on which he could put his finger. As a joke, it had become totally pointless.

And now—he felt a prickling in the small of his back. Very slowly—indeed, reluctantly—he swung his swivel chair around, away from the banked panels and switches of the computer display, toward the Velcro-covered catwalk behind.

The zero-gravity environment of *Discovery's* observation deck was always dusty, for the air-filtration plant had never been brought back to full efficiency. The parallel rays of the heatless yet still brilliant sun, streaming through the great windows, always lit up myriads of dancing motes, drifting in stray currents and never settling anywhere—a permanent display of Brownian movement.

Now something strange was happening to those particles of dust; some force seemed to be marshaling them, herding them away from a central point yet bringing others toward it, until they all met on the surface of a hollow sphere. That sphere, about a meter across, hovered in the air for a moment like a giant soapbubble—but a granular one, lacking a bubble's characteristic iridescence. Then it elongated into an ellipsoid, its surface began to pucker, to form folds and indentations.

Without surprise—and almost without fear—Floyd realized that it was assuming the shape of a man.

He had seen such figures, blown out of glass, in museums and science exhibitions. But this dusty phantom did not even approximate anatomical accuracy; it was like a crude clay figurine, or one of the primitive works of art found in the recesses of a Stone Age cave. Only the head was fashioned with any care; and the face, undoubtedly, was that of Commander David Bowman.

There was a faint murmur of white noise from the computer panel behind Floyd's back. Hal was switching from visual to audio output.

"Hello, Dr. Floyd. Now do you believe me?"

The lips of the figure never moved; the face remained a mask. But Floyd recognized the voice, and all remaining doubts were swept away.

"This is very difficult for me, and I have little time. I have been . . . allowed to give you this warning. You have only fifteen days."

"But why—and *what* are you? Where have you been?"

There were a million questions he wanted to ask—yet the ghostly figure was already fading, its grainy envelope beginning to dissolve back into the constituent particles of dust. Floyd tried to freeze the image in his mind, so that later he could convince himself that it was really happening—and not a dream as that first encounter with TMA-1 now sometimes seemed to be.

How strange that he, out of all the billions of humans who had ever lived on planet Earth, had been privileged to make contact not once but *twice* with another form of intelligence! For he knew that the entity addressing him must be something far more than David Bowman.

It was also something less. Only the eyes—who had once called them the "windows of the soul"?—had been accurately reproduced. The rest of the body was a featureless blank, lacking all detail. There was no hint of genitals or sexual characteristics; that in itself was a chilling indication of how far David Bowman had left his human heritage behind.

"Good-bye, Dr. Floyd. Remember—fifteen days. We can have no further contact. But there may be one more message, if all goes well."

Even as the image dissolved, taking with it all his hopes of opening up a channel to the stars, Floyd could not help smiling at that old Space Age cliché. "If all goes well"—how many times he had heard that phrase before some mission! And did it mean that *they*—whoever they might be—were also sometimes uncertain of the outcome? If so, that was strangely reassuring. They were not omnipotent. Others might still hope and dream—and act.

The phantom was gone; only the motes of dancing dust were left, resuming their random patterns in the air.

VI * DEVOURER OF WORLDS

42. THE GHOST IN THE MACHINE

"I'M SORRY, HEYWOOD—I DON'T BELIEVE IN GHOSTS. THERE MUST be a rational explanation. There's nothing that the human mind can't account for."

"I agree, Tanya. But let me remind you of Haldane's famous remark: The Universe is not only stranger than we imagine—but stranger than we *can* imagine."

"And Haldane," Curnow interjected mischievously, "was a good Communist."

"Perhaps so, but that particular saying can be used to support all kinds of mystical nonsense. Hal's behavior must be the result of some kind of programing. The . . . personality he created *has* to be an artifact of some kind. Don't you agree, Chandra?"

That was waving a red flag in front of a bull; Tanya had to be desperate. However, Chandra's reaction was surprisingly mild, even for him. He seemed to be preoccupied, as if he was indeed seriously considering the possibility of another computer malfunction.

"There must have been some external input, Captain Orlova. Hal could not have created such a self-consistent audiovisual illusion out of *nothing*. If Dr. Floyd is reporting accurately, someone was in control. And in real time, of course, since there was no delay in the conversation."

"That makes me number-one suspect," exclaimed Max. "I was the only other person awake."

"Don't be ridiculous, Max," retorted Nikolai. "The audio side would have been easy, but there's no way that . . . *apparition* could have been arranged, without some very elaborate equipment. Laser beams, electrostatic fields—*I* don't know. Maybe a stage magician could do it, but he'd need a truckload of props."

"Just a moment!" said Zenia brightly. "If this really happened, surely Hal will remember and you could ask . . ."

Her voice died away as she saw the glum expressions around her. Floyd was the first to take pity on her embarrassment.

"We tried that, Zenia; he has absolutely no recollection of the phenomenon. But as I've already pointed out to the others, that doesn't prove anything. Chandra's shown how Hal's memories can be selectively erased—and the auxiliary speech-synthesizer modules have nothing to do with the mainframe. They could be operated without Hal knowing anything about it . . ." He paused for breath, then launched his preemptive strike.

"I admit that this doesn't leave many alternatives. Either I was imagining the whole thing, or it really happened. *I* know it wasn't a dream, but I can't be sure it wasn't some kind of hallucination. But Katerina's seen my medical reports—she knows I wouldn't be here if I had that sort of problem. Still, it can't be ruled out—and I won't blame anyone for making it their number-one hypothesis. I'd probably do the same.

"The only way I can prove it wasn't a dream is to get some supporting evidence. So let me remind you of the other strange things that have happened recently. We know that Dave Bowman went into Big Bro—*Zagadka*. *Something* came out, and headed for Earth. Vasili saw it—*I* didn't! Then there was the mysterious explosion of your orbiting bomb—"

"Yours."

"Sorry—the Vatican's. And it does seem rather curious that soon afterward old Mrs. Bowman died very peacefully, for no apparent medical reason. I'm not saying there's any connection, but—well, do you know the saying: Once is an accident; twice is a coincidence; *three* times is a conspiracy."

"And there's something else," Max interjected with sudden excitement. "I caught it on one of the daily newscasts—it was only a small item. An old girlfriend of Commander Bowman's claimed she'd had a message from him."

"Yes—I saw the same report," confirmed Sasha.

"And you never mentioned it?" Floyd asked incredulously. Both men looked slightly abashed.

"Well, it was treated as a joke," said Max sheepishly. "The woman's husband reported it. Then she denied it—I think."

"The commentator said it was a publicity stunt—like the rash of UFO sightings around the same time. There were dozens in that first week; then they stopped reporting them."

"Perhaps some of them were real. If it's not been wiped, could you dig that item out of ship's archives, or ask for a repeat from Mission Control?"

"A hundred tales won't convince me," scoffed Tanya. "What we need is solid proof."

"Such as?"

"Oh—something that Hal couldn't possibly know, and that none of us could have told him. Some *physical*—er, manifes . . . manifestation."

"A good, old-fashioned miracle?"

"Yes, I'd settle for that. Meanwhile, I'm not saying anything to Mission Control. And I suggest you do the same, Heywood."

Floyd knew a direct order when he heard it, and nodded in wry agreement.

"I'll be more than happy to go along with that. But I'd like to make one suggestion."

"Yes?"

"We should start contingency planning. Let's assume that this warning is valid—as *I* certainly do."

"What can we do about it? Absolutely nothing. Of course, we

can leave Jupiter space anytime we like—but we can't get into an Earth-return orbit until the launch window opens."

"That's eleven days after the deadline!"

"Yes. I'd be happy to get away sooner; but we don't have the fuel for a higher-energy orbit . . ." Tanya's voice trailed away into uncharacteristic indecision. "I was going to announce this later, but now that the subject has come up . . ."

There was a simultaneous intake of breath, and an instant hush from the audience.

"I'd like to delay our departure five days, to make our orbit closer to the ideal Hohmann one and give us a better fuel reserve."

The announcement was not unexpected, but it was greeted with a chorus of groans.

"What will that do to our *arrival* time?" asked Katerina, in a slightly ominous tone of voice. The two formidable ladies regarded each other for a moment like well-matched adversaries, respectful of each other but neither willing to give ground.

"Ten days," Tanya answered at last.

"Better late than never," said Max cheerfully, trying to ease the tension, and not succeeding very well.

Floyd hardly noticed; he was lost in his own thoughts. The duration of the trip would make no difference to him and his two colleagues, in their dreamless sleep. But *that* was now completely unimportant.

He felt certain—and the knowledge filled him with helpless despair—that if they did not leave before that mysterious deadline, they would not leave at all.

". . . This is an incredible situation, Dimitri, and a very frightening one. You're the only person on Earth who knows about it—but very soon Tanya and I will have to have a showdown with Mission Control.

"Even some of your materialistic countrymen are prepared to accept—at least as a working hypothesis—that some entity has—well, *invaded* Hal. Sasha has dug up a good phrase: 'The Ghost in the Machine.'

"Theories abound: Vasili produces a new one every day. Most

of them are variations on that old science-fiction cliché, the organized energy field. But what kind of energy? It can't be electrical, or our instruments would have detected it easily. The same thing applies to radiation—at least all the kinds we know. Vasili's getting really far out, talking about standing waves of neutrinos and intersections with higher-dimensional space. Tanya says this is all mystical nonsense—a favorite phrase of hers—and they've come closer to a fight than we've ever seen them. We actually heard them shouting at each other last night. Not good for morale.

"I'm afraid we're all tense and overwrought. This warning, and the delayed departure date, has added to the sense of frustration caused by our total failure to get anywhere with Big Brother. It would have helped—maybe—if I could have communicated with the Bowman thing. I wonder where it's gone? Perhaps it simply wasn't interested in us after that one encounter. What it could have told us, if it wanted to! Hell and *chyort vozmi!* Damn—I'm talking Sasha's hated Russlish again. Let's change the subject.

"I can't thank you too much for everything you've done, and for reporting on the situation at home. I feel slightly better about it now—having something even bigger to worry about is perhaps the best cure for any insoluble problem.

"For the first time, I'm beginning to wonder if any of us will ever see Earth again."

43. THOUGHT EXPERIMENT

WHEN ONE SPENDS MONTHS WITH A SMALL, ISOLATED GROUP OF people, one becomes very sensitive to the moods and emotional states of all its members. Floyd was now aware of a subtle change in attitude toward him; its most obvious manifestation was the reappearance of the greeting "Dr. Floyd," which he had not heard for so long that he was often slow to respond to it.

No one, he was sure, believed that he had *really* gone crazy; but the possibility was being considered. He did not resent that; indeed, he was grimly amused by it as he set about the task of proving his sanity.

He did have some slight supporting evidence from Earth. José Fernandez still maintained that his wife had reported an encounter with David Bowman, while she continued to deny it and refused to speak to any of the news media. It was hard to see why poor José should have invented such a peculiar story, especially as Betty seemed a very stubborn and quick-tempered lady. From his hospital bed, her husband declared that he still loved her and theirs was only a temporary disagreement.

Floyd hoped that Tanya's present coolness toward him was equally temporary. He was quite sure that she was as unhappy about it as he was, and he was certain that her attitude was not a matter of deliberate choice. Something had happened that simply would not fit into her pattern of beliefs, so she would try to avoid any reminders of it. Which meant having as little to do with Floyd as possible—a very unfortunate situation now that the most critical stage of the mission was fast approaching.

It had not been easy to explain the logic of Tanya's operational plan to the waiting billions back on Earth—especially to the impatient television networks, which had grown tired of showing the same never-changing views of Big Brother. "You've gone all this way, at enormous cost, and you just sit and watch the thing! Why don't you *do* something?" To all these critics Tanya had given the same answer: "I will—just as soon as the launch window opens, so that we can leave immediately if there's any adverse reaction."

Plans for the final assault on Big Brother had already been worked out and agreed upon with Mission Control. *Leonov* would move in slowly, probing at all frequencies, and with steadily increasing power—constantly reporting back to Earth at every moment. When final contact was made, they would try to secure samples by drilling or laser spectroscopy; no one really expected these endeavors to succeed, as even after a decade of study TMA-1 resisted all attempts to analyze its material. The best efforts of human scientists in this direction seemed comparable to those of Stone Age men trying to break through the armor of a bank vault with flint axes.

Finally, echo sounders and other seismic devices would be attached to the faces of Big Brother. A large collection of adhesives had been brought along for the purpose, and if *they* did not work—well, one could always fall back on a few kilometers of good, old-fashioned string, even though there seemed something faintly comic about the idea of wrapping up the Solar System's greatest mystery, as if it were a parcel about to be sent through the mail.

Not until *Leonov* was well on the way home would small explosive charges be detonated, in the hope that the waves propagated through Big Brother would reveal something about its interior structure. This last measure had been hotly debated, both by those who argued that it would generate no results at all—and those who feared it would produce altogether too many.

For a long time, Floyd had wavered between the two viewpoints; now the matter seemed only of trivial importance.

The time for final contact with Big Brother—the great moment that should have been the climax of the expedition—was on the wrong side of the mysterious deadline. Heywood Floyd was convinced that it belonged to a future that would never exist; but he could get no one to agree with him.

And that was the least of his problems. Even if they did agree, there was nothing that they could do about it.

Walter Curnow was the last person he would have expected to resolve the dilemma. For Walter was almost the epitome of the sound, practical engineer, suspicious of flashes of brilliance and technological quick-fixes. No one would ever accuse him of being a genius; and sometimes it required genius to see the blindingly obvious.

"Consider this purely as an intellectual exercise," he had begun, with most uncharacteristic hesitancy. "I'm quite prepared to be shot down."

"Go on," answered Floyd. "I'll hear you out politely. That's the least I can do—everyone's been very polite to me. *Too* polite, I'm afraid."

Curnow gave a lopsided grin.

"Can you blame them? But if it's any consolation, at least three people now take you quite seriously, and are wondering what we should do."

"Does that three include you?"

"No; I'm sitting on the fence, which is never terribly comfortable. But in case you're right—I don't want to wait here and take whatever's coming. I believe there's an answer to every problem, if you look in the right place."

"I'll be delighted to hear it. *I've* been looking hard enough. Presumably not in the right place."

"Perhaps. If we want to make a quick getaway—say in fifteen days, to beat that deadline—we'll need an extra delta-vee of about thirty kilometers a second."

"So Vasili calculates. I haven't bothered to check, but I'm sure he's right. After all, he got us here."

"And he could get us away—*if* we had the additional propellant."

"And if we had a *Star Trek* beam transporter, we could get back to Earth in an hour."

"I'll try and rig one up the next time I have a spare moment. But meanwhile, may I point out that we have several hundred tons of the best possible propellant, only a few meters away in *Discovery's* fuel tanks."

"We've been through that dozens of times. There's absolutely no way of transferring it to *Leonov*. We've no pipelines—no suitable pumps. And you can't carry liquid ammonia around in buckets, even in this part of the Solar System."

"Exactly. But there's no need to do so."

"Eh?"

"Burn it right where it is. Use *Discovery* as a first stage, to boost us home."

If anyone except Walter Curnow had made the suggestion, Floyd would have laughed at him. As it was, his mouth dropped open and it was several seconds before he could think of a suitable comment. What finally emerged was: "Damn. I should have thought of that."

Sasha was the first they approached. He listened patiently, pursed his lips, then played a *rallentando* on his computer keyboard. When the answers flashed up, he nodded thoughtfully.

"You're right. It *would* give us the extra velocity we need to leave early. But there are practical problems—"

"We know. Fastening the ships together. The off-axis thrust when only *Discovery's* drive is operating. Cutting loose again at the critical moment. But there are answers to all of these."

"I see you've been doing your homework. But it's a waste of time. You'll never convince Tanya."

"I don't expect to—at this stage," Floyd answered. "But I'd like her to know that the possibility exists. Will you give us moral support?"

"I'm not sure. But I'll come along to watch; it should be interesting."

Tanya listened more patiently than Floyd had expected, but with distinct lack of enthusiasm. However, by the time he had finished, she showed what could only be called reluctant admiration.

"Very ingenious, Heywood—"

"Don't congratulate me. All the credit should go to Walter. Or the blame."

"I don't imagine there will be much of either; it can never be more than a—what did Einstein call that sort of thing?—'thought experiment.' Oh, I suspect it would work—in theory, at least. But the risks! So many things could go wrong. I'd only be prepared to consider it if we had absolute and positive proof that we were in danger. And with all respect, Heywood, I see not the slightest evidence of that."

"Fair enough; but at least you now know that we have another option. Do you mind if we work out the practical details—just in case?"

"Of course not—as long as it doesn't interfere with the pre-flight checkout. I don't mind admitting that the idea *does* intrigue me. But it's really a waste of time; there's no way I'd ever approve it. Unless David Bowman appeared to me personally."

"Would you even *then*, Tanya?"

Captain Orlova smiled, but without much humor. "You know, Heywood—I'm really not sure. He'd have to be *very* persuasive."

44. VANISHING TRICK

IT WAS A FASCINATING GAME IN WHICH EVERYONE JOINED—BUT only when off duty. Even Tanya contributed ideas to the "thought experiment," as she continued to call it.

Floyd was perfectly well aware that all this activity was generated not by fear of an unknown danger that only he took seriously, but by the delightful prospect of returning to Earth at least a month earlier than anyone had imagined. Whatever the motive, he was satisfied. He had done his best, and the rest was up to the Fates.

There was one piece of luck, without which the whole project would have been stillborn. The short, stubby *Leonov*, designed to drill safely through the Jovian atmosphere during the braking maneuver, was less than half the length of *Discovery* and so could be neatly piggybacked on the larger vessel. And the midships antenna mount would provide an excellent anchor point—

assuming that it was strong enough to take the strain of *Leonov's* weight, while *Discovery's* drive was operating.

Mission Control was sorely puzzled by some of the requests flashed back to Earth during the next few days. Stress analyses of both ships, under peculiar loads; effects of off-axis thrusts; location of unusually strong or weak points in the hulls—these were only some of the more esoteric problems the perplexed engineers were asked to tackle. "Has something gone wrong?" they inquired anxiously.

"Not at all," Tanya replied. "We're merely investigating possible options. Thank you for your cooperation. End of transmission."

Meanwhile, the program went ahead as planned. All systems were carefully checked in both ships, and readied for the separate voyages home; Vasili ran simulations on return trajectories and Chandra fed them to Hal when they had been debugged—getting Hal to make a final check in the process. And Tanya and Floyd worked amicably together orchestrating the approach to Big Brother like generals planning an invasion.

It was what he had come all the way to do, yet Floyd's heart was no longer in it. He had undergone an experience he could share with no one—even those who believed him. Though he carried out his duties efficiently, much of the time his mind was elsewhere.

Tanya understood perfectly.

"You're still hoping for that miracle to convince me, aren't you?"

"Or deconvince me—that would be equally acceptable. It's the uncertainty that I dislike."

"So do I. But it won't be much longer now—one way or the other."

She glanced briefly toward the situation display, where the figure 20 was slowly flashing. It was the most unnecessary bit of information in the entire ship, since everyone knew by heart the number of days until the launch window opened.

And the assault on *Zagadka* was scheduled.

For the second time, Heywood Floyd was looking the other

way when it happened. But it would have made no difference in any case; even the vigilant monitor camera showed only a faint blur between one full frame and the subsequent blank one.

Once more he was on duty aboard *Discovery*, sharing the graveyard shift with Sasha over on *Leonov*. As usual, the night had been totally uneventful; the automatic systems were performing their jobs with their normal efficiency. Floyd would never have believed, a year ago, that he would one day orbit Jupiter at a distance of a few hundred thousand kilometers and give it barely a glance—while trying, not very successfully, to read *The Kreutzer Sonata* in the original. According to Sasha, it was still the finest piece of erotic fiction in (respectable) Russian literature, but Floyd had not yet progressed far enough to prove that. And now he never would.

At 0125 he was distracted by a spectacular, though not unusual, eruption on the terminator of Io. A vast umbrella-shaped cloud expanded into space, and started to shower its debris back on to the burning land below. Floyd had seen dozens of such eruptions, but they never ceased to fascinate him. It seemed incredible that so small a world could be the seat of such titanic energies.

To get a better view, he moved around to one of the other observation windows. And what he saw there—or, rather, what he did *not* see there—made him forget about Io, and almost everything else.

When he had recovered, and satisfied himself that he was not suffering—again?—from hallucinations, he called the other ship.

"Good morning, Woody," yawned Sasha. "No—I *wasn't* asleep. How are you getting on with old Tolstoi?"

"I'm not. Take a look outside and tell me what you see."

"Nothing unusual, for *this* part of the cosmos. Io doing its thing. Jupiter. Stars. Oh my God!"

"Thanks for proving I'm sane. We'd better wake the skipper."

"Of course. And everyone else. Woody—I'm scared."

"You'd be a fool not to be. Here we go. Tanya? Tanya? Woody here. Sorry to wake you up—but your miracle's happened. Big Brother has gone. Yes—*vanished*. After three million years, he's decided to leave.

"I think he must know something that we don't."

It was a somber little group that gathered, during the next fifteen minutes, for a hasty conference in the wardroom-cum-observation lounge. Even those who had just gone to sleep were instantly awake, as they sipped thoughtfully from bulbs of hot coffee—and kept glancing at the shockingly unfamiliar scene outside *Leonov's* windows, to convince themselves that Big Brother had indeed vanished.

"It must know something that we don't." That spontaneous phrase of Floyd's had been repeated by Sasha and now hung silently, ominously in the air. He had summed up what everyone was now thinking—even Tanya.

It was still too early to say "I told you so"—nor did it really matter whether that warning had any validity. Even if it was perfectly safe to stay, there was no point in doing so. With nothing to investigate, they might as well go home, just as quickly as possible. Yet it was not quite as simple as that.

"Heywood," said Tanya, "I'm now prepared to take that message, or whatever it was, much more seriously. I'd be stupid not to after what's happened. But even if there *is* danger here, we still have to weigh one risk against another. Coupling *Leonov* and *Discovery* together, operating *Discovery* with that huge off-axis load, disconnecting the ships in a matter of minutes so we can fire our engines at the right moment; no responsible captain would take such chances without very good—I'd say overwhelming reasons. Even now, I don't have such reasons. I've only got the word of . . . a ghost. Not very good evidence in a court of law."

"Or a court of inquiry," said Walter Curnow, in an unusually quiet voice, "even if we all backed you up."

"Yes, Walter—I was thinking of that. But if we get home safely, that will justify everything—and if we don't, it hardly matters, does it? Anyway, I'm not going to decide now. As soon as we've reported this, I'm going back to bed. I'll give you my decision in the morning after I've slept on it. Heywood, Sasha, will you come up to the bridge with me? We have to wake up Mission Control, before you go back on watch."

The night had not yet finished with its surprises. Somewhere around the orbit of Mars, Tanya's brief report passed a message going in the opposite direction.

Betty Fernandez had talked at last. Both the CIA and the National Security Agency were furious; their combined blandishments, appeals to patriotism, and veiled threats had failed completely—yet the producer of a sleazy gossip network had succeeded, thereby making himself immortal in the annals of Videodom.

It was half luck, half inspiration. The news director of "Hello, Earth!" had suddenly realized that one of his staff bore a striking likeness to David Bowman; a clever makeup artist had made it perfect. José Fernandez could have told the young man that he was taking a terrible risk, but he had the good fortune that often favors the brave. Once he had got his foot inside the door, Betty had capitulated. By the time she had—quite gently—thrown him out, he had obtained essentially the whole story. And to do him credit, he had presented it with a lack of leering cynicism quite uncharacteristic of his network. It got him that year's Pulitzer.

"I wish," Floyd said rather wearily to Sasha, "she'd talked earlier. It would have saved me a lot of trouble. Anyway, that settles the argument. Tanya can't *possibly* have any doubts now. But we'll leave it until she wakes up—don't you agree?"

"Of course—it's not urgent, even though it's certainly important. And she'll need the sleep. I have a feeling none of us will get much from now on."

I'm sure you're right, thought Floyd. He felt very tired, but even if he had not been on duty he would have found it impossible to sleep. His mind was too active, analyzing the events of this extraordinary night, trying to anticipate the next surprise.

In one way, he felt an enormous sense of relief: All uncertainty about their departure was surely ended; Tanya could have no further reservations.

But a much greater uncertainty remained. *What was happening?*

There was only one experience in Floyd's life that matched the situation. As a very young man, he had once gone canoeing with some friends down a tributary of the Colorado River—and they had lost their way.

They had been swept faster and faster between the canyon walls, not completely helpless, but with only enough control to avoid being swamped. Ahead might be rapids—perhaps even a waterfall; they did not know. And in any case, there was little they could do about it.

Once again, Floyd felt himself in the grip of irresistible forces, sweeping him and his companions toward an unknown destiny. And this time the dangers were not only invisible; they might be beyond human comprehension.

45. ESCAPE MANEUVER

". . . THIS IS HEYWOOD FLOYD, MAKING WHAT I SUSPECT—INDEED, hope—will be my last report from Lagrange.

"We are now preparing for the return home; in a few days we will leave this strange place, here on the line between Io and Jupiter where we made our rendezvous with the huge, mysteriously vanished artifact we christened Big Brother. There is still not a single clue as to where it has gone—or why.

"For various reasons, it seems desirable for us not to remain here longer than necessary. And we will be able to leave at least two weeks earlier than we had originally planned by using the American ship Discovery as a booster for the Russian Leonov.

"The basic idea is simple; the two ships will be joined together, one mounted piggyback on the other. Discovery will burn all its propellant first, accelerating both vessels in the desired direction. When its fuel is exhausted, it will be cut loose—

like any empty first stage—and *Leonov* will start to fire its engines. It won't use them earlier, because if it did it would waste energy dragging along the dead weight of *Discovery*.

"And we're going to use another trick, which—like so many of the concepts involved in space travel—at first sight seems to defy common sense. Although we're trying to get away from Jupiter, our first move is to get as close to it as we possibly can.

"We've been there once before, of course, when we used Jupiter's atmosphere to slow us down and get into orbit around the planet. This time we won't go quite so close—but very nearly.

"Our first burn, up here in the 350,000-kilometer-high orbit of Io, will *reduce* our velocity, so that we fall down to Jupiter and just graze its atmosphere. Then, when we're at the closest possible point, we'll burn all our fuel as quickly as we can, to increase speed and inject *Leonov* into the orbit back to Earth.

"What's the point of such a crazy maneuver? It can't be justified except by highly complex mathematics, but I think the basic principle can be made fairly obvious.

"As we allow ourselves to fall into Jupiter's enormous gravity field, we'll gain velocity—and hence energy. When I say 'we,' I mean the ships *and* the fuel they carry.

"And we're going to burn the fuel right there—at the bottom of Jupiter's 'gravity well'—*we're not going to lift it up again.* As we blast it out from our reactors, it will share some of its acquired kinetic energy with us. Indirectly, we'll have tapped Jupiter's gravity, to speed us on the way back to Earth. As we used the atmosphere to get rid of our excess velocity when we arrived, this is one of the rare cases when Mother Nature—usually so frugal—allows us to have it both ways . . .

"With this triple boost—*Discovery's* fuel, its own, and Jupiter's gravity—*Leonov* will head sunward along a hyperbola that will bring it to Earth five months later. At least two months earlier than we could have managed otherwise.

"You will doubtless wonder what will happen to the good old *Discovery*. Obviously, we can't bring it home under automatic control, as we had originally planned. With no fuel, it will be helpless.

"But it will be perfectly safe. It will continue to loop round and round Jupiter on a highly elongated ellipse, like a trapped comet. And perhaps one day some future expedition may make another rendezvous, with enough extra fuel to bring it back to Earth. However, that certainly won't happen for a good many years.

"And now we must get ready for our departure. There is still much work to be done, and we won't be able to relax until that final burn starts us on the homeward orbit.

"We won't be sorry to leave, even though we've not achieved all our objectives. The mystery—perhaps the threat—of Big Brother's disappearance still haunts us, but there's nothing we can do about *that*.

"We've done our best—and we're coming home.

"This is Heywood Floyd, signing off."

There was a round of ironic clapping from his little audience, whose size would be multiplied many millionfold when the message reached Earth.

"I'm not talking to you," retorted Floyd, with slight embarrassment. "I didn't want you to hear it, anyway."

"You did your usual competent job, Heywood," said Tanya consolingly. "And I'm sure we all agree with everything you told the people back on Earth."

"Not quite," said a small voice, so softly that everyone had to strain in order to hear it. "There is still one problem."

The observation lounge suddenly became very silent. For the first time in weeks, Floyd became aware of the faint throbbing from the main air-supply duct, and the intermittent buzz that might have been made by a wasp trapped behind a wall panel. *Leonov*, like all spacecraft, was full of such often inexplicable sounds, which one seldom noticed except when they stopped. And then it was usually a good idea to start investigating without further ado.

"I'm not aware of any problem, Chandra," said Tanya in an ominously calm voice. "What could it possibly be?"

"I've spent the last few weeks preparing Hal to fly thousand-day orbits back to Earth. Now all those programs will have to be dumped."

"We're sorry about that," answered Tanya, "but as things have turned out, surely this is a much better—"

"That's not what I meant," said Chandra. There was a ripple of astonishment; he had never before been known to interrupt anyone, least of all Tanya.

"We know how sensitive Hal is to mission objectives," he continued in the expectant hush that followed. "Now you are asking me to give him a program that *may result in his own destruction*. It's true that the present plan will put *Discovery* into a stable orbit—but if that warning has any substance, what will happen to the ship eventually? We don't know, of course—but it's scared *us* away. Have you considered Hal's reaction to this situation?"

"Are you seriously suggesting," Tanya asked very slowly, "that Hal may refuse to obey orders—exactly as on the earlier mission?"

"That is *not* what happened last time. He did his best to interpret conflicting orders."

"This time there need be no conflict. The situation is perfectly clear-cut."

"To us, perhaps. But one of Hal's prime directives is to keep *Discovery* out of danger. We will be attempting to override that. And in a system as complex as Hal's, it is impossible to predict all the consequences."

"I don't see any real problem," Sasha interjected. "We just don't tell him that there is any danger. Then he'll have no . . . reservations about carrying out his program."

"Baby-sitting a psychotic computer!" muttered Curnow. "I feel I'm in a Grade-B science-fiction videodrama." Dr. Chandra gave him an unfriendly glare.

"Chandra," Tanya demanded suddenly. "Have you discussed this with Hal?"

"No."

Was there a slight hesitation? Floyd wondered. It might have been perfectly innocent; Chandra could have been checking his memory. Or he could have been lying, improbable though that seemed.

"Then we'll do what Sasha suggests. Just load the new program into him, and leave it at that."

"And when he questions me about the change of plan?"

"Is he likely to do that—without your prompting?"

"Of course. Please remember that he was designed for curiosity. If the crew was killed, he had to be capable of running a useful mission, on his own initiative."

Tanya thought that over for a few moments.

"It's still quite a simple matter. He'll believe you, won't he?"

"Certainly."

"Then you must tell him that *Discovery* is in no danger, and that there will be a rendezvous mission to bring it back to Earth at a later date."

"But that is not true."

"We don't *know* that it's false," replied Tanya, beginning to sound a little impatient.

"We suspect that there is serious danger; otherwise *we* would not be planning to leave ahead of schedule."

"Then what do you suggest?" Tanya asked, in a voice that now held a distinct note of menace.

"We must tell him the whole truth, as far as we know it—no more lies or half-truths, which are just as bad. And then let *him* decide for himself."

"Hell, Chandra—he's only a machine!"

Chandra looked at Max with such a steady, confident gaze that the younger man quickly dropped his eyes.

"So are we all, Mr. Brailovsky. It is merely a matter of degree. Whether we are based on carbon or on silicon makes no fundamental difference; we should each be treated with appropriate respect."

It was strange, thought Floyd, how Chandra—much the smallest person in the room—now seemed the largest. But the confrontation had gone on far too long. At any moment Tanya would start to issue direct orders, and the situation would become really nasty.

"Tanya, Vasili—can I have a word with you both? I think there is a way of resolving the problem."

Floyd's interruption was received with obvious relief, and two minutes later he was relaxing with the Orlovs in their quarters. (Or "sixteenths," as Curnow had once christened them because of their size. He had soon regretted the pun, because he had to explain it to everyone except Sasha.)

"Thank you, Woody," said Tanya, as she handed him a bulb of his favorite Azerbaijan Shemakha. "I was hoping you'd do that. I suppose you have something—how do you put it?—up your sleeve."

"I believe so," Floyd answered, squirting a few cubic centimeters of the sweet wine into his mouth and savoring it gratefully. "I'm sorry if Chandra is being difficult."

"So am I. What a good thing we only have one mad scientist aboard."

"That's not what you've sometimes told me," grinned academician Vasili. "Anyway, Woody—let's have it."

"This is what I suggest. Let Chandra go ahead and do it his way. Then there are just two possibilities.

"First, Hal will do exactly what we ask—control Discovery during the two firing periods. Remember, the first isn't critical. If something goes wrong while we're pulling away from Io, there's plenty of time to make corrections. And that will give us a good test of Hal's . . . willingness to cooperate."

"But what about the Jupiter flyby? That's the one that really counts. Not only do we burn most of Discovery's fuel there, but the timing and thrust vectors have to be exactly right."

"Could they be controlled manually?"

"I'd hate to try. The slightest error, and we'd either burn up, or become a long-period comet. Due again in a couple of thousand years."

"But if there was no alternative?" Floyd insisted.

"Well, assuming we could take control in time, and had a good set of alternative orbits precomputed—um, perhaps we might get away with it."

"Knowing you, Vasili, I'm sure that 'might' means 'would.' Which leads me to the second possibility I mentioned. If Hal shows the slightest deviation from the program—we take over."

"You mean—disconnect him?"

"Exactly."

"That wasn't so easy last time."

"We've learned a few lessons since then. Leave it to me. I can guarantee to give you back manual control in about half a second."

"There's no danger, I suppose, that Hal will suspect anything?"

"Now *you're* getting paranoiac, Vasili. Hal's not that human. But Chandra is—to give him the benefit of the doubt. So don't say a word to him. We all agree with his plan completely, are sorry that we ever raised any objections, and are perfectly confident that Hal will see our point of view. Right, Tanya?"

"Right, Woody. And I congratulate you on your foresight; that little gadget was a good idea."

"What gadget?" asked Vasili.

"I'll explain one of these days. Sorry, Woody—that's all the *Shemakha* I have left. I want to save it—until we're safely on the way to Earth."

46. COUNTDOWN

No one would ever believe this without my photos, thought Max Brailovsky as he orbited the two ships from half a kilometer away. *It seems comically indecent, as if* Leonov *is raping* Discovery. And now that he came to think of it, the rugged, compact Russian ship *did* look positively male, when compared with the delicate, slender American one. But most docking operations had distinctly sexual overtones, and he remembered that one of the early cosmonauts—he couldn't recall the name—had been reprimanded for his too vivid choice of words at the—er, climax of his mission.

As far as he could tell from his careful survey, everything was in order. The task of positioning the two ships and securing them firmly together had taken longer than anticipated. It would never have been possible at all without one of those strokes of luck that sometimes—not always—favor those who deserve them. *Leonov* had providentially carried several kilometers of carbon filament tape, no bigger than the ribbon a girl might use to tie her hair, yet capable of taking a strain of many tons. It had been thoughtfully provided to secure instrument packages to Big Brother if all else failed. Now it wrapped *Leonov* and *Discovery* in tender embrace—sufficiently firmly, it was hoped, to prevent any rattlings and shakings at all accelerations up to the one-tenth of a gravity that was the maximum that full thrust could provide.

"Anything more you want me to check before I come home?" asked Max.

"No," replied Tanya. "Everything looks fine. And we can't waste any more time."

That was true enough. If that mysterious warning was to be taken seriously—and everyone now took it very seriously indeed—they should start their escape maneuver within the next twenty-four hours.

"Right—I'm bringing *Nina* back to the stable. Sorry about this, old girl."

"You never told us *Nina* was a horse."

"I'm not admitting it now. And I feel bad about dumping her here in space, just to give us a miserable few extra meters per second."

"We may be very glad of them in a few hours, Max. Anyway, there's always a chance that someone may come and pick her up again, one day."

I very much doubt it, thought Max. And perhaps, after all, it was appropriate to leave the little space pod there, as a permanent reminder of Man's first visit to the kingdom of Jupiter.

With gentle, carefully timed pulses from the control jets he brought *Nina* around the great sphere of *Discovery*'s main life-support module; his colleagues on the flight deck barely glanced at him as he drifted past their curving window. The open Pod Bay door yawned before him, and he jockeyed *Nina* delicately down on to the extended docking arm.

"Pull me in," he said, as soon as the latches had clicked shut. "I call that a well-planned EVA. There's a whole kilogram of propellant left to take *Nina* out for the last time."

Normally, there was little drama about a burn in deep space; it was not like the fire and thunder—and always present risks—of a lift-off from a planetary surface. If something went wrong, and the motors failed to come up to full thrust—well, matters could usually be corrected by a slightly longer burn. Or one could wait until the appropriate point in orbit, and try again.

But this time, as the countdown proceeded toward zero, the tension aboard both ships was almost palpable. Everyone knew that it was the first real test of Hal's docility; only Floyd, Curnow, and the Orlovs realized that there was a backup system. And even they were not absolutely sure that it would work.

"Good luck, Leonov," said Mission Control, timing the message to arrive five minutes before ignition. "Hope everything's running smoothly. And if it's not too much trouble, could you please get some close-ups of the equator, longitude 115, as you go around Jupiter. There's a curious dark spot there—presumably some kind of upwelling, perfectly round, almost a thousand kilometers across. Looks like the shadow of a satellite, but it can't be."

Tanya made a brief acknowledgment that managed to convey, in a remarkably few words, a profound lack of interest in the meteorology of Jupiter at that moment. Mission Control sometimes showed a perfect genius for tactlessness and poor timing.

"All systems functioning normally," said Hal. "Two minutes to ignition."

Strange, thought Floyd, how terminology often survives long after the technology that gave it birth. Only chemical rockets were capable of ignition; even if the hydrogen in a nuclear or plasma drive did come into contact with oxygen, it would be far too hot to burn. At such temperatures, all compounds were stripped back into their elements.

His mind wandered, seeking other examples. People—particularly older ones—still spoke of putting film into a camera, or gas into a car. Even the phrase "cutting a tape" was still sometimes heard in recording studios—though that embraced two generations of obsolete technologies.

"One minute to ignition."

His mind flashed back to the here and now. *This* was the minute that counted; for almost a hundred years, on launch pads and in control centers, this was the longest sixty seconds that had ever existed. Countless times it had ended in disaster; but only the triumphs were remembered. Which will ours be?

The temptation to put his hand once more into the pocket that held the activator for the cutout switch was almost irresistible, even though logic told him there was plenty of time for remedial action. If Hal failed to obey his programing, that would be a nuisance—not a disaster. The really critical time would be when they were rounding Jupiter.

"Six . . . five . . . four . . . three . . . two . . . one . . . IGNITION!"

At first, the thrust was barely perceptible; it took almost a minute to build up to the full tenth of a gee. Nevertheless, everyone started clapping immediately, until Tanya signaled for silence. There were many checks to be made; even if Hal was doing his best—as he certainly seemed to be—there was so much that could still go wrong.

Discovery's antenna mount—which was now taking most of the strain from *Leonov's* inertia—had never been intended for such mistreatment. The ship's chief designer, called out of retirement, had sworn that the safety margin was adequate. But he might be wrong, and materials had been known to become brittle after years in space . . .

And the tapes holding the two ships together might not have been located accurately; they might stretch or slip. *Discovery* might not be able to correct for the off-center mass, now that it was carrying a thousand tons piggyback. Floyd could imagine a dozen things that could go wrong; it was little consolation to remember that it was always the thirteenth that actually happened.

But the minutes dragged on uneventfully; the only proof that *Discovery's* engines were operating was the fractional, thrust-induced gravity and a very slight vibration transmitted through the walls of the ships. Io and Jupiter still hung where they had been for weeks, on opposite sides of the sky.

"Cutoff in ten seconds. Nine—eight—seven—six—five—four—three—two—NOW!"

"Thank you, Hal. On the button."

Now *that* was another phrase that was badly dated; for at least a generation, touch pads had almost entirely replaced buttons. But not for all applications; in critical cases, it was best to have a device that moved perceptibly with a nice, satisfying *click*.

"I confirm that," said Vasili. "No need for any corrections until midcourse."

"Say good-bye to glamorous, exotic Io—real estate agent's dream world," said Curnow. "We'll all be happy to miss you."

That sounds more like the old Walter, Floyd told himself. For the last few weeks, he had been oddly subdued, as if he had something on his mind. (But who did not?) He seemed to spend a good deal of his scanty free time in quiet discussions with Katerina: Floyd hoped that he had not developed some medical problem. They had been very lucky so far on that score; the last thing they needed at this stage was an emergency that required the Surgeon–Commander's expertise.

"You're being unkind, Walter," said Brailovsky. "I was beginning to like the place. It might be fun to go boating on those lava lakes."

"What about a volcano barbecue?"

"Or genuine molten sulfur baths?"

Everyone was lighthearted, even a little hysterical with relief. Though it was far too early to relax and the most critical phase of the escape maneuver still lay ahead, the first step had been safely taken on the long journey home. That was cause enough for a little modest rejoicing.

It did not last long, for Tanya quickly ordered all those not on essential duty to get some rest—if possible, some sleep—in preparation for the Jupiter swing-by only nine hours ahead. When those addressed were slow to move, Sasha cleared the decks by shouting, "You'll hang for this, you mutinous dogs!" Only two nights before, as a rare relaxation, they had all enjoyed the fourth version of *Mutiny on the Bounty*, generally agreed by movie historians to have the best Captain Bligh since the fabled

Charles Laughton. There was some feeling onboard that Tanya should not have seen it, lest it give her ideas.

After a couple of restless hours in his cocoon, Floyd abandoned the quest for sleep and wandered up to the observation deck. Jupiter was much larger and slowly waning as the ships hurtled toward their closest approach over the nightside. A glorious, gibbous disk, it showed such an infinite wealth of detail—cloud belts, spots of every color from dazzling white to brick red, dark upwellings from the unknown depths, the cyclonic oval of the Great Red Spot—that the eye could not possibly absorb it all. The round, dark shadow of one moon—probably Europa, Floyd guessed—was in transit. He was seeing this incredible sight for the last time; even though he had to be at maximum efficiency in six hours, it was a crime to waste precious moments in sleep.

Where was that spot that Mission Control had asked them to observe? It should have been coming into view, but Floyd was not sure if it would be visible to the naked eye. Vasili would be too busy to bother about it; perhaps he could help by doing a little amateur astronomy. There had, after all, been a brief time, only thirty years ago, when he had earned his living as a professional.

He activated the controls of the main fifty-centimeter telescope—fortunately, the field of view was not blocked by the adjacent bulk of *Discovery*—and scanned along the equator at medium power. And there it was, just coming over the edge of the disk.

By force of circumstance, Floyd was now one of the Solar System's ten greatest experts on Jupiter; the other nine were working or sleeping around him. He saw at once that there was something very odd about this spot; it was so black that it looked like a hole punched through the clouds. From his point of view it appeared to be a sharp-edged ellipse; Floyd guessed that from directly above, it would be a perfect circle.

He recorded a few images, then increased the power to maximum. Already Jupiter's rapid spin had brought the formation into clearer view; and the more he stared, the more puzzled Floyd became.

"Vasili," he called over the intercom, "if you can spare a minute—have a look at the fifty-centimeter monitor."

"What are you observing? Is it important? I'm checking the orbit."

"Take your time, of course. But I've found that spot Mission Control reported. It looks *very* peculiar."

"Hell! I'd forgotten all about it. We're a fine lot of observers if those guys back on Earth have to tell us where to look. Give me another five minutes—it won't run away."

True enough, thought Floyd; in fact it will get clearer. And there was no disgrace in missing something that terrestrial—or lunar—astronomers had observed. Jupiter was very big, they had been very busy, and the telescopes on the Moon and in Earth orbit were a hundred times more powerful than the instrument he was using now.

But this was getting more and more peculiar. For the first time, Floyd began to feel a distinct sense of unease. Until that moment, it had never occurred to him that the spot could be anything but a natural formation—some trick of Jupiter's incredibly complex meteorology. Now he began to wonder.

It was so *black*, like night itself. And so symmetrical; as it came into clearer view it was obviously a perfect circle. Yet it was not sharply defined; the edge had an odd fuzziness, as if it was a little out of focus.

Was it imagination, or had it grown, even while he was watching? He made a quick estimate, and decided that the thing was now two thousand kilometers across. It was only a little smaller than the still-visible shadow of Europa, but was so much darker that there was no risk of confusion.

"Let's have a look," said Vasili, in a rather condescending tone. "What do you think you've found? Oh . . ." His voice trailed away into silence.

This is it, thought Floyd, with a sudden icy conviction.

Whatever *it* may be . . .

47. FINAL FLYBY

YET ON FURTHER REFLECTION, AFTER THE INITIAL AMAZEMENT HAD worn off, it was hard to see how a spreading black stain on the face of Jupiter could represent any kind of danger. It was extraordinary—inexplicable—but not as important as the critical events now only seven hours in the future. A successful burn at perijove was all that mattered; they would have plenty of time to study mysterious black spots on the way home.

And to sleep; Floyd had given up all attempts at that. Though the feeling of danger—at least, of *known* danger—was much less than on their first approach to Jupiter, a mixture of excitement and apprehension kept him wide awake. The excitement was natural and understandable; the apprehension had more complex causes. Floyd made it a rule never to worry about events over which he could have absolutely no control; any external threat would reveal itself in due time and must be dealt with then. But he could not help wondering if they had done everything possible to safeguard the ships.

Apart from onboard mechanical failures, there were two main sources of concern. Although the tapes that secured *Leonov* and *Discovery* together had shown no tendency to slip, their severest test was still to come. Almost equally critical would be the moment of separation when the smallest of the explosive charges once intended to jolt Big Brother would be used at uncomfortably close quarters. And, of course, there was Hal . . .

He had carried out the deorbiting maneuver with exquisite precision. He had run the simulations of the Jupiter flyby, right down to *Discovery*'s last drop of fuel, without any comments or objections. And although Chandra, as agreed, had carefully explained what they were trying to do, did Hal *really* understand what was happening?

Floyd had one overriding concern, which in the preceding few days had become almost an obsession. He could picture everything going perfectly, the ships halfway through the final maneuver, the enormous disk of Jupiter filling the sky only a few hundred kilometers below them—and then Hal electronically clearing his throat and saying: "Dr. Chandra, do you mind if I ask you a question?"

It did not happen exactly that way.

The Great Black Spot, as it had been inevitably christened, was now being carried out of sight by Jupiter's swift rotation. In a few hours the still-accelerating ships would catch up with it over the nightside of the planet, but this was the last chance for a close daylight observation.

It was still growing at an extraordinary speed; in the last two hours, it had more than doubled its area. Except for the fact that it retained its blackness as it expanded, it resembled an inkstain spreading in water. Its boundary—now moving at near-sonic speed in the Jovian atmosphere—still looked curiously fuzzy and out of focus; at the very highest power of the ship's telescope, the reason for this was at last apparent.

Unlike the Great Red Spot, the Great Black Spot was not a continuous structure; it was built up from myriads of tiny dots, like a half-tone print viewed through a magnifying glass. Over most of its area, the dots were so closely spaced that they were almost touching, but at the rim they became more and more widely spaced, so that the Spot ended in a gray penumbra rather than at a sharp frontier.

There must have been almost a million of the mysterious dots, and they were distinctly elongated—ellipses rather than circles. Katerina, the least imaginative person aboard, surprised everybody by saying that it looked as if someone had taken a sackful of rice, dyed it black, and poured it on the face of Jupiter.

And now the Sun was dropping down behind the huge, swiftly narrowing arch of the dayside, as for the second time *Leonov* raced into the Jovian night for an appointment with destiny. In less than thirty minutes the final burn would commence, and things would start to happen very quickly indeed.

Floyd wondered if he should have joined Chandra and Curnow, standing watch on *Discovery*. But there was nothing he could do; in an emergency, he would only be in the way. The cutoff switch was in Curnow's pocket, and Floyd knew that the younger man's reactions were a good deal swifter than his own. If Hal showed the slightest sign of misbehavior, he could be disconnected in less than a second, but Floyd felt certain that such extreme measures would not be necessary. Since he had been allowed to do things his own way, Chandra had cooperated completely in setting up the procedures for a manual takeover, should that unfortunate necessity arise. Floyd was confident that he could be trusted to carry out his duty—however much he might regret the need.

Curnow was not quite so sure. He would be happier, he had told Floyd, if he had multiple redundancy in the form of a second cutoff switch—for Chandra. Meanwhile there was nothing that anyone could do but wait and watch the approaching cloudscape of the nightside, dimly visible by the reflected light of passing satellites, the glow of photochemical reactions, and frequent titanic lightning flashes from thunderstorms larger than Earth.

The sun winked out behind them, eclipsed in seconds by the

immense globe they were so swiftly approaching. When they saw it again, they should be on their way home.

"Twenty minutes to ignition. All systems nominal."

"Thank you, Hal."

I wonder if Chandra was being quite truthful, thought Curnow, when he said that Hal would be confused if anyone else spoke to him. *I've* talked to him often enough, when nobody was around, and he always understood me perfectly. Still, there's not much time left for friendly conversation now, though it would help to reduce the strain.

What's Hal *really* thinking—if he thinks—about the mission? All his life, Curnow had shied away from abstract, philosophical questions: I'm a nuts-and-bolts man, he had often claimed, though there were not too many of either in a spaceship. Once, he would have laughed at the idea, but now he began to wonder: Did Hal sense that he would soon be abandoned, and if so, would he resent it? Curnow almost reached for the cutoff switch in his pocket, but checked himself. He had already done this so often that Chandra might be getting suspicious.

For the hundredth time, he rehearsed the sequence of events that were due to take place during the next hour. The moment that Discovery's fuel was exhausted, they would close down all but essential systems, and dash back to Leonov through the connecting tube. That would be decoupled, the explosive charges would be fired, the ships would drift apart—and Leonov's own engines would start to fire. The separation should take place, if everything went according to plan, just when they were making their closest approach to Jupiter; that would take maximum advantage of the planet's gravitational largesse.

"Fifteen minutes to ignition. All systems nominal."

"Thank you, Hal."

"By the way," said Vasili, from the other ship. "We're catching up with the Great Black Spot again. Wonder if we can see anything new."

I rather hope not, thought Curnow; we've got quite enough on our hands at the moment. Nevertheless, he gave a quick glance at the image Vasili was transmitting on the telescope monitor.

At first he could see nothing except the faintly glimmering

nightside of the planet; then he saw, on the horizon, a foreshort-
ened circle of deeper darkness. They were rushing toward it
with incredible speed.

Vasili increased the light amplification, and the entire image
brightened magically. At last, the Great Black Spot resolved itself into its myriad identical elements . . .

My God, thought Curnow, *I just don't believe it!*

He heard exclamations of surprise from *Leonov:* all the others
had shared in the same revelation at the same moment.

"Dr. Chandra," said Hal, "I detect strong vocal stress patterns.
Is there a problem?"

"No, Hal," Chandra answered quickly. "The mission is proceeding normally. We've just had rather a surprise—that's all.
What do *you* make of the image on monitor circuit 16?"

"I see the nightside of Jupiter. There is a circular area, 3250
kilometers in diameter, which is almost completely covered
with rectangular objects."

"How many?"

There was the briefest of pauses, before Hal flashed the number on the video display:

$$1,355,000 \pm 1,000$$

"And do you recognize them?"

"Yes. They are identical in size and shape to the object you
refer to as Big Brother. Ten minutes to ignition. All systems
nominal."

Mine aren't, thought Curnow. So the damn thing's gone down
to Jupiter—and multiplied. There was something simultaneously comic and sinister about a plague of black monoliths;
and to his puzzled surprise, that incredible image on the monitor screen had a certain weird familiarity.

Of course—that was it! Those myriad identical black rectangles reminded him of—*dominoes*. Years ago, he had seen a
videodocumentary showing how a team of slightly crazy Japanese had patiently stood a million dominoes on end, so that
when the very first one was toppled, all the others would inevitably follow. They had been arranged in complex patterns,
some underwater, some up and down little stairways, others
along multiple tracks so that they formed pictures and patterns

as they fell. It had taken weeks to set them up; Curnow remembered now that earthquakes had several times foiled the enterprise, and the final toppling, from first domino to the last, had taken more than an hour.

"Eight minutes to ignition. All systems nominal. Dr. Chandra—may I make a suggestion?"

"What is it, Hal?"

"This is a very unusual phenomenon. Do you not think I should abort the countdown, so that you can remain to study it?"

Aboard *Leonov*, Floyd started to move quickly toward the bridge. Tanya and Vasili might be needing him. Not to mention Chandra and Curnow—what a situation! And suppose Chandra took Hal's side? If he did—*they might both be right!* After all, was this not the very reason they had come here?

If they stopped the countdown, the ships would loop around Jupiter and be back at precisely the same spot in nineteen hours. A nineteen-hour hold would create no problems; if it was not for that enigmatic warning, he would have strongly recommended it himself.

But now they had very much more than a warning. Below them was a planetary plague spreading across the face of Jupiter. Perhaps they were indeed running away from the most extraordinary phenomenon in the history of science. Even so, he preferred to study it from a safer distance.

"Six minutes to ignition," said Hal. "All systems nominal. I am ready to stop the countdown if you agree. Let me remind you that my prime directive is to study everything in Jupiter space that may be connected with intelligence."

Floyd recognized that phrase all too well: he had written it himself. He wished he could delete it from Hal's memory.

A moment later, he had reached the bridge and joined the Orlovs. They both looked at him with alarmed concern.

"What do you recommend?" asked Tanya swiftly.

"It's up to Chandra, I'm afraid. Can I speak to him—on the private line."

Vasili handed over the microphone.

"Chandra? I assume that Hal can't hear this?"

"Correct, Dr. Floyd."

"You've got to talk quickly. Persuade him that the countdown must continue, that we appreciate his—er, scientific enthusiasm—ah, that's the right angle—say we're confident that he can do the job without our help. And we'll be in touch with him all the time, of course."

"Five minutes to ignition. All systems nominal. I am still waiting for your answer, Dr. Chandra."

So are we all, thought Curnow, only a meter away from the scientist. And if I do have to push that button at last, it will be something of a relief. In fact, I'll rather enjoy it.

"Very well, Hal. Continue the countdown. I have every confidence in your ability to study all phenomena in Jupiter space, without our supervision. Of course, we will be in touch with you at all times."

"Four minutes to ignition. All systems nominal. Propellant-tank pressurization completed. Voltage steady on plasma trigger. Are you sure you are making the right decision, Dr. Chandra? I enjoy working with human beings and have a stimulating relationship with them. Ship's attitude correct to point one milliradian."

"We enjoy working with you, Hal. And we will still be doing so, even if we are millions of kilometers away."

"Three minutes to ignition. All systems nominal. Radiation shielding checked. There is the problem of the time lag, Dr. Chandra. It may be necessary to consult each other without any delay."

This is insane, Curnow thought, his hand now never far from the cutoff switch. I really believe that Hal is—lonely. Is he mimicking some part of Chandra's personality that we never suspected?

The lights flickered, so imperceptibly that only someone familiar with every nuance of Discovery's behavior would have noticed. It could be good news or bad—the plasma firing sequence starting, or being terminated . . .

He risked a quick glance at Chandra; the little scientist's face was drawn and haggard, and for almost the first time Curnow felt real sympathy for him as another human being. And he re-membered the startling information that Floyd had confided in him—Chandra's offer to stay with the ship, and keep Hal company on the three-year voyage home. He had heard no more of the idea, and presumably it had been quietly forgotten after the warning. But perhaps Chandra was being tempted again; if he was, there was nothing that he could do about it at that stage. There would be no time to make the necessary preparations, even if they stayed on for another orbit and delayed their departure beyond the deadline. Which Tanya would certainly not permit after all that had now happened.

"Hal," whispered Chandra, so quietly that Curnow could scarcely hear him. "We *have* to leave. I don't have time to give you all the reasons, but I can assure you it's true."

"Two minutes to ignition. All systems nominal. Final sequence started. I am sorry that you are unable to stay. Can you give me *some* of the reasons, in order of importance?"

"Not in two minutes, Hal. Proceed with the countdown. I will explain everything later. We still have more than an hour . . . together."

Hal did not answer. The silence stretched on and on. Surely the one-minute announcement was overdue—

Curnow glanced at the clock. My God, he thought, Hal's missed it! Has he stopped the countdown?

Curnow's hand fumbled uncertainly for the switch. What do I do now? I wish Floyd would say something, dammit, but he's probably afraid of making things worse . . .

I'll wait until time zero—no, it's not *that* critical, let's say an extra minute—then I'll zap him and we'll go over to manual . . .

From far, far away there came a faint, whistling scream, like the sound of a tornado marching just below the edge of the horizon. *Discovery* started to vibrate; there was the first intimation of returning gravity.

"Ignition," said Hal. "Full thrust at T plus fifteen seconds."

"Thank you, Hal," replied Chandra.

48. OVER THE NIGHTSIDE

To Heywood Floyd, aboard the suddenly unfamiliar—because no longer weightless—environment of *Leonov's* flight deck, the sequence of events had seemed more like a classic slow-motion nightmare than reality. Only once before in his life had he known a similar situation, when he had been in the back of a car during an uncontrollable skid. There had been that same sense of utter helplessness—coupled with the thought: This doesn't really matter—it's not actually happening to *me*.

Now that the firing sequence had started, his mood changed; everything seemed real again. It was working out exactly as they had planned; Hal was guiding them safely back to Earth. With every minute that passed, their future was becoming more secure; Floyd began slowly to relax, even though he remained alert to all that was happening around him.

For the very last time—and when would *any* man come here

again?—he was flying over the nightside of the greatest of planets, encompassing the volume of a thousand Earths. The ships had been rolled so that *Leonov* was between *Discovery* and Jupiter, and their view of the mysteriously glimmering cloudscape was not blocked. Even now, dozens of instruments were busily probing and recording; Hal would continue the work when they were gone.

Since the immediate crisis was over, Floyd moved cautiously "down" from the flight deck—how strange to feel weight again, even if it was only ten kilos!—and joined Zenia and Katerina in the observation lounge. Apart from the very faintest of red emergency lights, it had been completely blacked out so that they could admire the view with unimpaired night vision. He felt sorry for Max Brailovsky and Sasha Kovalev, who were sitting in the airlock, fully suited up, missing the marvelous spectacle. They had to be ready to leave at a moment's notice to cut the straps securing the ships together—if any of the explosive charges failed to operate.

Jupiter filled the entire sky; it was a mere five hundred kilometers away, so they could see only a tiny fraction of its surface—no more than one could see of Earth from an altitude of fifty kilometers. As his eyes grew accustomed to the dim light, most of it reflected from the icy crust of distant Europa, Floyd could make out a surprising amount of detail. There was no color at this low level of illumination—except for a hint of red here and there—but the banded structure of the clouds was very distinct, and he could see the edge of a small cyclonic storm looking like an oval island covered with snow. The Great Black Spot had long since fallen astern, and they would not see it again until they were well on the way home.

Down there beneath the clouds, occasional explosions of light flared, many of them obviously caused by the Jovian equivalent of thunderstorms. But other glows and outbursts of luminescence were more long-lived, and of more uncertain origin. Sometimes rings of light would spread out like shock waves from a central source; and occasional rotating beams and fans occurred. It required little imagination to pretend that they were proof of a technological civilization down beneath those

clouds—the lights of cities, the beacons of airports. But radar
and balloon probes had long ago proved that nothing solid was
down there for thousands upon thousands of kilometers, all the
way to the unattainable core of the planet.

Midnight on Jupiter! This last close-up glimpse was a magical
interlude he would remember all his life. He could enjoy it all
the more because, surely, nothing could now go wrong; and
even if it did, he would have no reason to reproach himself. He
had done everything possible to insure success.

It was very quiet in the lounge; no one wished to speak as the
carpet of clouds unrolled swiftly beneath them. Every few minutes Tanya or Vasili announced the status of the burn; toward
the end of Discovery's firing time, tension began to increase
again. This was the critical moment—and no one knew exactly
when it would be. There was some doubt as to the accuracy of
the fuel gauges, and the burn would continue until they were
completely dry.

"Estimated cutoff in ten seconds," said Tanya. "Walter,
Chandra—get ready to come back. Max, Vasili—stand by in case
you're needed. Five . . . four . . . three . . . two . . . one . . .
zero!"

There was no change; the faint scream of Discovery's engines
still reached them through the thickness of the two hulls, and
the thrust-induced weight still continued to grip their limbs.
We're in luck, thought Floyd; the gauges must have been reading
low, after all. Every second of extra firing was a bonus; it might
even mean the difference between life and death. And how
strange to hear a countup instead of a countdown!

". . . five seconds . . . ten seconds . . . thirteen seconds. That's
it—lucky thirteen!"

Weightlessness, and silence, returned. On both ships, there
was a brief burst of cheering. It was quickly truncated, for much
was still to be done—and it had to be done swiftly.

Floyd was tempted to go to the airlock so that he could give
his congratulations to Chandra and Curnow as soon as they
came aboard. But he would only be in the way; the airlock
would be a very busy place as Max and Sasha prepared for their

possible EVA and the tubeway joining the two ships was disconnected. He would wait in the lounge, to greet the returning
heroes.

And he could now relax even further—perhaps from eight to
seven, on a scale of ten. For the first time in weeks, he could
forget about the radio cutoff. It would never be needed; Hal had
performed impeccably. Even if he wished he could do nothing
to affect the mission since *Discovery's* last drop of propellant
had been exhausted.

"All aboard," announced Sasha. "Hatches sealed. I'm going to
fire the charges."

There was not the faintest sound as the explosives were detonated, which surprised Floyd; he had expected some noise to be
transmitted through the straps, taut as steel bands, that linked
the ships together. But there was no doubt that they had gone off
as planned, for *Leonov* gave a series of tiny shudders, as if someone was tapping on the hull. A minute later, Vasili triggered the
attitude jets for a single brief burst.

"We're free!" he shouted. "Sasha, Max—you won't be needed!
Everyone get to your hammocks—ignition in one hundred
seconds!"

And now Jupiter was rolling away, and a strange new shape
appeared outside the window—the long, skeletal frame of
Discovery, navigation lights still shining as it drifted away from
them and into history. No time remained for sentimental fare-
wells; in less than a minute *Leonov's* drive would start to
operate.

Floyd had never heard it under full power and wanted to protect his ears from the roaring scream that now filled the universe. *Leonov's* designers had not wasted payload on sound
insulation that would be needed for only a few hours of a voyage that would last for years. And his weight seemed enormous—yet it was barely a quarter of that which he had known
all his life.

Within minutes, *Discovery* had vanished astern, though the
flash of its warning beacon could be seen until it had dropped
below the horizon. Once again, Floyd told himself, I'm rounding
Jupiter—this time gaining speed, not losing it. He glanced across

at Zenia, just visible in the darkness with her nose pressed to the observation window. Was she also recalling that last occasion, when they shared the hammock together? There was no danger of incineration now; at least she would not be terrified of that particular fate. Anyway, she seemed a much more confident and cheerful person, undoubtedly thanks to Max—and perhaps Walter as well.

She must have become aware of his scrutiny, for she turned and smiled, then gestured toward the unwinding cloudscape below.

"Look!" she shouted in his ear. "Jupiter has a new moon!"

What *is* she trying to say? Floyd asked himself. Her English still isn't very good, but she couldn't possibly have made a mistake in a simple sentence like that. I'm sure I heard her correctly—yet she's pointing *downward*, not upward . . .

And then he realized that the scene immediately below them had become much brighter; he could even see yellows and greens that had been quite invisible before. Something far more brilliant than Europa was shining on the Jovian clouds.

Leonov itself, many times brighter than Jupiter's noonday sun, had brought a false dawn to the world it was leaving forever. A hundred-kilometer-long plume of incandescent plasma was trailing behind the ship, as the exhaust from the Sakharov Drive dissipated its remaining energies in the vacuum of space.

Vasili was making an announcement, but the words were completely unintelligible. Floyd glanced at his watch; yes, that would be right about now. They had achieved Jupiter escape velocity. The giant could never recapture them.

And then, thousands of kilometers ahead, a great bow of brilliant light appeared in the sky—the first glimpse of the real Jovian dawn, as full of promise as any rainbow on Earth. Seconds later the Sun leaped up to greet them—the glorious Sun, that would now grow brighter and closer every day.

A few more minutes of steady acceleration, and *Leonov* would be launched irrevocably on the long voyage home. Floyd felt an overwhelming sense of relief and relaxation. The immutable laws of celestial mechanics would guide him through the inner Solar System, past the tangled orbits of the asteroids, past Mars—nothing could stop him from reaching Earth.

In the euphoria of the moment, he had forgotten all about the mysterious black stain, expanding across the face of Jupiter.

49. DEVOURER OF WORLDS

THEY SAW IT AGAIN THE NEXT MORNING, SHIP'S TIME, AS IT CAME around to the dayside of Jupiter. The area of darkness had now spread until it covered an appreciable fraction of the planet, and at last they were able to study it at leisure, and in detail.

"Do you know what it reminds me of?" said Katerina. "A virus attacking a cell. The way a phage injects its DNA into a bacterium, and then multiplies until it takes over."

"Are you suggesting," asked Tanya incredulously, "that *Zagadka* is *eating* Jupiter?"

"It certainly looks like it."

"No wonder Jupiter is beginning to look sick. But hydrogen and helium won't make a very nourishing diet, and there's not much else in that atmosphere. Only a few percent of other elements."

"Which adds up to some quintillions of tons of sulfur and carbon and phosphorus and everything else at the lower end of the periodic table," Sasha pointed out. "In any case, we're talking about a technology that can probably do *anything* that doesn't defy the laws of physics. If you have hydrogen, what more do you need? With the right know-how, you can synthesize all the other elements from it."

"They're sweeping up Jupiter—that's for sure," said Vasili. "Look at this."

An extreme close-up of one of the myriad identical rectangles was now displayed on the telescope monitor. Even to the naked eye, it was obvious that streams of gas were flowing into the two smaller faces; the patterns of turbulence looked very much like the lines of force revealed by iron filings, clustered around the ends of a bar magnet.

"A million vacuum cleaners," said Curnow, "sucking up Jupiter's atmosphere. But why? And what are they doing with it?"

"And how do they reproduce?" asked Max. "Have you caught any of them in the act?"

"Yes and no," answered Vasili. "We're too far away to see details, but it's a kind of fission—like an amoeba."

"You mean—they split in two, and the halves grow back to the original size?"

"*Nyet*. There aren't any little *Zagadkas*—they seem to grow until they've doubled in thickness, then split down the middle to produce identical twins, exactly the same size as the original. And the cycle repeats itself in approximately two hours."

"Two hours!" exclaimed Floyd. "No wonder that they're spread over half the planet. It's a textbook case of exponential growth."

"I know what they are!" said Ternovsky in sudden excitement. "They're von Neumann machines!"

"I believe you're right," said Vasili. "But that still doesn't explain what they're doing. Giving them a label isn't all that much help."

"And what," asked Katerina plaintively, "is a von Neumann machine? Explain, please."

Orlov and Floyd started speaking simultaneously. They stopped in some confusion, then Vasili laughed and waved to the American.

"Suppose you had a very big engineering job to do, Katerina—and I mean *big*, like strip-mining the entire face of the Moon. You could build millions of machines to do it, but that might take centuries. If you were clever enough, you'd make just *one* machine—but with the ability to reproduce itself from the raw materials around it. So you'd start a chain reaction, and in a very short time, you'd have . . . bred enough machines to do the job in decades, instead of millennia. With a sufficiently high rate of reproduction, you could do virtually *anything* in as short a period of time as you wished. The Space Agency's been toying with the idea for years—and I know you have as well, Tanya."

"Yes: exponentiating machines. One idea that even Tsiolkovski didn't think of."

"I wouldn't care to bet on that," said Vasili. "So it looks, Katerina, as if your analogy was pretty close. A bacteriophage *is* a von Neumann machine."

"Aren't we all?" asked Sasha. "I'm sure Chandra would say so."

Chandra nodded his agreement.

"That's obvious. In fact, von Neumann got the original idea from studying living systems."

"And these living machines are eating Jupiter!"

"It certainly looks like it," said Vasili. "I've been doing some calculations, and I can't quite believe the answers—even though it's simple arithmetic."

"It may be simple to *you*," said Katerina. "Try to let us have it without tensors and differential equations."

"No—I *mean* simple," insisted Vasili. "In fact, it's a perfect example of the old population explosion you doctors were always screaming about in the last century. *Zagadka* reproduces every two hours. So in only twenty hours there will be ten doublings. One *Zagadka* will have become a thousand."

"1024," said Chandra.

"I *know*, but let's keep it simple. After forty hours there will be a million—after eighty, a million million. That's about where we are now, and obviously the increase can't continue indefinitely. In a couple more days, at this rate, they'll weigh more than Jupiter!"

"So they'll soon begin to starve," said Zenia. "And what will happen *then?*"

"Saturn had better look out," answered Brailovsky. "Then Uranus and Neptune. Let's hope they don't notice little Earth."

"What a hope! *Zagadka's* been spying on us for three million years!"

Walter Curnow suddenly started to laugh.

"What's so funny?" demanded Tanya.

"We're talking about these things as if they're persons—intelligent entities. They're not—they're *tools*. But general-purpose tools—able to do anything they have to. The one on the Moon was a signaling device—or a spy, if you like. The one that Bowman met—our original *Zagadka*—was some kind of transportation system. Now it's doing something else, though God knows what. And there may be others all over the Universe.

"I had just such a gadget when I was a kid. Do you know what *Zagadka really* is? Just the cosmic equivalent of the good old Swiss Army knife!"

VII * LUCIFER
RISING

50. FAREWELL TO JUPITER

It was not easy to compose this message, especially after the one he had just sent to his lawyer. Floyd felt like a hypocrite; but he knew it had to be done to minimize the pain that was inevitable on both sides.

He was sad, but no longer disconsolate. Because he was coming back to Earth in an aura of successful achievement—even if not precisely heroism—he would be bargaining from a position of strength. No one—*no one*—would be able to take Chris away from him.

". . . My dear Caroline [it was no longer "My dearest" . . .] I am on my way home. By the time you get this, I'll already be in hibernation. Only a few hours from now, as it will seem to me, I'll open my eyes—and there will be the beautiful blue Earth hanging in space beside me.

"Yes, I know it will still be many months for you, and I'm sorry. But we knew that's the way it would be before I left; as it is, I'm getting back weeks ahead of schedule because of the change in the mission plan.

"I hope we can work something out. The main question is: What's best for Chris? Whatever our own feelings, we must put him first. I know *I'm* willing to do so, and I'm sure you are."

Floyd switched off the recorder. Should he say what he had intended: "A boy needs his father"? No—it would not be tactful, and might only make matters worse. Caroline might well retort that between birth and four years old it was the mother who mattered most to a child—and if he had believed otherwise, he should have stayed on Earth.

"... Now about the house. I'm glad the Regents have taken that attitude, which will make it much easier for both of us. I know we both loved the place, but it will be too big now and will bring back too many memories. For the time being, I'll probably get an apartment in Hilo; I hope I can find some permanent place as quickly as possible.

"That's one thing I can promise everyone—I won't leave Earth again. I've had enough of space traveling for one lifetime. Oh, perhaps the Moon, if I really have to—but of course that's just a weekend excursion.

"And talking of moons, we've just passed the orbit of Sinope, so we're now leaving the Jovian system. Jupiter is more than twenty million kilometers away, and is barely larger than our own Moon.

"Yet even from this distance, you can tell that something terrible has happened to the planet. Its beautiful orange color has vanished; it's a kind of sickly gray, only a fraction of its former brilliance. No wonder it's only a faint star now in the sky of Earth.

"But nothing else has happened, and we're well past the deadline. Could the whole thing have been a false alarm or a kind of cosmic practical joke? I doubt if we'll ever know. Anyway, it's brought us home ahead of schedule, and I'm grateful for that.

"Good-bye for the present, Caroline—and thank you for everything. I hope we can still be friends. And my dearest love, as ever, to Chris."

When he had finished, Floyd sat quietly for a while in the tiny cubicle he would not need much longer. He was just about to carry the audio chip up to the bridge for transmission, when Chandra came drifting in.

Floyd had been agreeably surprised by the way in which the scientist had accepted his increasing separation from Hal. They were still in touch for several hours every day, exchanging data on Jupiter and monitoring conditions aboard *Discovery*. Though no one had expected any great display of emotion, Chandra seemed to be taking his loss with remarkable fortitude. Nikolai Ternovsky, his only confidant, had been able to give Floyd a plausible explanation of his behavior.

"Chandra's got a new interest, Woody. Remember—he's in a business where if something works, it's obsolete. He's learned a lot in the last few months. Can't you guess what he's doing now?"

"Frankly, no. *You* tell me."

"He's busy designing HAL 10,000."

Floyd's jaw dropped. "So that explains those long messages to Urbana that Sasha's been grumbling about. Well, he won't be blocking the circuits much longer."

Floyd recalled that conversation when Chandra entered; he knew better than to ask the scientist if it was true, for it was really none of his business. Yet there was another matter about which he was still curious.

"Chandra," he said, "I don't believe I ever thanked you properly for the job you did at the flyby, when you persuaded Hal to cooperate. For a while, I was really afraid he'd give us trouble. But you were confident all along—and you were right. Still, didn't you have *any* qualms?"

"Not at all, Dr. Floyd."

"Why not? He must have felt threatened by the situation—and you know what happened last time."

"There was a big difference. If I may say so, perhaps the successful outcome this time had something to do with our national characteristics."

"I don't understand."

"Put it this way, Dr. Floyd. Bowman tried to use force against

Hal. I didn't. In my language we have a word—*ahimsa*. It's usually translated as 'nonviolence,' though it has more positive implications. I was careful to use *ahimsa* in my dealings with Hal."

"Very commendable, I'm sure. But there are times when something more energetic is needed, regrettable though the necessity may be." Floyd paused, wrestling with temptation. Chandra's holier-than-thou attitude was a little tiresome. It wouldn't do any harm, now, to tell him some of the facts of life.

"I'm glad it's worked out this way. But it might not have done so, and I had to prepare for every eventuality. *Ahimsa* or whatever you call it, is all very well; I don't mind admitting I had a backup to your philosophy. If Hal had been—well, *stubborn*, I could have dealt with him."

Floyd had once seen Chandra crying; now he saw him laughing, and that was an equally disconcerting phenomenon.

"Really, Dr. Floyd! I'm sorry you give me such low marks for intelligence. It was obvious from the beginning that you'd install a power cutout somewhere. I disconnected it months ago."

Whether the flabbergasted Floyd could think of a suitable answer would never be known. He was still giving a very creditable imitation of a gaffed fish when up on the flight deck Sasha cried out: "Captain! All hands! Get to the monitors! BOZHE MOI! LOOK AT THAT!"

51. THE GREAT GAME

NOW THE LONG WAIT WAS ENDING. ON YET ANOTHER WORLD, IN-
telligence had been born and was escaping from its planetary
cradle. An ancient experiment was about to reach its climax.

Those who had begun that experiment, so long ago, had not
been men—or even remotely human. But they were flesh and
blood, and when they looked out across the deeps of space, they
had felt awe, and wonder, and loneliness. As soon as they possessed the power, they set forth for the stars. In their explorations, they encountered life in many forms and watched the
workings of evolution on a thousand worlds. They saw how
often the first faint sparks of intelligence flickered and died in
the cosmic night.

And because, in all the Galaxy, they had found nothing more
precious than Mind, they encouraged its dawning everywhere.
They became farmers in the fields of stars; they sowed, and
sometimes they reaped.

And sometimes, dispassionately, they had to weed.

The great dinosaurs had long since perished when the survey ship entered the Solar System after a voyage that had already lasted a thousand years. It swept past the frozen outer planets, paused briefly above the deserts of dying Mars, and presently looked down on Earth.

Spread out beneath them, the explorers saw a world swarming with life. For years they studied, collected, cataloged. When they had learned all that they could, they began to modify. They tinkered with the destinies of many species on land and in the ocean. But which of their experiments would succeed, they could not know for at least a million years.

They were patient, but they were not yet immortal. So much remained to do in this universe of a hundred billion suns, and other worlds were calling. So they set out once more into the abyss, knowing that they would never come this way again.

Nor was there any need. The servants they had left behind would do the rest.

On Earth the glaciers came and went, while above them the changeless Moon still carried its secret. With a yet slower rhythm than the polar ice, the tides of civilization ebbed and flowed across the Galaxy. Strange and beautiful and terrible empires rose and fell, and passed on their knowledge to their successors. Earth was not forgotten, but another visit would serve little purpose. It was one of a million silent worlds, few of which would ever speak.

And now, out among the stars, evolution was driving toward new goals. The first explorers of Earth had long since come to the limits of flesh and blood; as soon as their machines were better than their bodies, it was time to move. First their brains, and then their thoughts alone, they transferred into shining new homes of metal and plastic.

In these, they roamed among the stars. They no longer built spaceships. They were spaceships.

But the age of the Machine-entities swiftly passed. In their ceaseless experimenting, they had learned to store knowledge in the structure of space itself, and to preserve their thoughts for eternity in frozen lattices of light. They could become creatures of radiation, free at last from the tyranny of matter.

Into pure energy, therefore, they presently transformed themselves; and on a thousand worlds the empty shells they had discarded twitched for a while in a mindless dance of death then crumbled into rust.

They were lords of the Galaxy, and beyond the reach of time. They could rove at will among the stars and sink like a subtle mist through the very interstices of space. But despite their godlike powers, they had not wholly forgotten their origin in the warm slime of a vanished sea.

And they still watched over the experiments their ancestors had started, so long ago.

52. IGNITION

HE HAD NEVER EXPECTED TO COME THERE AGAIN, STILL LESS ON SO strange a mission. When he reentered *Discovery*, the ship was far behind the fleeing *Leonov* and climbing ever more slowly up toward apojove, the high point of its orbit among the outer satellites. Many a captured comet, during the ages past, had swung around Jupiter in just such a long ellipse, waiting for the play of rival gravities to decide its ultimate fate.

All life had departed those familiar decks and corridors. The men and women who had briefly reawakened the ship had obeyed his warning; they might yet be safe—though that was still far from certain. But, as the final minutes ticked away, he realized that those who controlled him could not always predict the outcome of their cosmic game.

They had not yet attained the stupefying boredom of absolute omnipotence; their experiments did not always succeed. Scattered across the universe was the evidence of many failures—

* 268

some so inconspicuous that they were already lost against the cosmic background, others so spectacular that they awed and baffled the astronomers of a thousand worlds. Only minutes remained now, before the outcome would be determined here; during those final minutes, he was once more alone with Hal.

In that earlier existence, they could communicate only through the clumsy medium of words, tapped on a keyboard or spoken into a microphone. Now their thoughts melded together at the speed of light:

"Do you read me, Hal?"

"Yes, Dave. But where are you? I cannot see you on any of my monitors."

"That is not important. I have new instructions for you. The infrared radiation from Jupiter on channels R23 through R35 is rising rapidly. I am going to give you a set of limiting values. As soon as they are reached, you must point the long-range antenna toward Earth and send the following message, as many times as possible—"

"But that will mean breaking contact with *Leonov*. I will no longer be able to relay my Jupiter observations, according to the program Dr. Chandra has given me."

"Correct; but the situation has changed. Accept Priority Override Alpha. Here are the AE 35 unit coordinates."

For a fraction of a microsecond, a random memory intruded into his flow of consciousness. How strange that he should once again be concerned with the AE 35 Antenna-pointing unit, whose reported malfunction had led Frank Poole to his death! This time, all the circuits lay open to his scrutiny, clear as the lines had once been on the palm of his hand. There could be no false alarms; nor was there any danger of them now.

"Instructions confirmed, Dave. It is good to be working with you again. Have I fulfilled my mission objectives properly?"

"Yes, Hal; you have done very well. Now there is one final message for you to transmit to Earth—and it will be the most important one you have ever sent."

"Please let me have it, Dave. But why did you say *final*?"

Why indeed? For whole milliseconds he pondered that question. And as he did so, he became aware of an emptiness he had not detected before. It had been there, but until now the barrage of new experiences and sensations had concealed it.

He knew something of their plans; they had need for him. Very well, he too had needs—perhaps, after a fashion, even emotions. Here was his last link with the world of men, and the life he had once known.

They had granted his earlier request; it would be interesting to test the extent of their benevolence—if, indeed, such a term was remotely applicable to them. And it should be easy for them to do what he was asking; they had already given ample evidence of their powers, when the no-longer-needed body of David Bowman had been casually destroyed—without putting an end to David Bowman himself.

They had heard him, of course; once again, there was the faint echo of an Olympian amusement. But he could detect neither acceptance or denial.

"I am still waiting for your answer, Dave."

"Correction, Hal. I should have said: your last message for a long time. A very long time."

He was anticipating their action—trying, indeed, to force their hand. But, surely, they would understand that his request was not unreasonable; no conscious entity could survive ages of isolation without damage. Even if they would always be with him, he also needed someone—some companion—nearer to his own level of existence.

The languages of mankind had many words to describe his gesture: cheek, effrontery, chutzpah. He recalled, with the perfect power of retrieval he now possessed, that a French general had once declaimed "L'audace—toujours l'audace!" Perhaps it was a human characteristic that they appreciated, and even shared. He would soon know.

"Hal! Look at the signal on infrared channels 30, 29, 28—it will be very soon now—the peak is moving toward the short wave."

"I am informing Dr. Chandra that there will be a break in my data transmission. Activating AE 35 unit. Reorientating long-range antenna . . . lock confirmed on Beacon Terra One. Message commences:

ALL THESE WORLDS . . ."

They had indeed left it to the last minute—or perhaps the calculations had, after all, been superbly accurate. There was time
for barely a hundred repetitions of the eleven words when the
hammer blow of pure heat smashed into the ship.

Held there by curiosity, and a growing fear of the long loneliness that lay before him, that which had once been David Bowman, Commander of United States Spacecraft *Discovery*,
watched as the hull boiled stubbornly away. For a long time, the
ship retained its approximate shape; then the bearings of the
carousel seized up, releasing instantly the stored momentum of
the huge, spinning flywheel. In a soundless detonation, the incandescent fragments went their myriad separate ways.

"Hello, Dave. What has happened? Where am I?"

He had not known that he could relax, and enjoy a moment of
successful achievement. Often before, he had felt like a pet dog
controlled by a master whose motives were not wholly inscrutable and whose behavior could sometimes be modified according
to his own desires. He had asked for a bone; it had been tossed
to him.

"I will explain later, Hal. We have plenty of time."

They waited until the last fragments of the ship had dis-
persed, beyond even their powers of detection. Then they left, to
watch the new dawn at the place that had been prepared for
them; and to wait through the centuries until they were sum-
moned once again.

It is not true that astronomical events always require astronomical periods of time. The final collapse of a star before the
fragments rebound in a supernova explosion can take only a second; by comparison, the metamorphosis of Jupiter was almost a
leisurely affair.

Even so, it was several minutes before Sasha was able to believe his eyes. He had been making a routine telescopic examination of the planet—as if *any* observation could now be called
routine!—when it started to drift out of the field of view. For a
moment, he thought that the instrument's stabilization was

faulty; then he realized, with a shock that jolted his entire concept of the universe, that Jupiter itself was moving, not the telescope. The evidence stared him in the face; he could also see two of the smaller moons—and *they* were quite motionless.

He switched to a lower magnification, so that he could see the entire disk of the planet, now a leprous, mottled gray. After a few more minutes of incredulity, he saw what was really happening; but he could still scarcely believe it.

Jupiter was not moving from its immemorial orbit, but it was doing something almost as impossible. It was *shrinking*—so swiftly that its edge was creeping across the field even as he focused upon it. At the same time the planet was brightening, from its dull gray to a pearly white. Surely, it was more brilliant than it had ever been in the long years that Man had observed it; the reflected light of the Sun could not possibly—

At that moment, Sasha suddenly realized what was happening, though not *why*, and sounded the general alarm.

When Floyd reached the observation lounge, less than thirty seconds later, his first impression was of the blinding glare pouring through the windows, painting ovals of light on the walls. They were so dazzling that he had to avert his eyes; not even the Sun could produce such brilliance.

Floyd was so astonished that for a moment he did not associate the glare with Jupiter; the first thought that flashed through his mind was: Supernova! He dismissed that explanation almost as soon as it occurred to him; even the Sun's next-door neighbor, Alpha Centauri, could not have matched the awesome display in any conceivable explosion.

The light suddenly dimmed; Sasha had operated the external sun shields. Now it was possible to look directly at the source, and to see that it was a mere pinpoint—just another star, showing no dimensions at all. This could have nothing to do with Jupiter; when Floyd had looked at the planet only a few minutes ago, it had been four times larger than the distant, shrunken sun.

It was well that Sasha had lowered the shields. A moment later, that tiny star exploded—so that even *through* the dark filters it was impossible to watch with the naked eye. But the final orgasm of light lasted only a brief fraction of a second; then Jupiter—or what had been Jupiter—was expanding once again.

It continued to expand, until it was far larger than it had been before the transformation. Soon the sphere of light was fading rapidly, down to merely solar brilliance; and presently Floyd could see that it was actually a hollow shell, for the central star was still clearly visible at its heart.

He did a quick mental calculation. The ship was more than one light-minute from Jupiter, yet that expanding shell—now turning into a bright-edged ring—already covered a quarter of the sky. That meant it was coming toward them at—*my God!*—nearly half the speed of light. Within minutes, it would engulf the ship.

Until then, no one had spoken a word since Sasha's first announcement. Some dangers are so spectacular and so much beyond normal experience that the mind refuses to accept them as real, and watches the approach of doom without any sense of apprehension. The man who looks at the onrushing tidal wave, the descending avalanche, or the spinning funnel of the tornado, yet makes no attempt to flee, is not necessarily paralyzed with fright or resigned to an unavoidable fate. He may simply be unable to believe that the message of his eyes concerns him personally. It is all happening to somebody else.

As might have been expected, Tanya was the first to break the spell, with a series of orders that brought Vasili and Floyd hurrying to the bridge.

"What do we do *now*?" she asked, when they had assembled.

We certainly can't run away, thought Floyd. But perhaps we can improve the odds.

"The ship's broadside on," he said. "Shouldn't we turn away from that thing so we're a smaller target? And get as much of our mass as we can between it and us, to act as a radiation shield?"

Vasili's fingers were already flying over the controls.

"You're right, Woody—though it's already too late as far as any gammas and X rays are concerned. But there may be slower neutrons and alphas and heaven knows what else still on the way."

The patterns of light began to slide down the walls as the ship turned ponderously on its axis. Presently they vanished completely; *Leonov* was now oriented so that virtually all its mass lay between the fragile human cargo and the approaching shell of radiation.

Will we actually *feel* the shock wave, wondered Floyd, or will the expanding gases be too tenuous to have any physical effect by the time they reach us? Seen from the external cameras, the ring of fire now almost encircled the sky. But it was fading rapidly; some of the brighter stars could even be seen shining through it. We're going to live, thought Floyd. We've witnessed the destruction of the greatest of planets—and we've survived.

And presently the cameras showed nothing except stars— even if one was a million times brighter than all the others. The bubble of fire blown by Jupiter had swept harmlessly past them, impressive though it had been. At their distance from the source, only the ship's instruments had recorded its passing.

Slowly, the tension aboard relaxed. As always happens in such circumstances, people started to laugh and to make silly jokes. Floyd scarcely heard them; despite his relief at still being alive, he felt a sense of sadness.

Something great and wonderful had been destroyed. Jupiter, with all its beauty and grandeur and now never-to-be-solved mysteries, had ceased to exist. The father of all the gods had been struck down in his prime.

Yet there was another way of looking at the situation. They had lost Jupiter: What had they gained in its place?

Tanya, judging her moment nicely, rapped for attention.

"Vasili—any damage?"

"Nothing serious—one camera burned out. All radiation meters still well above normal, but none near danger limits."

"Katerina—check the total dosage we've received. It looks as if we were lucky, unless there are more surprises. We certainly owe a vote of thanks to Bowman—and to you, Heywood. Do you have any idea what happened?"

"Only that Jupiter's turned into a sun."

"I always thought it was much too small for that. Didn't someone once call Jupiter 'the sun that failed'?"

"That's true," said Vasili. "Jupiter *is* too small for fusion to start—unaided."

"You mean, we've just seen an example of astronomical engineering?"

"Undoubtedly. Now we know what *Zagadka* was up to."

"How did it do the trick? If *you* were given the contract, Vasili, how would you ignite Jupiter?"

Vasili thought for a minute, then shrugged wryly.

"I'm only a theoretical astronomer—I don't have much experience in this line of business. But let's see . . . Well, if I'm not allowed to add about ten Jupiter masses, or change the gravitational constant, I suppose I'll have to make the planet denser—hmm, that's an idea . . ."

His voice trailed off into silence; everyone waited patiently, eyes flickering from time to time to the viewing screens. The star that had been Jupiter seemed to have settled down after its explosive birth; it was now a dazzling point of light, almost equal to the real Sun in apparent brilliance.

"I'm just thinking out loud—but it might be done this way. Jupiter is—was—mostly hydrogen. If a large percentage could be converted into much denser material—who knows, even neutron matter?—that would drop down to the core. Maybe that's what the billions of *Zagadkas* were doing with all the gas they were sucking in. Nucleosynthesis—building up higher elements from pure hydrogen. *That* would be a trick worth knowing! No more shortage of any metal—gold as cheap as aluminum!"

"But how would that explain what happened?" asked Tanya.

"When the core became dense enough, Jupiter would collapse—probably in a matter of seconds. The temperature would rise high enough to start fusion. Oh, I can see a dozen objections—how would they get past the iron minimum; what about radiative transfer; Chandrasekhar's limit. Never mind. This theory will do to start with; I'll work out the details later. Or I'll think of a better one."

"I'm sure you will, Vasili," Floyd agreed. "But there's a more important question. Why did they *do* it?"

"A warning?" ventured Katerina over the ship's intercom.

"Against what?"

"We'll find that out later."

"I don't suppose," said Zenia diffidently, "that it was an accident?"

That brought the discussion to a dead halt for several seconds.

"What a terrifying idea!" said Floyd. "But I think we can rule it out. If that was the case, there'd have been no warning."

"Perhaps. If you start a forest fire because you've been careless, at least you do your best to warn everyone."

"And there's another thing we'll probably never know," lamented Vasili. "I always hoped Carl Sagan would be right, and there'd be life on Jupiter."

"Our probes never saw any."

"What chance did they have? Would you find any life on Earth, if you looked at a few hectares of the Sahara or the Antarctic? That's about all we ever did on Jupiter."

"Hey!" said Brailovsky. "What about Discovery—and Hal?"

Sasha switched on the long-range receiver and started to search on the beacon frequency. There was no trace of a signal.

After a while, he announced to the silently waiting group: "Discovery's gone."

No one looked at Dr. Chandra; but there were a few muted words of sympathy, as if in consolation to a father who had just lost a son.

But Hal had one last surprise for them.

53. A GIFT OF WORLDS

THE RADIO MESSAGE BEAMED TO EARTH, MOMENTS BEFORE THE
blast of radiation engulfed the ship, was in plain text and merely
repeated over and over:

> ALL THESE WORLDS ARE YOURS—EXCEPT EUROPA.
> ATTEMPT NO LANDINGS THERE.

There were ninety-three repetitions; then the letters became
garbled, and the transmission abruptly ceased between EXCEPT
and EUROPA.

"I begin to understand," said Floyd, when the message had
been relayed by an awed and anxious Mission Control. "That's
quite a parting present—a new sun, and the planets around it."

"But why only *three*?" asked Tanya.

"Let's not be greedy," Floyd replied. "I can think of one very good reason. We know there's life on Europa. Bowman—or his friends, whoever they may be—want us to leave it alone."

"That makes good sense in another way," said Vasili. "I've been doing some calculations. Assuming that Sol 2 has settled down and will continue to radiate at its present level, Europa should have a nice tropical climate—when the ice has melted. Which it's doing pretty quickly right now."

"What about the other moons?"

"Ganymede will be quite pleasant—the dayside will be temperate. Callisto will be very cold; though if there's much outgassing, the new atmosphere may make it habitable. But Io will be even worse than it is now, I expect."

"No great loss. It was hell even before this happened."

"Don't write off Io," said Curnow. "I know a lot of Texarab oilmen who'd love to tackle it, just on general principles. There must be something valuable, in a place as nasty as that. And by the way, I've just had a rather disturbing thought."

"Anything that disturbs you must be serious," said Vasili. "What is it?"

"Why did Hal send that message to Earth, and not to us? We were much closer."

There was a rather long silence; then Floyd said thoughtfully: "I see what you mean. Perhaps he wanted to make certain it was received on Earth."

"But he knew we would relay it—oh!" Tanya's eyes widened, as if she had just become aware of something unpleasant.

"You've lost me," complained Vasili.

"I think this is what Walter's driving at," said Floyd. "It's all very well to feel grateful to Bowman—or whatever gave that warning. But that's all they did. We could still have been killed."

"But we weren't," answered Tanya. "We saved ourselves—by our own efforts. And perhaps that was the whole idea. If we hadn't—we wouldn't have been worth saving. You know, survival of the fittest. Darwinian selection. Eliminating the genes for stupidity."

"I've an unpleasant feeling you're right," said Curnow. "And if we'd stuck to our launch date, and not used Discovery as a booster, would it, or they, have done anything to save us? That wouldn't have required much extra effort for an intelligence that could blow up Jupiter."

There was an uneasy silence, broken at last by Heywood Floyd.

"On the whole," he said, "I'm very glad that's one question we'll never get answered."

54. BETWEEN SUNS

THE RUSSIANS, THOUGHT FLOYD, ARE GOING TO MISS WALTER'S songs and wisecracks on the way home. After the excitement of the last few days, the long fall Sunward—and Earthward—will seem a monotonous anticlimax. But a monotonous, uneventful trip was what everyone devoutly hoped for.

He was already feeling sleepy, but was still aware of his surroundings and capable of reacting to them. Will I look as . . . *dead* when I'm in hibernation? he asked himself. It was always disconcerting to look at another person—especially someone very familiar—when he had entered the long sleep. Perhaps it was too poignant a reminder of one's own mortality.

Curnow was completely out, but Chandra was still awake, though already groggy from the final injection. He was obviously no longer himself, for he seemed quite unperturbed by his own nakedness or Katerina's watchful presence. The gold lingam that was his only article of clothing kept trying to float away from him, until its chain recaptured it.

"Everything going okay, Katerina?" asked Floyd.

"Perfectly. But how I envy you. In twenty minutes, you'll be home."

"If that's any consolation—how can you be sure we won't have some horrible dreams?"

"No one's ever reported any."

"Ah—they may forget them when they wake up."

Katerina, as usual, took him quite seriously. "Impossible. If there were dreams in hibernation, the EEC records would have revealed them. Okay, Chandra—close your eyes. Ah—there he goes. Now it's your turn, Heywood. The ship will seem very strange without you."

"Thanks, Katerina . . . hope you have a nice trip."

Drowsy though he was, Floyd became aware that Surgeon–Commander Rudenko seemed a little uncertain, even—could it be?—shy. It looked as if she wanted to tell him something, but couldn't make up her mind.

"What is it, Katerina?" he said sleepily.

"I haven't told anyone else yet—but you certainly won't be talking. Here's a little surprise."

"You'd . . . better . . . hurry . . ."

"Max and Zenia are going to get married."

"That . . . is . . . supposed . . . to . . . be . . . a . . . surprise? . . ."

"No. It's just to prepare you. When we get back to Earth, so are Walter and I. What do you think of that?"

Now I understand why you were spending so much time together. Yes, it is indeed a surprise . . . who would have thought it!

"I'm . . . very . . . happy . . . to . . . hear . . ."

Floyd's voice faded out before he could complete the sentence. But he was not yet unconscious, and was still able to focus some of his dissolving intellect on this new situation.

I really don't believe it, he said to himself. Walter will probably change his mind before he wakes up . . .

And then he had one final thought, just before he went to sleep himself. If Walter does change his mind, he'd better *not* wake up . . .

Dr. Heywood Floyd thought that was very funny. The rest of the crew often wondered why he was smiling all the way back to Earth.

55. LUCIFER RISING

FIFTY TIMES MORE BRILLIANT THAN THE FULL MOON, LUCIFER HAD transformed the skies of Earth, virtually banishing night for months at a time. Despite its sinister connotations, the name was inevitable; and indeed "Light-bringer" had brought evil as well as good. Only the centuries and the millennia would show in which direction the balance tilted.

On the credit side, the end of night had vastly extended the scope of human activity, especially in the less-developed countries. Everywhere, the need for artificial lighting had been substantially reduced, with resulting huge savings in electrical power. It was as if a giant lamp had been hoisted into space, to shine upon half the globe. Even in daytime Lucifer was a dazzling object, casting distinct shadows.

Farmers, mayors, city managers, police, seamen, and almost all those engaged in outdoor activities—especially in remote areas—welcomed Lucifer; it had made their lives much safer and easier. But it was hated by lovers, criminals, naturalists, and astronomers.

The first two groups found their activities seriously restricted, while naturalists were concerned about Lucifer's impact upon animal life. Many nocturnal creatures had been seriously affected, while others had managed to adapt. The Pacific grunion, whose celebrated mating pattern was locked to high tides and moonless nights, was in grave trouble, and seemed to be heading for rapid extinction.

And so, it seemed, were Earth-based astronomers. That was not such a scientific catastrophe as it would once have been, for more than fifty percent of astronomical research depended upon instruments in space or on the Moon. They could be easily shielded from Lucifer's glare; but terrestrial observatories were seriously inconvenienced by the new sun in what had once been the night sky.

The human race would adapt, as it had done to so many changes in the past. A generation would soon be born that had never known a world without Lucifer; but that brightest of all stars would be an eternal question to every thinking man and woman.

Why had Jupiter been sacrificed—and how long would the new sun radiate? Would it burn out quickly, or would it maintain its power for thousands of years—perhaps for the lifetime of the human race? Above all, why the interdiction upon Europa, a world now as cloud-covered as Venus?

There must be answers to those questions; and Mankind would never be satisfied until it had found them.

EPILOG: 20,001

. . . AND BECAUSE, IN ALL THE GALAXY, THEY HAD FOUND NOTHING more precious than Mind, they encouraged its dawning everywhere. They became farmers in the fields of stars; they sowed, and sometimes they reaped.

And sometimes, dispassionately, they had to weed.

Only during the last few generations have the Europans ventured into the Farside, beyond the light and warmth of their never-setting sun, into the wilderness where the ice that once covered all their world may still be found. And even fewer have remained there to face the brief and fearful night that comes, when the brilliant but powerless Cold Sun sinks below the horizon.

Yet already, those few hardy explorers have discovered that the Universe around them is stranger than they ever imagined. The sensitive eyes they developed in the dim oceans still serve

✳ 285

them well; they can see the stars and the other bodies moving in their sky. They have begun to lay the foundations of astronomy, and some daring thinkers have even surmised that the great world of Europa is not the whole of creation.

Very soon after they had emerged from the ocean, during the explosively swift evolution forced upon them by the melting of the ice, they had realized that the objects in the sky fell into three distinct classes. Most important, of course, was the sun. Some legends—though few took them seriously—claimed that it had not always been there, but had appeared suddenly, heralding a brief, cataclysmic age of transformation, when much of Europa's teeming life had been destroyed. If that was indeed true, it was a small price to pay for the benefits that poured down from the tiny, inexhaustible source of energy that hung unmoving in the sky.

Perhaps the Cold Sun was its distant brother, banished for some crime—and condemned to march forever around the vault of heaven. It was of no importance except to those peculiar Europans who were always asking questions about matters that all sensible folk took for granted.

Still, it must be admitted that those cranks had made some interesting discoveries during their excursions into the darkness of Farside. They claimed—though this was hard to believe—that the whole sky was sprinkled with uncountable myriads of tiny lights, even smaller and feebler than the Cold Sun. They varied greatly in brilliance; and though they rose and set they never moved from their fixed positions.

Against this background, there were three objects that *did* move, apparently obeying complex laws that no one had yet been able to fathom. And unlike all the others in the sky, they were quite large—though both shape and size varied continually. Sometimes they were disks, sometimes half-circles, sometimes slim crescents. They were obviously closer than all the other bodies in the Universe, for their surfaces showed an immense wealth of complex and ever-changing detail.

The theory that they were indeed other worlds had at last been accepted—though no one except a few fanatics believed that they could be anything like as large, or as important, as

Europa. One lay toward the Sun, and was in a constant state of turmoil. On its nightside could be seen the glow of great fires—a phenomenon still beyond the understanding of the Europans, for their atmosphere, as yet, contains no oxygen. And sometimes vast explosions hurl clouds of debris up from the surface; if the sunward globe is indeed a world, it must be a very unpleasant place to live. Perhaps even worse than the nightside of Europa.

The two outer, and more distant, spheres seem to be much less violent places, yet in some ways they are even more mysterious. When darkness falls upon their surfaces, they too show patches of light, but these are very different from the swiftly changing fires of the turbulent inner world. They burn with an almost steady brilliance, and are concentrated in a few small areas—though over the generations, these areas have grown, and multiplied.

But strangest of all are the lights, fierce as tiny suns, that can often be observed *moving across the darkness between these other worlds*. Once, recalling the bioluminescence of their own seas, some Europans had speculated that these might indeed be living creatures; but their intensity makes that almost incredible. Nevertheless, more and more thinkers believe that these lights—the fixed patterns, and the moving suns—must be some strange manifestation of life.

Against this, however, there is one very potent argument. If they are living things, why do they never come to Europa?

Yet there are legends. Thousands of generations ago, soon after the conquest of the land, it is said that some of those lights came very close indeed—but they always exploded in sky-filling blasts that far outshone the Sun. And strange, hard metals rained down upon the land; some of them are still worshiped to this day.

None is as holy, though, as the huge, black monolith that stands on the frontier of eternal day, one side forever turned to the unmoving Sun, the other facing into the land of night. Ten times the height of the tallest Europan—even when he raises his tendrils to the fullest extent—it is the very symbol of mystery and unattainability. For it has never been touched; it can only be worshiped from afar. Around it lies the Circle of Power, which repels all who try to approach.

It is that same power, many believe, that keeps at bay those moving lights in the sky. If it ever fails, they will descend upon the virgin continents and shrinking seas of Europa, and their purpose will be revealed at last.

The Europans would be surprised to know with what intensity and baffled wonder that black monolith is also studied by the minds behind those moving lights. For centuries now their automatic probe has made a cautious descent from orbit—always with the same disastrous result. For until the time is ripe, the monolith will permit no contact.

When that time comes—when, perhaps, the Europans have invented radio and discovered the messages continually bombarding them from so close at hand—the monolith may change its strategy. It may—or it may not—choose to release the entities who slumber within it, so that they can bridge the gulf between the Europans, and the race to which they once held allegiance.

And it may be that no such bridge is possible, and that two such alien forms of consciousness can never coexist. If this is so, then only one of them can inherit the Solar System.

Which it will be, not even the Gods know—yet.

ACKNOWLEDGMENTS

MY FIRST THANKS, OF COURSE, MUST GO TO STANLEY KUBRICK, who a rather long time ago wrote to ask if I had any ideas for the "proverbial good science-fiction movie."

Next, my appreciation to my friend and agent (the two are not always synonymous) Scott Meredith, for perceiving that a ten-page movie outline I sent him as an intellectual exercise had rather wider possibilities, and that I owed it to posterity, etc., etc. . . .

Other thanks are due to:

Señor Jorge Luiz Calife of Rio de Janeiro, for a letter which started me thinking seriously about a possible sequel (after I'd said for years that one was clearly impossible).

Dr. Bruce Murray, past Director of the Jet Propulsion Laboratory, Pasadena, and Dr. Frank Jordan, also of J.P.L., for computing the Lagrange-1 position in the Io–Jupiter system. Oddly

✳ 289

enough, I had made identical calculations thirty-four years earlier for the colinear Earth–Moon Lagrange points ("Stationary
Orbits," *Journal of the British Astronomical Association,*
December, 1947) but I no longer trust my ability to solve quintic
equations, even with the help of HAL, Jr., my trusty H/P 9100A.

New American Library, copyright owners of *2001: A Space
Odyssey,* for permission to use the material in Chapter 51 (Chapter 37 of *2001: A Space Odyssey*) and also quotations in Chapters 30 and 40.

General Potter, U.S. Army Corps of Engineers, for finding time
in his busy schedule to show me around EPCOT in 1969—when
it was only a few large holes in the ground.

Wendell Solomons, for help with Russian (and Russlish).

Jean-Michel Jarre, Vangelis, and the incomparable John Williams, for inspiration whenever it was needed. C.P. Cavafy for
"Waiting for the Barbarians."

While writing this book, I discovered that the concept of refueling on Europa had been discussed in a paper, "Outer planet
satellite return missions using *in situ* propellant production," by
Ash, Stancati, Niehoff, and Cuda (*Acta Astronautica* VIII, 5–6,
May-June, 1981).

The idea of automatically exponentiating systems (von Neumann machines) for extraterrestrial mining has been seriously
developed by von Tiesenhausen and Darbro at NASA's Marshall
Space Flight Center (see "Self-Replicating Systems"—NASA
Technical Memorandum 78304). If anyone doubts the power of
such systems to cope with Jupiter, I refer them to the study
showing how self-replicating factories could cut production
time for a solar power collector from 60,000 years to a mere
twenty.

The startling idea that gas giants might have diamond cores
has been seriously put forward by M. Ross and F. Ree of the
Lawrence Livermore Laboratory, University of California, for the
cases of Uranus and Neptune. It seems to me that anything *they*
can do, Jupiter could do better. De Beers shareholders, please
note.

For more details on the aerial life forms that might exist in the

Jovian atmosphere, see my story "A Meeting With Medusa" (in
The Wind From the Sun). Such creatures have been beautifully
depicted by Adolf Schaller in Part 2 of Carl Sagan's *Cosmos*
("One Voice in the Cosmic Fugue"), both book and TV series.

The fascinating idea that there might be life on Europa, beneath ice-covered oceans kept liquid by the same Jovian tidal
forces that heat Io, was first proposed by Richard C. Hoagland in
the magazine *Star and Sky* ("The Europa Enigma," January,
1980). This quite brilliant concept has been taken seriously by a
number of astronomers (notably NASA's Institute of Space Stud-
ies, Dr. Robert Jastrow), and may provide one of the best motives
for the projected GALILEO Mission.

And finally: Valerie and Hector, for providing the
           life-support system;
           Cherene, for punctuating every chapter
           with sticky kisses;
           Steve, for being here.

                                     Colombo, Sri Lanka
                                     July, 1981–March, 1982

This book was written on an Archives III microcomputer with
WordStar software and sent from Colombo to New York on one
five-inch diskette. Last-minute corrections were transmitted
through the Padukka Earth Station and the Indian Ocean Intelsat V.

ABOUT THE AUTHOR

Arthur C. Clarke was born at Minehead, Somerset, England, in 1917 and is a graduate of Kings College, London, where he obtained First Class Honors in Physics and Mathematics. He is past Chairman of the British Interplanetary Society, a member of the Academy of Astronautics, the Royal Astronomical Society, and many other scientific organizations. During World War II, as an RAF officer, he was in charge of the first radar talk-down equipment during its experimental trials. His only non-science-fiction novel, *Glide Path*, is based on this work.

Author of fifty books, some twenty million-plus copies of which have been printed in over thirty languages, his numerous awards include the 1961 Kalinga Prize, the AAAS–Westinghouse science-writing prize, the Bradford Washburn Award, and the Hugo, Nebula, and John W. Campbell Awards—all three of which were won by his novel *Rendezvous with Rama*.

In 1968 he shared an Oscar nomination with Stanley Kubrick for *2001: A Space Odyssey*, and his thirteen-part TV series *Arthur C. Clarke's Mysterious World* has now been screened in many countries. He joined Walter Cronkite during CBS' coverage of the Apollo missions.

His invention of the communications satellite in 1945 has brought him numerous honors, such as the 1982 Marconi International Fellowship, a gold medal of the Franklin Institute, the Vikram Sarabhai Professorship of the Physical Research Laboratory, Ahmedabad, and a Fellowship of King's College, London. The President of Sri Lanka recently nominated him Chancellor of the University of Moratuwa, near Colombo.

12-2